THE WITCH OF SHADOWMARSH

THE MOONSTONE CHRONICLES

BOOK ONE

SARA C ROETHLE

Character Art by Wojtek Depczyński

Cover Art by Amalia Chitulescu

❋ Created with Vellum

To Christina:
Brainstorming Buddy,
Shield Sister,
Capricorn Queen.

CHAPTER ONE

Elmerah

Elmerah checked the shackles on her wrists for the hundredth time. What a load of *dung*. How in Ilthune had lowly sea pirates been able to afford magic-nullifying wrist bonds? The ones on her ankles were just simple iron. She would free herself from *those* easily enough if she had access to her magic...which, she didn't.

The heavy iron hurt her wrists and squeezed her boots uncomfortably at her ankles, not to mention the steady *drip drip* of water leaking in from the deck above her head to add to her annoyance. She leaned her back against the wooden wall of the small cabin near the ship's bow, her temporary prison. Her long legs, clad only in thick tights, erupted in goosebumps.

A few other women shared the space with her, their heads slumped in the swinging lantern light. That her fellow captives were all women, and all young and fairly beautiful, told her one thing. They were on their way to be sold into slavery of the worst kind. Although, how the pirates intended to keep a witch like herself tethered for long was beyond her. The bigger question was, *why?* She was at least a decade older than the young girls, though she felt herself not horrible to look at. Her black hair and bronze skin hinted at her Arthali heritage, and she was curvy enough to be considered feminine, though her height and well-muscled frame scared off most male suitors.

Not that she'd been looking.

She shook her shackles again. The ship swayed gently, the sound of the choppy sea above muffling the soft weeping of her fellow prisoners.

Elmerah sneered. She'd never been one to weep, and she sure as Ilthune's lance didn't consider herself a victim. She was a temporary hostage, nothing more. As soon as she managed to rid herself of these shackles, she'd teach the sea pirates a lesson. They'd rue the day they decided it was a good idea to turn an Arthali swamp witch into a slave.

She glanced at her nearest fellow captive, barely illuminated by the swaying, lone lantern. The girl had long white hair like spider silk, and bony, angular features carved into perfect alabaster skin. Her downcast eyes dominated her small face, and pointed ears jutted out from beneath her hair. She was a Faerune elf, one of the Moonfolk. Elmerah knew that if the girl turned her large eyes upward, they would glint in the darkness. Faerune elves could see just as well at night as they could during the day. They were fast too, with incredibly agile hands that could send a dagger into your chest before you could even blink.

Agile hands, Elmerah thought, glancing once again at her shackles. Perhaps this girl could be of use to her.

"Psst," she whispered, scooting closer to the girl.

The girl startled and glanced upward, and sure enough, her eyes glinted like moonlight. Her loose white tunic made her look like a ghost.

"Yes?" she asked softly, seeming to regain her composure. Poor girl couldn't have been more than eighteen.

"Come over here," Elmerah whispered. "I need your help."

The girl narrowed her eyes, then clutching her shackled hands to her chest, she scooted along the floor until she was sitting side by side with Elmerah.

Elmerah lowered her head toward the girl. "Search my hair, I should still have some pins left in there." She *hoped* she'd had some pins left. Even after the pirate caught her unawares and cuffed her, she'd put up a fight. The man had ripped a clump of her hair out in the struggle. She'd made up for it by kicking out two of his teeth.

The girl's fingers tugged through Elmerah's matted hair.

She cringed. She needed a bath.

"You smell like a swamp," the girl muttered.

"Well you smell like fairy dung," Elmerah grumbled. Never mind that the girl actual smelled like a crystal clear brook surrounded by wildflowers. Elves always smelled pleasant, except perhaps the Akkeri. The sea-riders smelled a bit like rotten fish.

"There," the girl whispered, pulling a hairpin free. "Now what do you want me to do with it?"

Elmerah lifted her head, then held out her cuffed wrists. "Get these off me and I'll make these pirates *pay*."

The girl's eyes widened, as if finally just *really* seeing her. "You're Arthali," she gasped, retracting the pin toward her chest.

Elmerah fought the urge to sneer. Pureblood Arthali had

been exiled from the Ulrian Empire over three decades ago, but old fears ran as deep as the Kalwey Sea. "Yes," she hissed, "so you know I can back up my claims."

The elf girl met her gaze for several seconds, then lowered trembling hands to Elmerah's cuffs. "Arcale protect me," she muttered as she inserted the pin into the keyhole.

The girl's words inspired Elmerah to take a closer look at her garb. The white tunic, embroidered with little silver moons, topped fitted white pants. Her brows raised in recognition. These pirates really were idiots. They'd not only kidnapped an Arthali witch, but a Faerune priestess. If the elves ever found out about this, every last pirate would surely meet a swift end.

The pin clicked in the lock.

Elation filled her as she pulled off the cuffs, then hurriedly pumped magic into the benign shackles around her ankles, which soon clicked open. She stood, then looked down at the Faerune priestess.

Seeming to sense her hesitation, the girl glared. "You said you'd get us out of here."

"Actually, I said I'd make these pirates pay."

The girl's glare deepened.

She'd be a fool to get involved with the elves, but—she huffed out a long breath, then held a hand out to the girl. "Hold the cuffs away from your body."

Still staring up at her, the girl obeyed.

Elmerah pushed magic into the cuffs. They fell away from the girl's wrists, then clattered to the wooden planks, followed by the ones at her ankles.

The girl stood, a full head shorter than Elmerah "Now the others," she demanded.

Elmerah glared down at her. "Weren't you just trembling

in your boots about freeing an Arthali witch? Are you sure you should be making demands?"

Her glare did not waver.

"Fine," Elmerah hissed. "They'll prove a worthwhile distraction, if nothing else."

She made her way around the small cabin, freeing the other women one by one. There were six in total, eight counting herself and the elven priestess. Some of the women stood, but others remained slumped on the floor, *broken*.

The elf girl watched her expectantly.

"I've freed them," she grumbled. "If they're not willing to help themselves now, there's nothing I can do. Now I'm off to murder some pirates."

After a moment, the elf girl nodded. She marched across the small space away from the lantern's light and retrieved something from a dark corner, then returned to Elmerah with a long oar in hand, taller than the girl holding it.

"You Moonfolk really can see in the dark, can't you?"

She nodded. "Yes, now let us go enact our vengeance."

Elmerah smirked. Perhaps she'd made a wise choice in allying herself with the girl after all. She made her way toward the rickety wooden steps leading up to the deck. A heavy padlock dangled from the trapdoor above.

She made quick work of it, overwhelming the metal components with magic until they snapped. Leave it to pirates to only buy enchanted shackles and not a padlock. They were in *way* over their heads.

The women had all herded together behind her, those who'd stood on their own now supporting those who'd refused.

"What's your name?" Elmerah asked the elven girl as she reached her side.

She gripped the oar tightly in her hands. "Saida Fenmyar."

"Elmerah Volund," she introduced. "Are you ready, Saida?"

Saida nodded.

Elmerah tossed the trap door open, landing with a loud *thwack* on the deck above. She rushed up the final steps, angry magic coursing through her veins. Only three of the men were on deck, all turned toward her with jaws agape.

She kicked the nearest one right in his hanging jaw, darting in and stealing his cutlass before he hit the deck.

"I thought you'd use magic to attack them," Saida said, facing the other two men just a few paces off as the other women ascended behind her.

"I'm saving it for their leader," Elmerah explained. "Plus, I was really feeling like I needed to kick someone in the face."

The other two men neared, weapons drawn. Their dirty faces and ragged loose clothing hinted to their status as lowly crewman. "Oi!" one of them called out, "the prisoners are loose!"

More men would be on deck soon. They needed to act fast so they wouldn't be overwhelmed. Elmerah lifted her cutlass, ready to fight, but Saida was way ahead of her. She launched herself at the men in a graceful leap, swinging the oar like a staff, her white hair streaming behind her. One man tried to counter, but his weapon was effortlessly flicked away, right before the oar swooped back around and smacked him with the broad side on the back of his head. The other man got the narrow side straight in his gut, knocking the wind from his lungs.

Elmerah would have liked to continue watching but

more men had swarmed the deck, their legs braced wide against the swaying of the ship. She counted them, weighing their odds before realizing she'd be out of magical energy by the time this fight was over. The other women huddled together near the trap door, their eyes squinted against the occasional gust of heavily salted air. *Useless.*

She lifted the cutlass toward the cloudy sky, filling it with more of her magic than she should have been expending, but she wasn't about to risk someone shackling her once more. Her power surged into the blade to the point of bursting as the first man charged her.

A rumble in the sky echoed her guttural growl. She really shouldn't be doing this, but it was too late to go back now. If she moved the sword, the lightning might be attracted to her instead.

The bolt hit the blade, absorbing into the metal. The man stumbled away, eyes wide. Too late for him as well. She whipped the blade downward, sending a bolt of lightning straight toward his chest. It hit its mark, then bounced to the next man before hitting the far wall of the above-deck cabin where it dissipated.

She spared a quick glance toward Saida, who'd stayed near the women, protecting them with her oar, then turned back as more men charged her. One had a new set of shackles in hand.

"Get them 'round her wrists!" a finely dressed man shouted from a safe distance.

Her lip quivered with a snarl. She'd found the captain.

Still bursting with energy, she whipped the sword toward the men, tossing them aside with electrical currents. She surged forward, slicing any who'd not fallen with her blade.

7

One man's cutlass neared her throat, then fell away as an oar thunked down upon his sweaty brow.

"My thanks!" Elmerah shouted, slamming her shoulder into another pirate and sending him overboard.

She turned toward another, brandishing her blade flickering with elemental sparks. She must have looked quite the sight, given a wet spot soon formed on his breeches. He tossed his cutlass aside and willingly followed his fellow pirate into the sea.

Her snarl still in place, she turned toward the captain. He was attempting to unlock the cabin door behind him, but his trembling hands were fumbling the key. She stalked toward him. Saida stood back with her oar in hand and several men lying broken at her feet.

The captain glanced over his shoulder at her approach. His blue eyes widened. With his shiny black hair and clear complexion he was almost handsome. Unfortunately, the stain of capturing slaves made him ugly.

His little metal key clattered to the deck.

Cutlass still in hand, Elmerah knelt to retrieve it. She stood, dangling the key in front of his face. "I believe you dropped this."

"Please don't kill me," he whimpered.

Her smile broadened. "Did you really think it was a good idea to kidnap an Arthali witch? My people are well known for showing little mercy."

"I was just following orders. Please, I'll tell you everything. I'll tell you who hired me and you can go after her."

Her? Now that was interesting.

"I'm guessing any information I might want is contained in the cabin behind you," she gestured to the locked door with her cutlass. "I'm not seeing any reason to spare you."

Footsteps sounded behind her, then Saida appeared at her side. "We'll take him back to my people. He will stand trial for his crimes."

Elmerah snorted. "I'm not going anywhere near the elves." She turned back to the captain, offering him the key. "Unlock it. Let's see what you have inside."

The captain snatched the key, then unlocked the door with still trembling hands. "Thank you," he muttered. "Thank you for not bringing me to the elves." He pushed the door open.

His thanks sent a disgusted shiver down Elmerah's spine. She turned and gave Saida a subtle nod.

The oar came down. The captain crumpled.

Elmerah glanced back at the waiting women, then to Saida. "Have them tie up any who still live. I'm going to take a look around."

Saida nodded, then returned to the women as Elmerah stepped over the prostrate captain into the office.

The furnishings were sparse, but high quality. A heavy oak writing desk dominated the far wall, stationed next to a bed with a proper mattress topped with vibrant silks and fluffy feather pillows. While the bed appealed to her tired body, she was more interested in the desk, and what information its drawers might contain.

She marched across the room, fighting her sluggishness as her adrenaline seeped away. She'd used far too much magical energy calling lightning to her new cutlass. It would have been easier with an enchanted sword, but her weapons had been left behind when she was kidnapped.

Swapping the cutlass to her left hand, she opened the middle drawer. Ink, bitterroot with a pipe, and blank sheets of parchment. Useless. She opened the next drawer. Empty.

Why even have a desk? When the third drawer revealed only a few clean handkerchiefs, she turned back to the rest of the cabin. She could hear Saida outside directing the other women to bind all the men, but she still wanted to act fast. She'd like to be far away on one of the smaller boats long before the ship reached shore. *If* it reached shore. She would be highly surprised if any of the women actually knew how to sail.

She narrowed her gaze at one of the floorboards near the bed. It was slightly raised from the others.

She stepped toward it, then halted, feeling dizzy. She'd used *far* too much power. She'd be lucky to make it to shore on her own at all.

"Are you well?" a woman's voice asked.

She turned to see Saida peeking into the cabin.

"All the men are bound, but we should decide what to do soon. If I'm not mistaken, we are headed toward Galterra."

"The Capital?" Elmerah balked, swaying on her feet. She shook her head. "It doesn't matter. Could you check that floorboard?" she pointed. "I'll take whatever is hidden down there and depart on one of the smaller boats."

Saida marched across the room and knelt, easily prying up the floorboard with her fingertips. She withdrew a stack of rolled documents, set them aside, then withdrew three large leather pouches of coin.

Elmerah stepped forward, then snatched two pouches of coin from Saida's hands and affixed them to her belt. Next she retrieved the folded documents from the floor and placed them under her arm. After a moment of debate, she tossed her new cutlass aside with a dull *clang*, then approached the unconscious captain in the doorway. Sure enough, a far finer cutlass was at his hip. She slid it from his belt, considering skewering the man with his own blade, but walked out into the open air instead. A storm was brewing further out to sea, and she really wanted to start paddling before it was too late.

Saida hurried out after her, then past her. "There are four extra boats," she explained. "We should all be able to reach shore easily enough." She retrieved her oar from one of the women, then turned back to Elmerah. "It would be best to have four women per boat, everyone can row."

Elmerah stalked past her toward the lower cabin where they'd been held prisoner, the pouches of coin jangling at her hips. "I told you, I'll be leaving on my own. The rest of you would be wise to take only one boat, and take turns rowing. It is more tiring than you think."

Saida followed her as she descended the stairs into the cabin. "If that is true, then how do you intend to man a boat on your own?"

"It's tiring for weak young girls," Elmerah muttered, groping about in the darkness for the oars. "Not for me."

Saida stomped a few paces past her, reached into the darkness, then handed Elmerah an oar. Her elven eyes glinted in the near dark. "There's no need to be difficult. We're all in this together. Surely once we reach Galterra we will be offered aid."

Elmerah raised an eyebrow at her. "Have you ever *been* to Galterra?"

Saida lifted her nose into the air. "Once, with an envoy. My clan was signing a new trade agreement."

Elmerah held out her hand expectantly for another oar, which Saida soon offered her. "You saw the Capital on its best behavior," she explained. "I advise you to don a hood as soon as you reach shore. Keep your hair and ears covered, and don't let anyone see your eyes at night."

Saida's dainty jaw dropped, but Elmerah had no more time to explain things to her. She herself would wear a hood if she decided to enter the Capital. While she might not stand out quite as much as an elf, her height and coloring would give away exactly what she was, a pure-blooded Arthali, not the half-breeds still allowed in the Empire. Many would steer clear of her, but others would view her as a challenge. Oars in hand, she turned and walked back up the stairs.

She heard the clatter of oars behind her, then thunks coming up the stairs after her, but didn't turn to look. If the girl wanted to carry oars and make herself responsible for the other women, that was her choice.

Her own oars in hand, she strode toward the side of the ship, then stopped in her tracks. She would have palmed her face if she had a free hand. She'd need someone to help her lower her boat down to the sea.

She turned back with a huff to see Saida handing out oars to the other women. A few of the men still alive had come to, and were groaning and pleading to be set free. She would have kicked them into silence if she had the energy. Cursed Ilthune her limbs were tired.

"Hey elf girl!" she called out. "Why don't you let the others row into Galterra to report what has happened, and you and I can find some quiet place far from the docks from which to disappear."

Saida approached, her brow furrowed. "I thought you wanted to go alone."

Elmerah shifted her oars to lean against the deck, then brushed a clump of salt-saturated hair from her face. "If you'd like to take your chances in Galterra, be my guest. I'm just trying to help you."

Her gaze narrowed. "Show me how to lower a boat for the other women, then I'll go with you, but only to the shore. After that I'll head toward Galterra to send word to my mother."

Elmerah fought her shoulders as they threatened to slump in relief. Saida was a bit scrawny, but she could still help her row . . . not that she'd *ever* openly admit to needing the help.

"Please," a nearby man groaned. "Just untie us. We can help you lower the boats."

Elmerah found she suddenly had enough energy to land her boot against his ribs.

After a pained *oof*, he kept his mouth shut.

"Let's go. I want to reach the shore before the storm hits."

Saida nodded, then moved past her toward the waiting women.

Elmerah watched her go, though her thoughts were no longer on the elf girl. Rather, her thoughts were on what in the name of Arcale she was going to do when she reached shore. Without the use of a ship, it would take her weeks to reach home again. She had no food or travel supplies, and no time to search the ship for such things if she didn't want to get stuck in a tiny boat in a storm.

She patted her belt pouch. At least she had coin, and if she could find a place to rest, she could regain enough energy to protect herself. She just needed to get through a single night, then she'd be fine . . . At least, that's what she kept telling herself.

CHAPTER TWO

Saida

Saida's arms pumped rhythmically, propelling the small boat across the choppy water. Her shoulders were already aching, but she was quite sure she was their only hope of reaching shore.

Elmerah slumped against the bow, her eyes half closed, her long legs stretched out across the wooden plank where Saida perched. She'd spent the first leg of their journey reading through the rolled parchments she'd found in the pirate's cabin, before eventually tossing them overboard. She hadn't commented on anything she'd learned.

Saida paused her rowing to wipe the sweat from her brow.

One of Elmerah's eyes opened. "If you don't keep rowing, we'll not beat the storm."

She was right, an angry black storm was right on their tail. She hoped the other women would make it to Galterra safely, though they'd likely have little trouble with six of them to take turns rowing. It was probably foolish of her to leave with the Arthali witch, but she hadn't been sure of the mechanism to lower the boats. She'd needed Elmerah's help, and this was the price.

"You could always *help*," she chided.

Elmerah's eye fluttered closed. "Sorry, I'm a bit tired from saving your bony rump."

Saida sucked her teeth in irritation, but continued rowing despite her body's protests. "I've never seen someone summon lightning like that. Not even the high priests of Faerune are capable of such a feat."

"Well you've clearly never met one of the Arthali. My magic is a flickering spark compared to some."

Saida suppressed a shiver. Elmerah was right, she'd never met one of the Arthali before, and she'd never hoped to. The Arthali were beyond brutal, feared pirates who'd conquered entire nations. It was only through the treaties of the elves with the Empire that the Arthali were finally pushed back, exiled to terrorize distant lands instead of this one.

Of course, this had all happened long before Saida was born. Given Elmerah appeared only a bit older than her, she doubted the witch had ever seen the Arthali at their full power.

"So you know others of your kind?" Saida pressed, her curiosity getting the better of her.

One eye cracked open again. "Not for a very long while." The eye shut again.

With a huff, Saida focused on her rowing. She had half a mind to toss the witch overboard, but quickly dismissed the idea. Though Elmerah seemed exhausted now, her light-ning had been quite the sight, as had her swordwork. The cutlass was still strapped to the witch's belt, and she'd have trouble wielding an oar to protect herself in the small vessel.

She breathed a sigh of relief as a sandy inlet came into view, leading back to ancient trees taller than the temples in her homeland. She aimed the boat toward it, just as the first raindrops tickled her cheeks.

Finally, both of Elmerah's eyes opened. She gazed past Saida's head toward the storm, then sat up enough to peer over her shoulder at the inlet. She seemed to scan the trees for several long moments, then turned back to Saida. "If we're lucky we'll find an inn along the Emperor's Path. I'll cover the cost of a room," she glanced at Saida's trembling arms, still working the oars, albeit slowly, "to show my thanks," she finished. "We can part ways in the morning."

Saida wasn't about to argue with her. Her arms felt like sweet plum jelly, and her belly was cramped and empty. Not thinking properly, she'd given the third coin purse to the other women, not bothering to take a few coins for herself. Elmerah still had the other two strapped to her belt.

Greedy woman.

"Is there a problem?" Elmerah questioned.

Thinking once again of the lightning, Saida shook her head. She'd let the witch buy her a room, then in the morning she'd head for Galterra. There she'd send word to her mother, who'd surely deploy an envoy to rescue her. Of course, then she'd have to explain to her mother what she'd been doing so far from home, but she could easily cover up her actions. Given her satchel—stuffed with a change of clothes and enough food to last a week—had been taken by the pirates, she could simply tell her mother she'd been out gathering burrberries when she'd been attacked, not running away from home.

Realizing Elmerah was still watching her, she shifted uncomfortably, giving a final painful heave of the oars to send them into the rolling surf.

The bounce of the boat finally prompted the witch to give up her lounging. She moved to the small bench beside Saida and took one of the oars. "Try and keep the bow pointed straight toward shore," she instructed. "If we get too far misaligned the waves will capsize us, and we'll be wet enough with the rain as it is."

Saida did as instructed, working her oar whenever the boat drifted a bit too far to the left. Her stomach lurched every time they crested a wave, then dropped back down to her feet as she was pelleted with sharp droplets of seawater.

The boat hit sand with a dull thud, eliciting a sigh of relief.

Before she could react further, Elmerah dropped her oar and hopped out the boat, wetting her boots as she tugged the vessel more firmly ashore.

Saida hopped out after her. She stumbled as her boots sunk into the sand, landing on her rump at the edge of the water. Though she'd mainly been using her arms, it seemed the effect of bracing herself had taken a toll on her legs as well. She was utterly exhausted, and now the damp sand was soaking through her thick tights.

Elmerah stood over her, hands on hips, her head blocking out the last rays of sun that would soon be swallowed up by the storm. "Can you stand?"

A flurry of stinging rain drops whipped across her cheeks. She nodded, though she wasn't sure. She'd try in a moment . . .

"We need to head inland," Elmerah pressed. Though her face was in shadow from the blinding sun rays hitting the back of her head, Saida imagined Elmerah was raising an eyebrow and smirking at her, the weak little elf girl.

Elmerah's hand extended downward.

With an internal cringe, Saida took it. She could not wait for this day to end. If she ever made it home, she was quite sure she'd *never* leave again.

THE RAIN PELLETED DOWN AROUND THEM, SPLASHING across the puddles formed in ruts on the road, and ricocheting off tree branches to fall in all directions. Saida's hair was plastered to her head, and her ear tips had long since gone numb. Her boots were heavy with water and mud.

Elmerah marched on beside her, her longer legs setting a brisk pace. Her black hair was thick enough to not look limp, though it was as soaked as Saida's.

"Do you smell that?"

Saida sniffed the air, catching the scent of woodsmoke a moment later. They'd been traveling down the Emperor's Path, the main route leading into and away from Galterra, for roughly an hour, heading away from the city rather than toward it.

Elmerah had claimed the inns further from the Capital would be safer for both their kinds, though they'd also likely be rickety dung heaps. At this point, Saida didn't care either way as long as she had a roof over her head and a meal in her belly.

They rounded a bend in the road, and the inn came into view. Perhaps she *did* care. The inn had an almost . . . evil feel to it, with its dark, uneven planks glistening with moisture. The surrounding fence had eroded in places, overtaken by dense vines reaching out from the surrounding forest. The establishment had no sign bearing the symbol of its name. In fact, the only thing telling Saida it was an inn at all was its location, and the individual stable stalls lining one exterior wall. Only two were filled, one with a shiny black horse that looked just as evil as the inn, and the other with a skinny mule that would likely drop dead at any moment.

"Are you coming?" Elmerah asked.

Saida realized she had stopped in her tracks. "Are you sure this is where you want to stay?"

Elmerah smirked. "Do you see anywhere else, princess?"

Though Saida didn't appreciate being called *princess*, she supposed Elmerah was right. It was only one night, and she was beginning to shiver from the rain.

Fully resigned, she followed Elmerah off the road and through the opening in the fence that no longer had a gate. Reaching the inn, Elmerah pulled open the heavy wood and iron door without so much as a knock, striding confidently inside.

Saida scurried in after her, her eyes darting back and forth for signs of danger. When nothing attacked her, she relaxed, soothed by the warmth of a blazing fire in the nearby hearth. Past the hearth was a small, gleaming bar, tended by an elderly man in modest, yet clean clothing. He looked her up and down suspiciously, and remembering Elmerah's words, she tugged her limp hair over her ear tips.

There was only one other person in the small common room, a seemingly male figure with a deep cowl obscuring his features. His clothing was all muted browns and greens that would easily blend in with the woods outside. He sat in the far corner, a boiled leather mug at his fingertips.

Elmerah approached the innkeep, withdrawing a few

coins from one of the purses at her belt. "A room for a single night," she ordered, "one with two beds, and two meals."

The innkeep stared long and hard at Elmerah, then down to the coins on the counter, then back up. "Aye, that will cost you double what you're offering."

Elmerah snorted. "Really? What did *he* pay?" she nodded toward the man in the corner.

The innkeep licked his wrinkly lips. "*He* doesn't come with the same risks as an Arthali witch and one of the Elderfolk. It'll cost me a lot more if my inn gets burned to the ground for harboring your kind."

Elmerah let out an exaggerated sigh, then placed three more coins on the counter. "Our meals had better come with wine."

The innkeep snatched up the coins, then nodded toward the vacant tables. "Sit anywhere you like, and keep your heads down if anyone else comes in."

Saida followed Elmerah toward a table near the hearth. Elmerah slouched into one of the rickety chairs, leaning it back so it rested on only two legs, placing her a bit closer to the fire.

Saida dragged another chair so her back would be to the wall, then sat. She leaned across the table, closer to Elmerah. "Do you really think someone would burn the inn down just because we're here?"

Elmerah snorted. "Because of you? Probably not. Me? Well, old grudges tend to cling through generations."

Saida shook her head. She'd had few experiences with non-elf races, but she could hardly believe Elmerah would be attacked just for the bronze color of her skin.

The innkeep, who'd disappeared into what Saida assumed was the kitchen, reemerged with two steaming bowls of soup. He placed one in front of Saida, then left the other at the edge of the table for Elmerah to pull toward herself. He left, then returned with two boiled leather mugs of wine and a small metal key. "You'd be wise to leave at first light. A few of the militia men often come in for a meal first thing."

"They patrol this far from the Capital?" Elmerah asked.

The innkeep nodded. "There have been several sightings of Akerri ships in the night, and a few of the nasty mongrels near the gates. There have even been a few attacks. The militia has many new volunteers."

Saida shivered. The Akerri were a race of elves detested by most. They lived almost entirely at sea, not being overly welcome in any of the cities, and for good reason. Not only did they reek of rotten fish, they worshipped Ilthune, the tentacled goddess of the Underworld. They were blood-thirsty, vile creatures.

The innkeep excused himself, retreating back behind the small bar.

Saida looked to Elmerah. "What do you think the Akerri want?"

Elmerah slurped down a spoonful of her soup, then took a hearty swig of her wine. She shrugged. "What does anyone want? Riches or revenge."

She looked down at the small, hard turnips and grayish meat in her stew, feeling ill. "Well I don't want either of those things, so perhaps the Akerri don't either."

With another shrug, Elmerah drank more wine. "Well you're the elf here. You tell me what the Akerri want."

She frowned. Her people were nothing like the Akerri, but she imagined arguing the point would do little good with Elmerah. "So what was on those parchments you found in the captain's quarters? Why did you toss them in the ocean?"

Elmerah's mug paused halfway to her lips. "What does it matter to you?"

"Simple curiosity?"

She sighed. "They were the acquisition orders. Someone was looking to buy foreign races of slaves along with the normal shipment. You and I would have fetched a pretty penny."

Saida stirred her stew, debating testing it. "But why?"

"Who knows?" She smirked. "Who *cares*? We're free now, and I'm sure the militia will be heading out in the morning to fetch some very wet, cold pirates."

Saida finally braved the stew, then wished she hadn't. The meat had the texture of tree bark, and the underripe turnips were incredibly bitter. "Did you at least learn who placed the order for us? Who would want an Arthali witch?"

Elmerah lifted her brow. "Am I meant to be insulted now?"

Saida dropped her spoon, panic lancing through her. "I didn't mean to insult," she blurted. "I only meant anyone would be a fool to think they could keep one of the Arthali as a servant."

"In that case, you are correct. And keep your voice down. Our friend in the corner is eavesdropping."

She whipped her gaze to the side without thinking, but the cowled man's face was turned away.

"How very subtle you are," Elmerah chided. "Now finish your stew so we can get some rest. You'll want to leave first thing in the morning to reach Galterra by the evening without a horse."

With a nod, Saida forced another bite of stew into her mouth, washing it down with wine almost as bitter as the turnips. She glanced a few more times at the cowled man as she ate, but he seemed to be paying them little mind. She wasn't sure why Elmerah thought he was eavesdropping, but she supposed it didn't matter. In the morning she would make for Galterra to send word to her mother. Within one moon cycle, she'd be home. Far away from pirates, Akerri, and disgruntled swamp witches.

CHAPTER THREE

Elmerah

E lmerah woke with the dawn. While she didn't feel
fully recharged, she was sure she'd at least be able to
protect herself during her first day of travel . . . unless she
ran into any witch hunters. Enchanted armor and weapons
could be used to nullify her magic, and many of the witch
hunters had both. Ironically, such technology had been
stolen from her own people to be used against them.
Without it, the Arthali would likely be ruling the Ulrian
Empire, not that snake-tongued criminal, Egrin Dinoba.

Shaking away her thoughts, she climbed out of her
rickety bed, glancing across the room at Saida's still sleeping
form. It didn't matter who was emperor. Soon Elmerah
would be back in her swamp, far from the politics she so
detested.

She tugged her dirty loose blouse over the hips of her
thick black tights, then padded barefoot across the floorboards toward the few remaining embers in the hearth. The

room's small window was foggy from the chilly, damp morning air. She shivered, not looking forward to leaving behind the warmth of the inn. At least she had plenty of coin should she happen upon another establishment before nightfall. Coin that had paid for her capture, and Saida's.

More disconcerting still was the signature at the bottom of the contracts she'd found. Rissine Volund was a despicable woman. Cruel, cold, and selfish. Truly, she was utter pond scum.

She was also Elmerah's older sister.

Yes, Rissine had orchestrated her kidnapping, *and* Saida's. They were the only two women on the ship requested by name. The others had likely just been in the wrong place at the wrong time.

She glanced over her shoulder again at Saida. Why would Rissine want *her*? Just who was this brazen little elf girl?

As she watched, Saida sat up in bed. She started to lift her arms over her head, then winced and brought them back down.

Elmerah almost felt guilty about making her do all the rowing . . . *almost*. "What is your standing amongst your clan?"

Saida paused halfway through a yawn, blinking bleary eyes at her. "What?"

"Your standing," Elmerah repeated. "I'm wondering why the pirates wanted you."

"Perhaps they just wanted an elf."

She narrowed her gaze. She wasn't willing to reveal what had been on the contracts, not yet. "Pretty as you may be, I think there's something more. Why *you* out of all the other elves? You wear the garb of a priestess, and you know how to fight. I imagine one of your lowly surfs would have been much easier to acquire."

Saida's pale face turned pink. "I am no one special, I assure you."

Elmerah crossed her arms. "Is this how you repay someone for saving your neck? Someone who has provided you with a hot meal and a bed?"

"With money you stole!"

Her arms still crossed, she tapped her bare foot on the floorboards.

Saida glowered. "As you've already realized, I am a priest-ess, but a lowly one. I cannot work the magic of crystals like our elders. I am nothing special." Her cheeks turned a slightly darker shade of pink.

The girl was clearly lying, but that was all she really needed to know. Saida was a Faerune priestess, but there were many priestesses. Why her specifically?

"You know," she began, slumping into a more casual stance, "I'm having second thoughts about fleeing so quickly. Perhaps I will accompany you to Galterra to resupply before my long journey."

Saida climbed out of bed, still in her dirty tunic and white pants, then gathered her boots from the floor. "Really? You were quite insistent on running the other way only last night."

"I changed my mind." She watched as Saida hurried toward the door. "Where are you going?"

"To the latrine if you must know."

Elmerah nodded. If the girl was trying to flee, she could find her again. They were going to the same place now, after all, and the fastest way was the Emperor's Path. She'd need to find a cloak somewhere first though. Perhaps she could search through the innkeep's belongings while he was busy preparing the morning meal he'd mentioned. In fact, she would be wise to obtain something to conceal herself before then, if militia men would be visiting. While the large clans of the Arthali had been exiled, it wasn't illegal for a single witch to step foot in the Empire, but most acted like it was. Things would only be worse in Galterra, but if her sister was somehow surviving, she could too.

Her mind made up, she quickly donned her boots, then left the small room in search of a cloak.

Saida

SAIDA STOOD AT THE TOP OF THE STAIRS, WONDERING IF what Elmerah had said was true. She could hear the militia men below, taking their morning meal while speaking amongst themselves. If the innkeep was to be believed, they were on the lookout for the Akerri . . . but the innkeep had also warned her and Elmerah against being seen. Would these men truly attack her for being a Faerune elf? Her people had been welcomed in the Capital just three seasons prior. Was it all an act to ensure the trade treaties were signed?

Clinging to the hem of her white tunic, she shook her head. The moon embroidery would give her away as a priestess. Surely these men wouldn't dare harm one of her status.

She took a step down the stairs.

"I wouldn't do that if I were you."

She whipped around to find the cloaked man from the

night before. "W-what do you want?" she gasped, her heart-beat strangling her words.

"Nothing," the man replied. He still wore his cowl, though with daylight streaming in through the window below, she could see the outline of his strong jaw, a well-formed nose, and light colored eyes.

With a smirk, he walked past her. "Just cautioning you. I'd find a hood to wear, and keep your head down. Your kind might be welcomed down South, but old hatreds linger in the Capital."

With that, he was gone, disappearing into the common room. A moment later, the front door opened and shut. After a momentary silence, the militia men resumed their conversation.

Something plunked on her shoulders and she nearly screamed.

"Wear this," Elmerah instructed, straightening the cloak she'd unceremoniously tossed upon her.

She turned to see Elmerah already hidden within her own stolen cloak. It was charcoal gray, and in far better condition than the ratty tan fabric she'd given her. "Will they truly attack us?"

Elmerah shrugged. "Perhaps. You, they would hold for ransom. Me," she smirked, "they would beat into a bloody pulp just to prove their breeches aren't filled with empty space. Well, they would *try* at least. I, however, would prove that's exactly what their breeches are filled with." She tugged Saida's hood over her head. "Now let's go."

Saida's stomach growled. "What about food? We'll need supplies if we are to survive."

Elmerah patted a satchel hanging from her opposite

shoulder. "This will see us to the Capital. After that, you are on your own."

She glared at Elmerah's back as she flounced down the stairs, then at the pause in the militia men's conversation, quickly hurried after her.

She reached the common room to find two of four men had risen from their seats, and were moving to block the door.

"I told you," the innkeep grumbled from her left, "you should have left before the sun."

A few paces ahead of her, Elmerah placed her hands on her hips, draping her cloak like the wings of a raven. "Can I assist you, gentlemen?"

Saida wasn't sure how the innkeep knew they were militia men. They wore no uniforms, just clean breeches and linen shirts, topped by heavy coats. Perhaps it was the weapons at their belts that gave them away, short swords on the right, and sword-breakers on the left.

"We're looking for the Akkeri," one of the men near the door stated. "Now kindly remove your hoods and we'll allow you to be on your way."

"First," Elmerah said, lifting a finger into the air, "you know very well we are not Akerri." She moved her hand toward her face, "my skin is far from sickly and mottled like the underbelly of a wyrm, and as you see, I am diurnal."

"Remove the hood," the man said again, "and you can be on your way."

"You didn't make that other traveler remove his hood," Saida accused, stepping forward. "Why hinder us?"

"Two of my men went after him," one of the men still seated explained. He leaned back in his chair, clearly bored.

"Is that my cloak?" the innkeeper asked from behind them. "Hey!"

Her face burning with a blush, Saida walked toward the door past Elmerah.

"Hey!" the innkeep said again.

"Oh bloody pig filth," Elmerah growled, tossing back her hood.

The innkeep had come around the bar, and now tugged at Saida's cloak.

"What do we do?" she hissed, bunching her hands around her cloak at her shoulder and tugging back.

Elmerah whirled on the four men, now all on their feet and slowly approaching.

"I'll need to see your papers," one of the men said, his eyes on Elmerah. "You look a bit *dark* to be from the Capital."

"And you look a bit stupid to be carrying a sword," she spat. She hooked a nearby chair with her foot and flung it at the man who'd spoken.

He shrieked and dove aside, and the chair thwacked against the front door before clattering to the floorboards.

She crossed her arms like she hadn't just flung a chair with enough force to knock a man unconscious. "And it's no longer illegal to be Arthali."

The innkeep had loosened his hold on Saida's cloak and backed away. "Take what you stole," he grumbled, "just don't destroy my inn."

"Stole?" the man who'd lounged so casually asked. "Why thank you for such a lovely excuse." Stalking toward them, he drew his sword.

"Why does this always happen to me?" Elmerah sighed, then withdrew her stolen cutlass.

Things were about to get ugly. Saida glanced around for a weapon. While she was trained in hand to hand combat, with her size she was much more proficient with a staff. The room erupted into motion around her.

She raced toward a table, grabbing the only weapon she could see, a pewter mug, then flung it at the militia man who'd lunged for her. It hit him right between the eyes, causing a rather stupid expression moments before he hit the ground.

The next thing she knew, a full satchel was sailing toward her. "Get outside and meet me on the road!" Elmerah shouted.

She caught the satchel and hurried toward the door, sparing a glance for Elmerah fighting off three men at once. She debated assisting her, but she'd proven the previous day she could fend off a few armed men all on her own. She kicked the door open and hurried outside, clutching the satchel against her chest.

She almost instantly skidded to a halt.

The cloaked man was standing right in front of her. He leaned around her, peeking into the inn as something slammed against the wall. Before she could react, he grabbed her shoulder and tugged her aside. A chair shot out the door and bounced across the dirt path.

"Do you think she needs any help?" he asked, his hands still on her shoulders.

"No," she muttered, tugging away from him. She hurried past the broken chair toward the main road. She'd wait in the woods for Elmerah, and if she didn't show up . . . well, she was probably better off continuing toward the Capital on her own.

Luckily, the man didn't follow her.

CHAPTER FOUR

Elmerah

"I didn't *need* your help," Elmerah grumbled to the man beside her. She limped down the rutted dirt road, favoring her left ankle. Now where was that blasted elf girl with her supplies?

"Yes," the man replied, "I imagine you had them right where you wanted them."

She glared at him, though the side of his cowl obscured his line of sight toward her. He'd walked in just as one of the militia men had his sword at her throat. She'd underestimated their training, and had overestimated her level of recovery from the previous day's escapades. She hadn't been able to summon a lick of magic.

"Why would you help someone like me anyway?" she muttered. "Most men would rather fight me, or run the other way."

"Arthali may not be overly common in the Capital, but

I've run into them further north. Some regions have put old prejudices aside more than others."

She hadn't been north to the Draiderin Province in ages. Perhaps that was where Rissine was hiding, running slaves through the Capital to be shipped to other areas of the continent. "Well you have my thanks, but I'm fine now, so you can be on your way." She scanned the tall pines for signs of Saida. By now, she was quite sure the little whelp had made off with her supplies.

"I *am* on my way," he gestured to the road ahead. "I'm traveling to the Capital to meet an old friend."

"Of course you are," she sighed. She narrowed her gaze to the distance where three men had come to view, short swords on their right hips, and sword breakers on their left.

"Ah," the man walking to her right observed, "I imagine they're on their way to check in with the other patrol. You know, the ones you left bloody and beaten on the floor of that inn."

"Well *you* beat one of them," she growled, "and two others were allegedly sent after you."

Not waiting for a response, and hearing the men ahead shouting their way, she darted off the road and into the woods. She ran through the trees, hoping to escape *questioning*.

She sighed loudly as the annoying man caught up to her, casually weaving around trees as he jogged at her side. That blasted cowl was still up, obscuring his face from her.

He smirked at her as they ran. "Are you a wanted criminal or something?"

She darted around a tree, careful to not slip on the slick moss covering the loamy earth. The men wouldn't bother chasing them far into the deep woods. Most men wouldn't risk running into Fossegrims or Trolls. It was safer on the path.

"You know very well why I must run," she panted.

"They probably would have let you pass if you would have simply removed your hood."

She skidded to a halt. The men were shouting for them to come back and show themselves, but were not following.

Cowards.

She turned toward her stalker. "How long were you watching me?"

His gaze on the surrounding woods, he shrugged. "You came downstairs just moments after I did. I was still outside when you decided to challenge those men with your charming bravado."

Now she *really* wanted to see his face, if only to slap it. "I will not be treated as inferior simply because a man thinks he can order me about."

The sunlight hit his face enough to reveal his smirk, though his eyes were mostly shadowed. "They are the Emperor's Militia. They treat *everyone* as inferior. Now we should continue on before those men realize their cowardice is showing."

"There is no *we*," she growled, stalking further into the woods. She'd traverse the border of the deeper forest for a time, then make her way back to the Emperor's Path. With Saida missing, she'd be a little hungry by the time she reached the Capital, but she'd survive.

Not long after she'd made her choice, she caught sight of something white through the trees.

"There you are!" Saida called out, hurrying toward them.

Elmerah winced at the volume of her voice, but waited patiently for Saida to reach them. "I was waiting further up the road, but when I saw more militia men I thought it best to hide—" she turned her gaze to the man standing a few paces behind Elmerah, as if just realizing his presence.

Elmerah held her hand out for the satchel. "You shouldn't go running and shouting around these woods, girl. You might get eaten."

Her expression now wary, she handed Elmerah the satchel. At least she'd kept her hood over her ears. The ugly tan fabric made her look even paler than usual.

Elmerah slung the satchel over her shoulder then started walking, her boots hissing across lichen and soggy pine needles.

Saida hurried to her side, leaning in toward her shoulder. "Why is he following us?" she whispered.

She shrugged. "Maybe he's looking for new friends." She pulled a shriveled apple from the satchel, offered it to Saida, then withdrew another for herself.

"Don't I get an apple for saving your life?" the man behind them questioned.

"No." She took a bite of the mealy apple, giving it a few light chews before forcing it down her throat. There hadn't been much else in the storeroom she'd raided, other than some rock-hard bread and more of the turnips they'd *enjoyed* in their soup the previous night.

"What is your name?" Saida questioned, glancing back at the man.

"Don't engage the madman," Elmerah lectured.

"Alluin," he replied, ignoring her comment. "And I must say, I'm quite surprised to see one of the Moonfolk traveling on her own, and a priestess no less."

Elmerah glanced at Saida covered fully in her cloak, then

realized Alluin had seen them the previous night, though they were yet to really see *him*.

She whirled on him, hand on the pommel of her cutlass, partially hidden under her gray cloak. "You've made it clear you know what we both are, now either tell us what you want, or be on your way."

Finally, he removed his cowl, revealing rich brown hair well past his shoulders, vibrant green eyes, and artfully pointed ears.

"A Valeroot elf?" Saida questioned.

Of course he was one of the Forest Children, Elmerah thought. What was one more elven thorn in her side?

He nodded in response to Saida's question. "Yes, and if the two of you hope to enter the Capital, you'll need my help."

"We do not need, nor want your help," Elmerah snapped.

"Oh?" he asked, his eyebrow raised. "Then you have traveling papers? You know the militia will ask for them at the gates."

She glowered. It had been so many years since she'd been to the Capital, she'd forgotten she'd need papers until the militia man had asked for them.

Apple still in hand, she crossed her arms. "And how do you intend to *help* us?"

He crossed his arms, mirroring her. "I know another way into the city."

"And what will it take for you to show us?"

He grinned. "Just a bit of kindness, and a bit of *food*. I didn't have time for a morning meal, and it's a long walk to the Capital."

She chucked her partially eaten apple at him, hoping it

would smack him in the face, but his hand darted out and caught it.

He took a bite, then gestured roughly northward. "Shall we?"

She turned and continued walking. If this elf knew a secret way into the Capital, perhaps he knew other things about the less legal goings on. Perhaps he even knew Rissine. She wanted to find her older sister sooner rather than later so she could return to her swamp in peace. The elves could accompany her as long as they proved useful, and no longer.

Saida

SAIDA WALKED ALONG BESIDE ELMERAH, HER BACK STIFF with nerves that had only grown as the sky grew dark. Her parents had told her of the Woodfolk. They were sly tricksters, and could not be trusted. In fact, they were almost as bad as the Akkeri, except they didn't worship the dark goddess Ilthune. Alluin was probably planning on robbing them, or selling them out to the militia.

Of course, he had gone back into the inn to aid Elmerah, while she'd fled into the woods, so maybe not.

"We should veer east here," Alluin instructed.

They'd been traveling along the edge of the deeper woods for some time now, and she could hear distant workers and animals on the farms leading up to the gates. The Capital had to be near, though she could not see the walls through the dense trees.

"Why?" Elmerah questioned.

"If you go anywhere near the gates, you'll be detained.

When the militia learns you have no papers, you will be turned away. I'd rather not waste any time with that. I can show you another way into the city, then we can all be on our way."

Saida watched as Elmerah turned toward him, more cranky than she'd been at any point on their journey thus far, *including* their time on the pirates' ship. "I wasn't asking why we should avoid the gates. I'm not daft. I was asking why we should veer *here*." She gestured to the shadowy woods. "Are you sure you're not taking us off to rob us? I cannot fathom why you'd go so far out of your way for a mealy apple and bread hard enough to crack teeth."

Alluin looked them both up and down, his green eyes glinting with mischief as they lingered on Elmerah's coin purses partially visible beneath her cloak. "While that is a thought, I don't quite like my odds. I saw what you did to those men at the inn, and knowing your race, I imagine you have more tricks up your sleeve than flinging chairs." He gestured eastward. "Now if you don't mind, I'd like to be out of these woods before nightfall. The things out here won't care a lick about your coin."

With a heavy sigh, Elmerah turned in the direction he'd gestured, and Saida followed, noting the sound of running water nearby.

"Is there a river?" she asked after a time, her throat parched. Elmerah had only procured a single water skin, and it hadn't lasted long.

"It's a manmade waterway," Elmerah explained. "It spans the perimeter of the Capital. Surely you saw it on your previous visit?"

Saida was glad the growing darkness hid her blush.

She'd been in a covered carriage when they'd entered the city, and had spent most of her stay within the central castle.

"Speaking of the waterway," Elmerah began before Saida could think of a reply, "how do you propose we get past it and into the city if we're not using the gates?" She stopped and turned toward Alluin.

"You'll see," he said simply.

"I don't like this," Saida muttered, closing in against Elmerah's side as Alluin ventured ahead.

Elmerah side-stepped away. "Do you want to enter the city or not?"

She widened her eyes at Elmerah's tone. "You really wouldn't know camaraderie if it bit you on the bottom, would you?"

"Not all of us were raised within the shelter of an elven temple."

"Speak for yourself!" Alluin called back. "I for one have spent a great deal of time in temples."

"Why do I sincerely doubt that?" Elmerah growled.

Saida rubbed her tired eyes. This journey couldn't end soon enough.

Her dragging feet kicked into something hard, yet brittle feeling. She moved to kick it completely out of her way, then yipped in surprise. The bone could have belonged to an animal, but there was something distinctly . . . human about it.

Noticing her hesitation, Elmerah marched back toward her. She kicked the bone, peering down at it in thought, then scanned the surrounding ground.

"Is that a human bone?" Saida asked, her voice hitching in panic. The bone appeared aged, not from someone freshly killed, but still, if some murderer was hiding his victims out here . . .

"Look," Elmerah pointed as Alluin joined them.

Saida followed her outstretched finger. Nearby was a patch of brambles, partially obscuring a circle made out of palm sized stones. Within the circle were more human bones. A shiver went up her spine.

Alluin took a step toward the circle. "The Akkeri, I'd imagine. We shouldn't touch anything."

Elmerah walked past him. Reaching the circle, she kicked one of the stones out of place. "You don't know that this was the Akkeri." She stepped into the circle, kicking aside a bundle of partially burnt, dried herbs that had been left beside a pile of glistening red . . . parts, now going gray from sitting in the open air.

"This is clearly death magic," Alluin argued. "Perhaps necromancy."

Elmerah snorted. "And the Akkeri are not the only race skilled in such arts. This close to the city, it could have been anyone."

"There have been Akkeri attacks on some of the farms," Alluin explained. "They even tried to get into the city. That's why there are so many militia men on patrol."

"Does it really matter who did this?" Saida asked, her voice strained. "Shouldn't we make our way into the city? It will be full dark soon, and I don't want to be here to meet any Akkeri *or* necromancers." She swallowed the lump in her throat. No, she did not want to be *anywhere* near the site of a dark ritual in the pitch black night.

Elmerah perused the circle a moment longer, then nodded, turning her gaze to Alluin. "You better not have anything to do with this," she gestured downward. "If you try to sacrifice us to some dark god, you'll wish I'd killed you quickly." She stomped out of the circle, paying no mind to what she trampled.

It was clear to Saida now that she had taken up with a madwoman.

"You're the Arthali here," Alluin quipped. "If anyone is in danger of being sacrificed, it's *me*."

He turned and continued walking in the direction they'd been headed, though Saida didn't miss the new stiffness to his shoulders. The ritual site had made him nervous. It made *her* nervous too, but she wasn't the one who'd led them right past it. Had he truly not noticed it, or had he simply been hoping they wouldn't?

Elmerah

FULL DARK HAD FALLEN BY THE TIME ALLUIN STOPPED walking. Elmerah had kept an eye out for any more signs of necromancy, but had seen none. While she was suspicious of Alluin's intentions, she was far more curious about the small cave he'd led them to.

"There's no way I'm going in there," Saida balked. "He'll kill us as soon as we're trapped."

Elmerah snorted. The girl had some self-preservation instincts after all. "You go first. If you meet your end, I will avenge you."

Saida glared at her. Maybe she wasn't *that* naive either.

"If you're worried," Alluin interrupted, standing near the inky black cave entrance, "I'll go first."

"So you can spring the trap as soon as we enter?" Saida hissed.

He sighed. "Truly, what happened to you women to make you so distrusting? In case you haven't realized, I'm risking my neck even showing you this place. For all I know, you'll run off and report its existence to the militia."

Saida crossed her arms. "Not if we're dead."

Elmerah flinched at the sound of a branch breaking not far off. They really did need to get out of these blasted woods. It would soon be hunting hour for some of the larger creatures, and the three of them would be ideal prey.

She sighed. "I'll go in." She turned to Saida. "If he makes a move, shout." She walked toward the cave, its top lip not much taller than her. Before she entered into the darkness, she aimed a steady glare at Alluin.

He lifted his hands in surrender. "I won't move, I swear it. There are lanterns deeper inside. Be a sweet peach and fetch one."

Her glare deepened, then she turned and stepped into the complete blackness of the cave. She felt at least a shred of magic returning to her, and she had her cutlass. If someone, or *something*, attacked, she'd at least take them down with her.

The stone beneath her boots was slick with moisture. The same moisture made the air dense and uncomfortable to breathe. Her stomach clenched. She hated caves and underground passages at the best of times.

This was not the best of times.

Sensing no imminent attack, she ventured further into the cave, groping along in the darkness until her hands hit solid stone. She continued feeling her way along the wall until her fingertips grazed a wooden shelf mounted straight into the stone, then across cool metal and glass. A lantern. Now to figure out how to light it.

She felt her way down the lantern to the small shelf it sat upon, then smoothed her fingers across until she found a fire-striker. A loud groan of metal made her jump, dropping the fire-striker. It clattered across the cave floor, bouncing several times before landing somewhere far off. *Wonderful.*

Not liking how suddenly the groaning metal sound had come and gone, she focused what little magic energy she had gathered onto the lantern, willing a small flame to life.

Smoke hit her nostrils, then the tiniest hint of flame illuminated the lantern's wick. With a final push that left her sweating, she forced the flame to life.

Once she had light, her shoulders relaxed. She lifted the lantern and peered around the cave. It was mostly just a long, empty space. Another lantern rested upon a lower shelf . . . with three more fire-strikers.

Sucking her teeth in irritation, she crept further into the cave until she reached the end where a grated metal gate was mounted into the wall. Past it was empty darkness, but she had a feeling these tunnels went on for a while. The metal groaning she'd heard before must have been a gate further in, which meant someone might soon be headed her way.

Having seen enough, she turned and left the cave.

She reached the entrance to find Saida and Alluin huddled shoulder to shoulder just outside.

She smirked. "Afraid of the dark?"

"Yes," Alluin replied, "and I'd be a fool not to be. Can we go inside now?"

She nodded. "I imagine you have a key to that gate?"

"You imagine right."

Elmerah turned and led the way back through the cave

until they reached the gate. "I heard another gate opening deeper in. Someone might be headed this way."

Alluin nodded as he searched his breeches pockets, presumably for the key. "This path is often used to get people in and out of the city . . . for a price."

"Are you taking us through a smuggler's path?" Saida hissed.

Alluin, knelt to put the key in the lock. "Would it matter?"

She snorted. "At this point, I suppose not."

The lock turned over, and Alluin pulled the gate outward, gesturing for Elmerah to walk through.

"I think *not*."

He sighed. "Can I at least have the lantern?"

She shook her head. She wasn't about to get locked in a dreary, moist cave, nor was she about to have him run off with their only source of light.

"So untrusting," he tsked, then walked through ahead of them.

Elmerah gestured for Saida to go next, then finally walked through herself. She waited while Alluin shut the gate and locked it once more, fighting the feeling of panic in her chest. The only thing worse than underground caverns were underground caverns with gates that locked you inside.

With the gate locked, Alluin began to lead the way deeper in, but soon stopped to look back at her. "If you refuse to relinquish the lantern, might you at least walk by my side?" His gaze flicked to Saida and her oddly reflective eyes, then back to her. "*Some* of us can't see in the dark."

"Fine," she huffed, stepping forward. Though the ground was still slick with moisture this far in, it was smooth and easy to traverse. She could hear a steady stream of water somewhere within the cave, and sincerely hoped there would be no swimming in her near future.

Eventually they reached another gate, though there'd been no sign of other people. Perhaps what she'd heard had been someone going in ahead of them, not coming out. "Where exactly does this lead?" she asked as Alluin knelt to unlock the second gate.

"There's a small area where goods, and sometimes people are stored," he explained, opening the gate. "We'll pass a guard before we reach that place, and there will be guards on the other end too, where it lets out into a house."

"So you *are* a smuggler then," she stated blandly, following him through the gate.

"In a way," he replied vaguely.

Elmerah caught Saida's eye as she walked through the gate.

Saida shrugged, apparently just as perplexed as she.

Alluin locked the second gate, then they continued onward.

By this point, Elmerah had no idea what she was walking into, nor what she'd find in Galterra if she actually made it out the other side.

When she finally found Rissine, she had better have an excellent excuse for having her kidnapped . . . not that Elmerah would listen.

Alluin

ALLUIN KNEW HE WAS TAKING A RISK BRINGING THE TWO women through the tunnels, but he was no fool. Judging by her garb, which was now wisely covered by a cloak, Saida was a Faerune priestess. The Faerune elves never traveled in these parts alone, unless they were exiles, which he doubted Saida was. Did her people know their trade treaties were about to be tossed to the wind?

Once again, he doubted it. She seemed to be lost, with no idea what she should do next. It would be difficult to see her returned to her people, but if he could convince her to trust him, he could send word to the Faerune elves . . . word they might actually believe if it wasn't straight from Valeroot lips.

He flexed his fingers, belying his nerves as they approached the guard standing under a lone hanging lantern at the next gate. He hoped Elmerah would keep her big mouth shut. If he was unsure about Saida, he was utterly perplexed by the Arthali woman. While there were other Arthali within the city, they tended to keep to the slums. Elmerah did *not* seem the *slum* type.

The guard, a tall elf with thin gray hair named Merley, looked them up and down, his steel-gray eyes finally settling on Alluin. "I hope you have a worthwhile excuse for bringing strangers through these tunnels," he grumbled.

He was glad the women both had their hoods tugged up. In the low light, they would be difficult to identify.

"Trust me, the boss will understand."

Merley nodded, taking Alluin at his word, as expected. He unlocked the gate with a different key than the one Alluin possessed, opened it, then stepped aside.

Alluin had to crouch to make it through the narrow walkway, then straightened into a much more comfortable space. Beds lined one wall, still composed of solid stone though they were near the cavern's end, and a small bar well-stocked with various drinks and other supplies took up the other. The room was currently void of inhabitants, though at times it would be packed. A few burning lanterns hinted someone had passed through recently.

"What in Ilthune is this place?" Elmerah asked, reaching his side.

Saida stood nearby, silently observing their surroundings.

"It doesn't matter," he explained. "Through that door is the house I mentioned. We'll pass two more guards, then you'll be free to do as you please within the city."

Her dark eyes narrowed in suspicion.

He supposed he couldn't blame her. Arthali still alive after the exile were dealt a poor hand in life. She likely trusted no one, because no one had *ever* trusted her . . . except, apparently, Saida.

"So you'll just let us leave? Just like that?" Elmerah asked, lifting her hand into the air. "You do not fear we'll speak of this place?"

He smirked. "I find it highly unlikely you'll be reporting to the emperor or his militia any time soon." Though she *could* . . . but there were people in place ready to dissuade any who posed the threat of a search.

"Let's get out of here," Saida muttered. "I need to reach the castle."

Alluin did his best not to balk. Perhaps she *did* know what she was doing, but then why would a lone Faerune elf want to reach the castle?

Elmerah glanced at Alluin, then back to Saida. "We can discuss that *later,* away from prying elven ears."

Alluin sucked his teeth. Cursed Arthali.

"This way ladies," he gestured to the wooden door at the other end of the room.

He followed Elmerah as she led the way, then held out his hand for her lantern. "You won't need that the rest of the way."

There was that suspicious glare again.

Finally, she handed him the lantern, which he extinguished and set aside, then knocked on the wooden door. A moment later, it opened outward, revealing an elf twice as muscled as Merley. Alluin couldn't quite recall his name, though the elf clearly recognized him. He gave a nod and stepped aside.

Alluin lead the way up a narrow set of wooden stairs, barely lit by two sconces in the wall. He reached the top, then knocked on the trap door above him, which was opened by another nameless guard who looked each of them up and down as they ascended into the basement of a large house, lit by several more sconces.

Elmerah crossed her arms and gave him that suspicious look again. Perhaps he'd have to be more wary of her than he'd originally thought. He wouldn't be surprised if he found her snooping around the next day.

With a heavy sigh, he led the two women to another set of stairs up into the house. They passed a few more faces vaguely familiar to him, though none stopped to question them. Soon enough, they were back out in the cold night. It was early enough in the evening that people would still be milling about on the main street, but the narrow alley in which they stood appeared deserted.

Elmerah crossed her arms again, though this time he suspected it was from the cold. The cloak she wore was thin, but with the coin at her belt she'd have no trouble acquiring something heavier. "Well," she began, "I suppose we owe you our thanks."

He wondered if he should simply let them go, or offer to escort them further. He needed to keep an eye on Saida, but he might be better off simply tracking her for a while to learn her true intentions. "You could also offer me an apology. You've thoroughly questioned my character today."

She snorted, then shoved a lock of black hair back into her hood. "And it is still in question, so you have my thanks, but not my apology." She turned to Saida. "Shall we? I don't want to waste my efforts by letting you get murdered on your first night in the city."

Alluin couldn't help a small smile. The Arthali woman might have been crude, but at least she was honest.

Saida nodded. "I suppose one more night together won't kill me . . . hopefully."

With that, both women gave him a polite nod, then walked away. He waited for several heartbeats, then took to the shadows and followed.

CHAPTER FIVE

Elmerah

After another restful night at a far nicer inn, Elmerah felt some of her magic returning. She'd fallen out of practice during the years hiding in her swamp. She hoped next time it would come back to her more quickly, that she'd start absorbing magic from the earth like a sea sponge, but she wasn't sure.

She took a deep breath of thin morning air, then looked at Saida standing next to her in front of the inn. She could admit, if only to herself, that the elf girl had grown on her a bit, but it was time to part ways. She didn't need the girl becoming any more involved with Rissine than she already was.

"I suppose you can find your way to the castle?" she asked cooly. "Be sure to keep your hood up."

Saida nodded, glancing around the street in front of the inn, quickly filling with people. Mostly humans, but also a few Forestfolk like Alluin. There were occasional hints of more olive skin like Elmerah's, though none looked as purely Arthali as she.

"Well then," she muttered. "Good luck." She turned to leave.

"Where will you go?" Saida's voice cut through the din of early morning greetings and conversation.

Elmerah turned back to her. "I have a bit of information I'd like to gather, then I'll head back to the swamps of Outer Crag."

Saida nodded at her explanation. "Well, if you ever come to—" she cut herself off, then mouthed *Faerune*.

Elmerah nodded. "It's unlikely I'll find myself there, but if I do, perhaps I'll seek you out."

Saida nodded again, then turned and walked away, quickly disappearing amongst the bustling crowd.

Elmerah felt a little pang of loneliness, which she quickly pushed away. She needed to find Rissine. She turned and made her way down the street, keeping her head down and her hood up. No one was likely to bother her in such a bustling area, but once she reached the slums things would change. She'd have to travel through dark alleys filled with vagrants and criminals all too willing to look the other way while she was robbed or beaten, because information about Rissine would surely be found at the end of one such alley.

Saida

Saida had the distinct feeling she was being watched. She glanced over her shoulder repeatedly, but was overcome by the chaos of the crowd. She needed to reach a more quiet area. Then she'd be able to see if someone was indeed watching her, or if it was just her nerves overcoming her senses.

She glanced again, then had her shoulder slammed painfully.

"Move!" a man growled, barely even looking at her.

Rubbing her sore shoulder, she ducked her head and cut across the crowd toward the nearest intersection, then plastered her back against the stone foundation of a shop. Now that she was out of the crowd, she took a moment to scan the people heading this way and that. Most were dressed modestly in muted wool and linen, though she spotted a few flashes of fine silks and glittering gowns. The silks were usually accompanied by at least one armed man, ready to protect his mistress should her day of shopping be interrupted.

She let out a heavy sigh, wondering if she could stop anyone long enough to gain directions to the castle. So far, her impression of the Capital stood in stark contrast to the serene streets of Faerune. If someone bumped into her there, they would bow and beg forgiveness.

She watched the crowd for a moment more, then gave up on the idea of asking for directions. The castle was stationed near the center of the city, that much she knew, so perhaps if she continued heading in the opposite direction of the gates, she'd catch a glimpse of it.

She'd turned to walk further down the intersection, away from the main crowd, when the spot between her shoulder blades began to itch. She was *definitely* being watched. She might not have the innate magic of the high priests and priestesses, but her instincts were strong enough to at least tell her that.

She halted for a moment, debating rejoining the main crowd . . . but that was surely where the watcher lurked. With a shaky breath, she tensed her legs, steeled her gaze, and ran. A few people glanced at her as she sped by, her boots barely making a sound on the cobblestones. She thought she heard the gentle tap of footsteps aways behind her, matching her pace. Someone capable of following her a great distance if the grace of their footfalls was any indicator.

A woman walked out from a shop with a two-handled basket of apples. Saida saw her too late. She tried to dart around her, but clipped the basket with her hip, sending green apples flying everywhere.

"My apologies!" she shouted as she spun to right herself. She resumed her run before the final apple hit the cobblestones.

"Come back here!" the woman shouted, followed by a loud screech.

Saida glanced back long enough to note a cloaked man skidding to a halt right before he would have trampled the apples. She turned forward and continued running, darting down every new turn she could find, silently thanking her apple-carrying savior.

Eventually she reached a dark backstreet where she stopped to rest against a stack of large wooden storage crates. The crates shielded her from sight in the direction she'd come, though she was quite sure she'd lost her watcher at the site of the apple incident.

"Are you lost?" a melodious voice inquired.

She whipped around, then her jaw dropped. A woman with alabaster skin and gray eyes approached. Her white-blonde hair fell in a shimmery curtain to her waist, not fully hiding the pointed tips of her ears. She'd expected a lot of things in the city, but one of her people wasn't one of them.

"What are you doing here?" Saida gasped. She didn't recognize the woman from Faerune, and she wore the muted linens that seemed common in the city, but she was most definitely a pure-blood Faerune elf.

"I own this shop." The elf gestured to the back door from which she'd emerged. "I was coming to move my shipment inside." She patted the crates.

"You own a shop here?" She knew she sounded like an idiot, but she was utterly baffled. Why would this woman live in the Capital, unless . . . "You're an exile?" she gasped.

The woman raised a blonde brow. "And you, apparently, are not. Still, it's been a long while since I met one of my kind. Why don't you help me with these crates, then we can have a meal together."

Saida shook her head, stepping back. It took a great offense to merit exile from Faerune. This woman was likely a murderer, or *worse*.

The woman sighed. "I live in exile because of my mother. *She* was the criminal. I was born here in Galterra."

Saida lifted a hand to her thundering heart. "My apologies. I'm a bit on edge. I'm trying to reach the castle." She looked at the elf more closely. She was clearly making no attempt to hide what she was, so . . . "Forgive me, but aren't you afraid to so openly show what you are? A friend of mine claimed such actions are risky."

"There are ways to protect oneself," she replied with a small smile. "Life for a lone elf is perhaps risky, but I have good . . . *friends*. I can introduce you to them if you like. I'm sure they'll help you find what you're looking for."

Saida clutched her cloak where it fastened near her

throat. She didn't quite like the way the woman said *friends*, but if they could help get her home . . .

The woman took a step toward her. "What is your name?"

She resisted the urge to step back. "Elmerah," she lied, giving the first name that popped into her head. She couldn't risk this elf recognizing her name and holding her for ransom. Any who knew the elves of Faerune well knew Saida Fenmyar would fetch a pretty penny.

The elf seemed surprised by her answer, but quickly recovered. "I'm Thera. Now come inside." she gestured to the still open door. "We'll have a nice meal, and talk about how to get you home."

She licked her dry lips. "Why would you assume I want to go home?"

Thera chuckled. "You're not an exile. Any Faerune elf not living in exile will always return to Faerune."

She supposed she was right. With a hesitant nod, she allowed Thera to guide her into the shop. She wasn't sure she trusted her new *friend*, but she could always run away later.

Elmerah

AFTER SEVERAL LONG HOURS OF QUESTIONING ANYONE who would listen, Elmerah returned to the inn where she and Saida had stayed the previous night. Her feet were tired and her belly was empty. She'd have a nice meal, a tankard of Galterran ale, and would resume her search after nightfall.

The door to the establishment was propped open, letting

in the balmy air enjoyed at the start of the growing season. She walked inside, barely glancing at the mostly empty tables as she headed toward the tired, slouched barkeep. She almost debated pulling back her hood in the quiet establishment, but decided against it. If Rissine was in the city, she didn't want to risk being found before she could figure out just what her sister was up to.

Reaching the barkeep, she placed two silver gulls on the rough wood in front of him. "A tankard of ale and whatever food you're serving."

He lifted his gaze, then stared at her face as if memorizing every detail.

"Is there an issue?"

He swiped the two coins from the bar into his waiting palm, then turned away.

"Dusty old sea crab," she muttered once he'd gone into the kitchen. She turned around to take a seat at the nearest table, then paused. She recognized that cowl. "Has Arcale cursed me? Why are you here?"

Alluin lifted his head from his palm at her words. He'd been slouched in the corner adjacent the door, escaping her initial notice.

He tapped the boiled leather tankard in front of him. "I've as much right to sit here as you."

With hands on hips, she looked him up and down. "Isn't it a bit early to be drinking ale?"

The barkeep chose just that moment to walk up behind her with a tankard of ale and plate of roasted fish and leeks, both of which he set on the bar beside her without a word before walking away.

"Isn't it a bit early to be drinking ale?" Alluin echoed.

With a sigh she retrieved her plate and tankard, then

approached his table, slumping into the wooden chair across from him. "So are you following me? Change your mind about selling me out to the militia?"

He drained the remnants of his tankard, then met her gaze. "You weren't the only one who left those men battered and bruised."

She glanced down at her unappealing fish, then reached for her tankard. "So what is it then? Why are you here?"

"Can a man not simply have a drink?"

"No," she snapped. "Not when the man was left an hour's walk from here, with plenty of other taverns in between. I don't believe in coincidences."

He traced his finger across the woodgrain on the table. "Perhaps my curiosity got the better of me, and now I'm wondering just what you're planning here in Galterra. Since I'm the one who let you in, that would make me responsible for any nefarious deeds you might commit."

She sucked her teeth. Of course he thought *she* was the one who was up to no good. Never mind that she was actually the victim, kidnapped from her cozy hut to be hauled across the ocean. "I didn't realize smugglers felt so much responsibility for a city's wellbeing."

"I'm not a smuggler."

"And I'm not here to commit nefarious deeds."

"Where's Saida?" he asked abruptly.

Did he really want her to punch him? "Why do you care?"

He placed his hands on the table and leaned back. "Are you always this suspicious?"

"Yes."

He sighed. "Fine, I was worried about her. A Faerune elf

left on her own in Galterra is sure to find trouble. Saida doesn't seem the type to join a guild."

"A guild?" she pressed, wondering what he meant.

"You really haven't been to Galterra in a while, have you?"

She shook her head. "It's been more than a few years."

"The slums are run by guilds," he explained. "Sort of a counterbalance to the militia. The larger guilds govern the streets, and offer certain protections to their own. Almost any elf, halfling, or Arthali in the city is a member of a guild. They wouldn't survive otherwise."

She sipped her ale, deep in thought. "So," she began, setting down her cup. "What guild are you part of? I imagine the *boss* I heard mentioned runs it?"

He hesitated at her question. Clearly she was making him uncomfortable. *Good.*

"That's none of your concern," he grumbled.

"And Saida is none of yours, though given that you must have followed us here last night, I'm surprised you're not off questioning *her*."

He didn't reply.

Realization dawned on her. "You lost her?" She grinned. "Some Valeroot elf you are. Aren't your people supposed to be excellent trackers?"

He grimaced. "Yes, and apparently Faerune elves are excellent . . . escapers."

She chuckled as she pulled her plate in front of her to start picking at her fish. "So tell me more of these guilds. Do their leaders have names?" *Guildmaster* seemed exactly like the type of occupation Rissine would enjoy.

He narrowed his eyes, clearly suspicious. "Some. Why does it matter? Are you hoping to join?"

She took a bite of her fish. It was too salty, but at least it was food. "Hardly," she answered as she chewed. "I'm actually looking for someone. I wouldn't put it past her to be involved with one of these . . . *guilds*."

He gestured to the barkeep for another ale, then turned back to her. "What's her name?"

She began absentmindedly mutilating her fish with her two-pronged fork while she debated her answer. He seemed harmless enough, and seemed to know a decent amount about the goings on in the slums, but he was most certainly trying to pluck information from her, for purposes unknown.

"Let's play a little game," she decided. "A question for a question."

He raised a brow at her from within the shadows of his cowl. "What makes you think I want information from you?"

"Well, you're still sitting here, aren't you?"

The barkeep arrived with a fresh tankard of ale. He took Alluin's offered coin, then stomped away.

Alluin took a sip, then set down his tankard. "Deal."

Saida

Saida sat in the back of the building nestled in a cushy chair with a cup of hot tea. Thera had left her to tend a customer up front in her textile shop. She could hear the murmur of voices in the next room, but she was unable to distinguish the words. Saida couldn't help but wonder how many textiles it would take to fill the large crates she'd helped carry inside, and how they could possibly be so heavy.

She had almost gained the courage to go back into the

storage room and take a look inside one of the crates, when Thera returned, shutting the interior door behind her.

"My apologies," she said as she sat across from her. "I didn't mean to leave you alone back here for so long."

Saida sipped her tea to hide her irritation. "Please don't apologize. I appreciate your kindness, but I really must head toward the castle if I hope to make it before dark."

Thera picked up her own cup from the nearby tray. "I fear I cannot in good conscience allow you to venture off alone. If you'll wait until tomorrow, I'll escort you to the castle myself. I have a few friends who will offer us protection."

Saida was growing increasingly sure she didn't want to meet these *friends*. Something wasn't quite right about Thera. She stood, then set down her empty cup. "Truly, I appreciate the offer, but I must go today. I've made it this far, I'm sure I'll be fine." She lifted a finger to her painfully throbbing brow. Was the room suddenly hotter than before?

She looked down at Thera. "I think I need some fresh air." She took a staggering step away, swaying on her feet. The room seemed to be moving.

"Now, now," Thera soothed, guiding her back to her seat. "You're clearly not well. You must rest."

Panic shot through her, exploding into tiny stars dancing across her vision. She forced her eyes to focus on Thera. "What was in that tea?" she rasped.

"Nothing fatal," Thera chuckled. "Now rest. My friends will be here soon."

Saida fought her heavy eyelids, though they seemed to be all she could feel. The rest of her body had gone numb. She couldn't move. She couldn't—

CHAPTER SIX

Saida

Someone was hovering over Saida when she awoke, but the room seemed too bright for her to focus. Or maybe it was just the inside of her head that was too bright. It felt like someone had driven a pick through her skull.

She squeezed her eyes shut, then opened them again, more slowly this time. Her vision came back in increments as her eyes adjusted to the room's lighting. It wasn't terribly bright after all, just a lantern and a few candles.

She focused on the lone woman in the room. Thick, dark hair, coiled into a long braid. Large eyes, the irises almost as dark as the hair. Olive skin, the same color as Elmerah's. "Who—" she croaked, swallowing to wet her dry throat. "Who are you?"

The woman straightened. She seemed as tall as Elmerah too, perhaps a bit taller. She wore a tight suede vest over a loose white blouse, and the hips of her breeches shimmered with small bells and jewels.

"I could ask you the same question," the woman replied, her full lips curving into a smile.

Saida tried to lift her hands, but something dug painfully into her wrists. She looked down to see she was tied to a wooden chair. Her feet were bound to the legs too. She glanced around, but did not recognize the room in which she sat. The plain wood walls gave nothing away.

She cleared her throat. "I'm Elmerah," she answered, figuring she'd be wise to stick with the same lie she'd given Thera.

The woman placed her hands on her hips. "How odd. I've been looking for an Elmerah, but you are not she. Thera was perplexed as well. Perhaps it's just coincidence, but I don't think so."

Saida tried to put the pieces together, but it felt like a drum circle was occurring inside her brain. Could this woman be looking for the same Elmerah she knew? It seemed likely. They looked similar enough to be sisters.

"I'm sorry," she began, wishing she at least had her hands free. "I don't think I know you, nor can I imagine any reason you'd be looking for me."

The woman's pleasant smile turned ugly. She placed a hand over each of Saida's wrists then leaned forward, grinding her bones against the chair arms. A wash of strong spices and herbs hit her nostrils as the woman leaned in even further. "Do not lie to me, girl. I know there was an elven priestess on that ship. Now *where* is my sister?"

Everything fell into place all at once. "You had something to do with us being taken, didn't you?"

The woman snorted, then straightened. "You're in no position to ask questions, girl. Tell me where my sister is and I'll let you go. I can always fetch another elf for my buyer."

Saida's stomach clenched. She was going to be sick. This woman wanted to *sell* her. "I don't know where she is," she answered honestly. "We parted ways."

The woman leaned in again, her movements too fast for Saida's bleary eyes to follow. "For your sake, I hope that's a lie. If you don't know where she is, I only have one use left for you, and you're *not* going to like it."

"I could help you find her!" she blurted. "I know where she might be."

"Tell me," the woman demanded.

Saida shook her head. "It would do you little good. Correct me if I'm wrong, but I get the feeling she would run if she saw you? Allow me to approach her while you lie in wait. Once you capture her, I get my freedom. Deal?"

The woman drummed her fingers over Saida's wrists. "Fine," she decided, "but be warned, you are now a tiny little minnow on my hook. If you forget your role, I'll feed you to the sharks . . . *literally*."

Saida's heart pounded in her throat, but she managed to nod. She saw no other choice. She only hoped Elmerah could forgive her.

Elmerah

ELMERAH LIFTED HER TANKARD TO HER LIPS, THEN scowled upon realizing it was empty. She peered across the table at Alluin, who seemed to be in a similar predicament. The windows had grown dark, and most of the tables were now filled, but the ale was still flowing and that was all that really mattered right now. At some point her hood had fallen back, but no one had given her any trouble . . . yet.

"So tell me truly," she slurred, lifting a finger to signal the barkeep, "can your kind really track your prey by scent?"

Alluin chuckled. "Yes, though sight is a more reliable tool."

She giggled. "So you're just like a dog then? Do you like to be scratched behind the ears?"

He scowled. "I wouldn't try it if I were you."

She waved him off. She knew she'd long since gotten any useful information out of him, but now she was a bit too drunk to do anything about it. He'd heard of a growing slave trade within the Capital, but did not know which guild was running it, nor had he heard of Rissine.

The barkeep appeared with more ale. He'd become a bit more friendly since he'd become the owner of nearly half the coin in Elmerah's purse. Luckily, she still had a second pouch hidden at the back of her belt beneath her cloak.

She sipped her fresh ale, then sighed. She really should have stopped sooner. She needed to find Rissine, then get out of Galterra before it was too late.

She turned her gaze back to Alluin, another snide remark on the end of her tongue, but he was looking right past her. She glanced over her shoulder, spotting a female Valeroot elf with shoulder length hair the same earthy brown as Alluin's, and with eyes just as green.

She turned back to him, but he was still staring at the girl. "Old lover?" she questioned.

He startled, then shook his head. "Sister, actually. If you really want to know about the slave trade, she's the one to ask. I can almost guarantee she's somehow involved."

Elmerah raised an eyebrow at him. "I take it you two don't get along?"

"Hardly," he huffed.

She leaned forward. "Call her over here," she tried to whisper, though her voice came out a bit louder than intended. "Let's hold her down and question her."

"Too late," he sighed, once again looking past her. "She's coming this way."

Elmerah turned to watch the elf girl's sauntering approach, flanked by two men, one another Valeroot elf and one human.

"Alluin," the girl purred, leaning her hands against the tabletop near Elmerah. "Are you actually out having fun? How . . . unusual."

Elmerah scooted her chair back to put the girl fully in her sights.

"And you are?" the girl questioned.

She smiled, though she had a feeling it probably looked more like a snarl. "I could be your new friend if you tell me what I want to know."

The girl stepped back, looking her up and down. "I'm not sure I want you to be my friend. Arthali are usually more trouble than they're worth."

Alluin sighed loudly. "Vessa, do you know anything about young girls being sold into servitude?"

Vessa's expression faltered. Perhaps Alluin would prove useful after all.

"I've heard a few rumors," she said casually, "nothing more."

The human half of Vessa's male escort shifted uncomfortably.

Elmerah watched him closely. There was no way she was

letting this trio get away. They could probably lead her right to Rissine.

If only the room wasn't spinning.

She stood, wedging herself between Vessa and the two men.

Vessa turned with her, trying to back away, but ended up trapped between Elmerah and the table.

She leaned in, knowing Vessa and the men were all furiously deciding whether or not she possessed the fearsome Arthali magic recorded in all the histories. "Now Vessa," she whispered. "I think we should be friends, because being my enemy is not good for one's health. All I need to know is where to find Rissine."

She audibly gulped.

Elmerah felt a hand on her upper arm through her cloak. She gave Alluin a warning look, willing him to step away. She was just seconds away from catching her sister's trail. She would *not* let it go.

"Rissine has a warehouse by the southern docks," Vessa blurted. "That's where she hides the girls when they first arrive. It's a huge warehouse with no windows, and a big lock on the door. You can't miss it."

"Vessa!" one of the men chided.

Elmerah lifted her hands in surrender and backed away. "Thank you Vessa. I'm glad we could be friends."

The men tugged Vessa away while she glared at Alluin, as if he were the one who'd made her speak.

Vessa rejoined her table, where her other *friends* were beginning to rise, their gazes all firmly locked on Elmerah.

"Something tells me we'd better go," Alluin muttered.

She nodded. Drunken bravado got her into trouble every

cursed time. She skirted around the table, edging toward the door.

She didn't wait for Vessa's friends to give chase, she had no doubt they would. She vaulted over an empty table and barreled out the door, followed by angry shouts.

She took a sharp left as soon as the night air closed around her, then sprinted down the main street, prepared to dart off as soon as an alley caught her eye. She flinched as footsteps raced up beside her, then relaxed when she realized it was Alluin.

Moments later, the angry shouts made their way out into the street, quickly spotting them judging by their change in tone.

"This way!" Alluin urged, shoving her into a narrow space between two buildings she would have otherwise passed right by.

The space was too narrow to run full out, but she managed to shimmy her way through, emerging into a pitch black back alley.

"Go right!" Alluin hissed, coming out of the space behind her.

She didn't question him, and instead continued running, her ale-filled belly protesting every step. She realized too late she was running full speed toward a dead end.

"Up on the crates," Alluin instructed, quickly mounting stacked storage crates against one of the adjacent walls of the dead end. He climbed them so effortlessly she had to stop and stare in awe for a moment.

"My mistake," she mused. "You're not a flea-ridden dog, you're an alley cat."

He looked down at her from atop the roof. "And you'll be a dead sow if you don't get up here."

She could hear their pursuers emerging from the narrow space behind them, so she didn't argue. She hopped up onto the crates, climbing onto the taller end of the stack before pulling herself up onto the roof.

"This way," Alluin instructed.

She followed him, cursing him all the while for being so graceful while drunk. Personally, she was ready to keel over.

He ran to the edge of the long roof, then crept across a thick wooden beam meant to hold the Capital's purple and white flag on festival days. It conveniently connected to the next building across the street.

She approached the beam, staring down at it dubiously. Alluin was already on the next roof.

"If I break my neck," she muttered, "I'm coming back to haunt you."

She placed her boot on the beam, careful not to look down beyond the beam itself. Barely breathing, she put one foot in front of the other. She could hear their pursuers climbing up the crates, but she doubted they'd have the manhood to follow her across the beam.

She exhaled a loud sigh of relief as she reached the next roof, then eyed Alluin. "You know, I'm quite sure I don't like you."

"The feeling is mutual. Now come this way."

He took off at a run again, and she followed, though at this point she was ready to turn around and face whoever had made it this far and greet them with her cutlass. Still, it was probably best to avoid a confrontation. If someone ended up dead, Vessa would likely have to explain to Rissine what had happened. If no one died, she'd likely keep her mouth shut and hope for the best. Elmerah wanted Rissine to be surprised when she showed up to throttle her.

Alluin swung down off the roof ahead of her onto a narrow walkway bordering the second story of the building. He obviously knew his way around, because she never would have spotted the barely visible edge of the walkway otherwise. She knelt and gripped the edge of the roof, then swung down after him. She nearly shrieked when he grabbed her and shoved her in through an open door.

Releasing her, he gently shut the door behind them, then held a finger to his lips.

One set of footsteps sounded across the roof above. She *really* wanted to see who'd had the guts to follow them across the beam, but instead she crouched down and waited.

A male voice shouted something unintelligible, then the footsteps retreated.

She breathed a sigh of relief, then peered across the small space at Alluin. Other than the two of them, there were only a few pieces of furniture covered in heavy sheets, and a staircase leading downward.

Once she was sure the person above wasn't coming back, she whispered, "What is this place? Or were we simply lucky enough to find an abandoned home at the right moment?"

He stood from his crouch. "My employer owns many buildings across the Capital. I've stayed here a few times."

"What would a smuggler want with an empty home in the middle of town?" She glanced around. "I don't see any goods."

He walked across the wooden floorboards and peered out the window facing the back alley. "I never said I was a smuggler."

"Well you didn't deny it." She leaned against the wall. The ale was wearing off, leaving her with a splitting headache. "So you're not a smuggler, but you have a secret way into the city, and your sister works for slavers."

He glared at her. "If you think for a second I condone my sister's actions—"

She held up a hand. "I don't, which is why I'm confused. If you're not after Faerune moonliquor or exotic slaves, why do you want Saida?"

He laughed. "You thought I was hoping to acquire moonliquor from Saida? That stuff is poison to anyone but the Faerune elves."

"Yes, poison," she chuckled, "but *fun* poison. If you were a smuggler, that's exactly what you'd want from a Faerune elf."

"But I'm not a smuggler."

She sighed. "No, you're not, and you're also avoiding the question. What do you want with Saida?"

He stepped away from the window and leaned against the adjacent wall. Though the room was mostly dark, there was enough moonlight to see his pensive expression. "I'll tell you what I want with Saida, if you tell me what you want with Rissine Volund."

Her jaw dropped. "So you *do* know who she is! You lied to me."

"I wanted to be sure you weren't part of her . . . flock."

Her face burned. Damn sly elves. "Tell me what you want with Saida, and I'll tell you what I want with Rissine."

He stared at her for several long moments, then answered, "You first."

She shook her head. "No."

He pushed off the wall and took a step toward her.

She bristled, ready should he choose to attack.

He sighed. "Look, you already know much more about

me than I do about you. You know about the secret tunnel and the storehouse. If you want to know more, you're going to have to give me a reason to trust you."

She gritted her teeth. She didn't like it, but she understood where he was coming from. If he betrayed her, she had little at stake. If she betrayed him, well, she already knew a very big secret.

"Rissine is my sister," she grumbled. "My full name is Elmerah Volund. We parted ways after our mother was killed, and haven't spoken in nearly a decade."

He didn't seem surprised by her explanation, but then again, there weren't many Arthali in Galterra, and she and Rissine looked a lot alike . . . or at least they used to. She had no idea what her sister looked like now.

"Why seek her out now?" he questioned.

"I didn't," she growled. "The snake-tongued witch had me kidnapped by pirates. That's how I met Saida. She was another victim. I've come to Galterra to make sure it doesn't happen again. I just want to live out my days in my swamp in peace."

"You live in a swamp?"

She glared. "Yes. It's *peaceful,* and now you know my secret. It's time to tell me yours."

He continued to watch her, as if debating telling her the truth.

She crossed her arms and tapped her foot. She'd give him a moment to decide, but if he chose wrong . . . well, she was not above beating the information out of him.

Finally, he asked, "Do I have your word that you are not part of the slave trade, nor will you ever be?"

"My role in the slave trade began and ended with my

kidnapping. Well, except for the boot I plan to shove against a certain slaver's face."

He took another step toward her. "If you breathe word of this to anyone, many lives will be at stake."

Her throat went dry in anticipation. She had a feeling she was about to learn another very big secret.

He stood just a single pace away. "I'm not a smuggler of goods," he explained, keeping his voice low, "but a smuggler of people. We've been helping elves out of the city, many of whom were caught up in the slave trade like you and Saida. They're sending word to the Valeroot clans that the trade treaties with the empire are about to fall through."

She blinked at him. She hadn't expected a secret *that* big. "How can you possibly know that?"

"We've been watching Rissine for a long time. She's not running a small-time operation. We believe she's in league with the emperor. He's shipping slaves to the East, and signing new treaties with the Dreilore and Nokken."

"But what about Faerune?" she hissed. "These treaties have kept the peace since the Arthali and Akkeri were exiled."

He shook his head. "I don't know. I can't say all that the emperor plans, but why keep these new treaties a secret from Faerune unless he plans to break the old ones?"

She took a steadying breath. "And Rissine is a part of this? Are you sure? She has allied herself with a man who detests our race?"

He nodded. "So you see why I had to be sure of this before telling you. I wanted to find Saida again to gain her trust, and send her with word back to Faerune. We've tried to send other messages, but the Faerune elves are untrusting, especially of my kin. Allying ourselves with one of their priestesses could prove invaluable, especially one of her standing."

"Her standing?" she questioned distantly, still in a state of shock.

He nodded. "I may be mistaken, but I believe she is the daughter of one of the high priestesses. Faerune is always ruled by six. Saida stands to take over her mother's role."

Elmerah leaned back against the wall, then slid against it to the floor. What in Ilthune had she gotten herself into? She looked up at him. "The contracts," she breathed.

"Contracts?"

"On the ship," she explained, "I found the contract with my name on it, signed by Rissine. That's how I knew I wasn't just taken by coincidence. There was a contract for Saida too, not just for a Faerune elf. Rissine requested her by name."

Alluin crouched in front of her. "But why would a slaver want to acquire the daughter of a high priestess?"

She shook her head. "I don't know, but we're going to find out."

CHAPTER SEVEN

Saida

S aida groaned as light hit her face. At first she thought she'd been moved somewhere with a window, then she realized a lantern was being held before her eyes.

She scowled at the woman dangling the lantern, now in focus. *Thera.* It was the first time she'd seen her since she'd been drugged. Although, in the pitch dark of her long night tied to the chair, she hadn't been able to see *anything*. "You should be ashamed," she rasped, "to so betray one of your people."

Thera retracted the lantern. "*My* people? I've never even been to Faerune, nor would I be allowed within the crystalline walls. Rissine has done more for me than the elves ever will. Now are you ready?"

"Ready for what?" Saida flexed her bound hands against the chair arms. Her bones were cold and achy. She'd hardly be in a fighting state when she was finally untied.

"To be bait," Thera explained. "You will help us lure in Elmerah, then you will be granted your freedom."

Oh yes, *that*. "Why do you want her? Do you intend to hurt her?"

"That is none of your concern," Thera snapped.

"Ah," Saida observed, "so you don't know either?"

Thera glared at her, though it had little effect. As far as Saida was concerned, Thera was *filth*. If her mother was truly exiled, it was for good reason. She had no justification for selling out her own kind.

Thera glanced over her shoulder to the room's dark back end. It was only then Saida noticed the two large, muscular men standing there.

"As you can see," Thera said, turning back to her, "any attempts at escape will only end in your misery. Play nice with me, and you'll not be harmed."

For some reason, she doubted that. Slavers had no honor. As soon as she helped them, they'd turn around and sell her to the highest bidder. "You swear you'll let me go after you have her?" she asked meekly, playing along.

Thera grinned. "Of course. We have no reason to betray you."

Saida would have laughed in her face if she wasn't so busy concocting a way to escape that wouldn't involve betraying Elmerah and using her as a distraction. Of course, Elmerah herself might be the solution. She'd seen her display of power on the ship, but suspected Elmerah had overextended herself, and needed time to recover. Hopefully she'd had long enough.

The two men stepped forward as Thera knelt and began tugging at the knots securing Saida's wrists to the chair.

She'd tried to tug at them herself most of the night, but had been unable to maneuver her hands to the base of the chair arms.

The ropes came free, leaving a stinging sensation at her wrists. Once both hands were free, she rubbed them together, hoping the feeling would return soon. The men stood near, watching her every move while Thera untied her feet.

Once they were free, one of the men tugged her up by her arm, hauling her to her feet.

Her bladder cramped painfully. "Um, I might need to use the latrine before we depart."

Thera stared at her as if she suspected a trick.

"Unless you'd like to walk around with an elf in wet breeches," Saida added.

Thera nodded at the man to release her arm, as her own hand took its place. "I'll take you. You need to change your clothes anyway. We don't need anyone gawking at the elven priestess."

She towed her to a closed door, opened it, then shoved Saida inside, closing the door behind her.

Saida had a moment of elation when she thought perhaps she'd been presented with an opportunity to escape, but it was quickly quashed. The natural light that had her momentarily excited filtered in through a window high up in the wall, far out of reach. The small latrine was sparsely furnished, with nothing she could move to stand on.

The door opened suddenly behind her, and a pile of clothing was tossed in, then the door slammed shut once again.

She knelt to unwrap the bundle of clothing, then

frowned at what she found. Within a finely woven magenta cloak was a ruby red silk gown. Surely she would stand out in this far more than she would have in her dirty white tunic and tattered cloak.

With the dress were fresh white underpinnings and new stockings. She assumed she was intended to keep her same boots, as they would hardly show beneath the long, flowing gown.

She glanced at the door, then around the small latrine with a heavy sigh. She'd have to play along for now, and hope the opportunity to escape presented itself once the feeling had fully returned to her limbs.

Elmerah

ELMERAH PEERED OUT AT THE OCEAN, SOOTHED BY THE damp air caressing her face. She always felt content near the sea. Unfortunately, the rough wood of the dock was beneath her feet, not the pure white sands of a home she barely remembered.

She brushed her hands down her new fitted black coat, held in place by three brass buttons down the center. The hem reached her knees, flapping gently with the ocean breeze. A slit up the side allowed for easy access to her cutlass at her belt. She pulled up the coat's black hood, hiding her hair and shadowing her face.

Alluin stepped up beside her, his own features shadowed by his ever-present cowl. "I believe I found the building Vessa described, though I'm not sure we should approach."

She whipped her gaze to him. She was more than ready to find her wretched sister. "*Why?*"

"It's being watched," he explained. "My guess is the men with Vessa are hoping to silence us before Rissine learns of her slip up."

"The men, but not Vessa herself?"

He shrugged, turning his gaze out toward the sea. "I have hope Vessa would not wish me harm, though part of me feels that might not be true."

Elmerah stroked the cutlass at her belt, ready to be imbued with the magic that had finally returned to her. "Blood loyalty only goes so far amongst the morally corrupt."

He chuckled. "I suppose that means your blood loyalty is nearly non-existent."

She glared at him, though she couldn't quite argue. She knew she might have to kill Rissine in the end, if she hoped to be free of her. Such an act would label her both disloyal *and* morally corrupt, but if it meant she could return to her swamp in peace, then so be it.

"Let us trigger their trap then be done with this," she decided.

"You believe we can best them?"

She smiled, though it was more of a snarl. "I take it you've never fought with a pure-blood Arthali witch?"

He looked her up and down. "I sincerely hope you can live up to the name. The warehouse is the last one at the end of the dock. You can't miss it."

She raised an eyebrow. "Will you not be joining me?"

He smirked. "Oh I don't want to miss this, but I think I'll let *you* lead the way."

With a snort, she turned and walked further south down

the dock. She knew he was using her to take the first blow, but she didn't mind. She'd never been much of a follower.

Her boots echoed down the dock, past men unloading the morning's catch from small fishing boats, and others unloading crates from larger vessels. She found it telling that no militia men were in sight. They'd be out in droves at the main docks where sea-faring ships brought goods from Faerune and beyond, but here, there existed a different kind of law. According to Alluin, the larger guilds were nearly as powerful as the emperor himself.

The warehouse Vessa had mentioned came into Elmerah's sight, and sure enough, she spotted movement by the far wall. She debated skirting off that way and silencing the waiting men one by one, but she'd always been better suited to facing threats head on.

She reached the front door with Alluin following a few steps behind. She lifted the heavy padlock, then dropped it with a sneer.

"What's wrong?" Alluin muttered behind her.

"It's enchanted," she hissed. "My magic won't work on it."

He stepped up beside her. "Watch my back."

She looked a question at him, but soon obeyed, moving to shield him from sight as he knelt in front of the padlock. A faint clicking sound hit her ears and she smiled. He knew how to pick locks. Perhaps he'd be of more use than she'd originally thought.

A few moments later, the padlock clicked open. She waited, scanning their quiet surroundings while Alluin removed the lock and opened the door. Apparently the ambush would wait until they went inside, which was just as well, she would be a fool to use her magic out in the open.

With a final glance down the docks, she turned and slipped into the warehouse ahead of Alluin. She moved a few steps in, then stopped. Crates, oars, furniture, and bolts of silk and linen were stacked around haphazardly, providing numerous hiding places for would-be ambushers.

Alluin came inside, shutting the door behind him, then stopped by her side. "Are we just going to wait for the ambush here," he whispered, "or should we have a look around?"

She leaned near his shoulder and hissed, "My magic will do little good if I receive a dagger in the back."

"Your back will be fine, because I will be watching it."

She smirked. "Somehow I don't find that comforting."

She walked forward, keeping her distance from the nearest crates. She knew Valeroot elves had superior hearing and sense of smell, and wondered if Alluin could hear their watchers breathing, or if they were wrong about everything and were actually alone in the warehouse.

She walked toward a neat stack of rolled silks. Perhaps this really was just a storage warehouse. She didn't see any signs of inhabitance, though Vessa had claimed slaves were kept here before being sent off to meet their fates.

Alluin tapped her shoulder, then pointed to the area past a stack of crates. A dusty rug was spread across the floorboards. Conspicuous, as only that one area was covered.

She glanced at him, assuring herself that he'd watch her back, then approached the rug. With one hand on her cutlass, she reached down and flipped it aside, revealing a trap door. Judging by the height of the docks, any room below would be nearly at water level. Another dark, damp space. *Wonderful*.

"Elmerah," Alluin hissed.

There was a loud *thud*, then the nearby stack of crates shifted. Before she could react, Alluin grabbed her upper arm and tugged her away, flinging her right past him moments before the crates toppled near the trap door.

"You shouldn't have come here!" a female voice called from above.

Righting herself, Elmerah glanced upward to see Vessa standing on one of the beams spanning the width of the ceiling. Her hand still held a rope attached to a heavy sack of grain or sand. The sack had been let down onto a board wedged underneath the crates, toppling them.

Elmerah backed away as three men emerged from their hiding places within the storeroom. "You really thought to get rid of me by flattening me with crates?" she balked. "How unoriginal."

Vessa sneered. "Whatever gets the job done."

Alluin had withdrawn a gleaming sliver dagger from his belt. He moved protectively to Elmerah's back, facing the two men edging in from that part of the room.

Elmerah drew her cutlass, debating whether or not to give the men a fighting chance.

One man drew his sword then spat at her feet.

It was a short debate.

She focused on her cutlass. It was difficult to wield elements indoors, and she didn't want to push herself as far as she had on the pirate's ship, but she was quite sure she could manage. She thought of flames, the feeling of heat on her skin and the sharp sting of a burn.

A flicker of orange surged across her blade.

The two men who'd been nearing her stepped back.

"Your blades will protect you, you fools!" Vessa called out. "Now attack!"

Elmerah frowned. *Of course* they had enchanted blades. If they worked for Rissine, they'd already had a taste of Arthali magic.

She extinguished her blade as one of the men charged. There was no reason to expend her extra magic if her attacker's blade was made to nullify it. He swung his short sword in a well-practiced arc. She parried, swooping her blade around his and flinging it from his hand. He knew how to swing, but had obviously never faced a skilled opponent.

She caught a glimpse of Alluin gracefully fending off attacks with twin daggers, then turned back as her second attacker lunged for her. This one was more skilled. Their blades connected with a *clang*, sending a jolt up Elmerah's arm.

She parried his next attack, then sensing someone approaching her back, she shifted her grip on her cutlass and stabbed through the circle of her left arm behind her. Her blade sunk into flesh, and the knife poised to stab her in the back clattered to the floorboards.

She tore her cutlass free, then parried another attack from her still-living attacker.

"Cursed Arthali," Vessa muttered from above, just before hopping down onto another stack of crates.

Elmerah parried another attack, cringing at a whiff of sweaty odor wafting from the scarred man. She needed to force him onto the defensive, but without her magic she was relying on sword skill alone, and he was *good*.

She continued to block his attacks, then instinctively rolled aside as Vessa launched herself from the crates, intent on kicking her in the head. Elmerah quickly stood as Vessa effortlessly rolled with her momentum then hopped to her feet, drawing a pair of daggers. It seemed she and Alluin had been trained by the same mentor.

Thinking of Alluin, she backed away from her attackers and called, "Are you alright back there?"

"Fine!" he replied, echoed by the clang of steel on steel.

Vessa twirled one of her daggers, then crouched in a fighting position beside the scarred man. "My apologies, but I cannot let Rissine find out about my mistake. You never should have threatened me."

Elmerah tightened her grip on her cutlass. "And you'll kill your own brother to cover this up?"

Vessa frowned. "He will not be killed. I know *he* would never sell me out."

Okay, so she didn't have to worry about Alluin, they didn't want him dead. They obviously didn't know just who she was though, as she was quite sure Rissine wanted her alive. She could tell them she was Rissine's sister, but she really didn't want to spoil the surprise.

"Are your daggers enchanted as well?" she asked.

Vessa's smug expression faltered.

With a wicked grin, Elmerah relit her blade.

"Get her," Vessa hissed, stepping behind the thug.

He charged Elmerah, but his movements were a bit slower than before. Lots of muscle, but no endurance if he was already tired. She darted around him and went for Vessa, increasing the fire on her blade as she flung it forward. The fire whipped outward, hitting Vessa in the chest and knocking her to the ground.

Vessa shrieked, rolling across the floorboards to extinguish the flames from her clothing.

Elmerah used the distraction to slice her still flaming

blade through the air at the scarred thug. If his blade truly was enchanted, it would easily extinguish the flames, but in his moment of terror he seemed to forget. He threw himself out of the path of her flaming sword, his back landing hard on the floorboards. He was nowhere near as graceful as Vessa as he tried to hop to his feet, and she quickly disarmed him.

Contact with his blade extinguished her flames, but it didn't matter now that she had the pointed tip at his throat.

Alluin trotted up from the other side of the room, a little mussed and bloody, but none the worse for wear. He stopped in front of his sister.

Elmerah wished she could see his expression and not just his back, but there was no way she'd be taking her attention off the thug.

"Where is Rissine?" Alluin demanded.

"She'll kill me if I tell you!" Vessa cried.

Elmerah was glad Alluin didn't seem to have much in common with his sister. All this moaning and whining was getting annoying. "And we'll kill you if you don't tell us," she growled, speaking to Vessa though her eyes were on the thug, "so out with it."

"Never!"

Elmerah momentarily turned toward Vessa and rolled her eyes. "Don't be so dramatic."

She whipped around and eyed the thug dangerously as he shifted to the side, his fingertips scrambling for his sword. His scrambling quickly ceased.

"What are you going to do?" Vessa asked, clearly speaking to her brother. "Will you kill me in defense of an Arthali witch?"

"Why not?" he questioned. "You're clearly willing to die

for one, though I'm not sure why. You know you have protection if you want it."

"Yes protection," Vessa spat, "and a life of always hiding, always being looked down on for our heritage. I cannot live like you, brother."

"This is getting boring," Elmerah interrupted, "and my arm is tired." She looked down at the thug past the tip of her cutlass indenting the skin of his throat. "Tell me where Rissine is, or I'll drive my blade through your throat, then I'll incinerate your body and give the ashes to the Akkeri for their dark rituals."

The thug's eyes widened. "I don't know where she is, but a Faerune elf named Thera does. She runs a textile shop near the main square. If you want to find Rissine, she's the one you need to see."

"Now was that so difficult?" Elmerah quipped.

Keeping her blade at his throat, she moved to his side and retrieved his discarded sword. The enchanted metal seemed to suck the life out of her, though she knew that wasn't the case. It was simply the nullification of magic she was feeling. It felt as if she lacked a little sliver of her soul.

She secured the blade beneath her arm, then drew back the tip of the cutlass from the man's throat. "Off you go. I suggest you leave Galterra at once. Rissine has quite a temper."

"You'll tell her it was me?" he whimpered.

"Sorry," she replied, "I don't do favors for people who kidnap young girls and sell them to the highest bidder. Be thankful you'll leave here with your life."

He nodded a little too quickly, stumbled to his feet, and ran. Once he was out the door, he slammed it behind him, and his footsteps could be heard echoing down the docks.

Elmerah moved to Alluin's side to look down at Vessa. Her tunic was missing its center, surrounded by fabric charred black. She'd extinguished the flames before they ate through her underpinnings, though areas of her flesh were badly burned.

"The other two men?" Elmerah questioned, flicking her gaze to Alluin.

"Taken care of," he replied cooly.

"Well," Vessa began, "you have what you want, so can I go now?"

Elmerah raised an eyebrow at her. "Do you intend to flee the city as well?"

She glared up at her. "Tomas was the one who betrayed Rissine, and now that he's leaving the city, I can easily blame it all on him."

Elmerah took a step forward. "Unless I tell Rissine it was *you*."

Vessa's eyes widened. "Just who exactly are you?"

Elmerah squatted down in front of her. "I'm one of the very last Shadowmarsh witches. If you know Rissine well, you know just what that means."

Vessa's green eyes were now wide enough Elmerah thought they might pop out of her head. "But Rissine said she was the last one, the *only* one. She never spoke of a sister."

She smiled. "Rissine is a liar. Now, since you seem to finally comprehend the situation, I'm going to offer you a deal. Go into hiding, take whatever protection your brother can offer, and I'll deal with my sister."

Vessa looked to Alluin, then back to Elmerah. Finally, she nodded. "Okay. I'll hide. Just please don't tell Rissine I was involved. I won't speak a word about you being here to *anyone*."

Elmerah stood, then made a shooing gesture. "Off you go."

Vessa scrambled to her feet, took one last look at her brother, then fled.

Alluin stepped up beside her. "I'm surprised you let her go."

She turned to him. "You mean you wouldn't have protested me killing her?"

He shook his head. "No, I would have protested, but if you truly are a Witch of Shadowmarsh . . . "

"Don't believe everything you hear," she sighed. "I for one have never put my enemy's head on a pike." She turned away, ready to see what was hidden under that trap door.

On her way, she glimpsed the two men who'd attacked Alluin, bound and gagged with strips of silk.

She glanced back at him with a wry smile as he walked up behind her. "Have you? The pike I mean."

He smirked. "On a pike, no. The Forestfolk tend to be a little more discreet."

She pushed a fallen crate aside, then knelt by the trap-door to find another lock, this one smaller than the enchanted one outside. This one was also benign, unlike the enchanted blade still braced under her arm. She set it aside, then sent a trickle of air magic into the lock until she'd built enough pressure to turn the mechanism over with a faint *click*. She tossed the lock and gave the door a tug.

It was heavier than it looked. She stood and crouched down, bracing with her knees. Once it was lifted Alluin darted in to help her flip it over to the opposite side.

She walked back to the opening and peered into the

pitch blackness. The space below smelled foul, like rotten wood and sweat. There was a rickety staircase leading down.

She turned to Alluin. "Care to take the lead?"

"*Now* you want me to take the lead?"

She sighed. "Yes, Alluin, if I have a chance to avoid going into the small dark space, I'm going to take it."

"I thought you seemed a little skittish in the cavern."

She scowled at his back as he crept down the stairs, creaking loudly with every step. He didn't comment about having only the light from above to see by, though she knew Valeroot elves did not possess superior night-vision.

She waited above, glancing occasionally toward the front door. She doubted Vessa or Tomas would return, but one couldn't be too careful.

Finally, Alluin climbed back up the stairs. "Just sleeping mats, water skins, and a bit of refuse. It seems Vessa told the truth. The women are likely kept here for a time before being moved through the city."

She glanced again at the bound men. "I suppose my next step is to find this Thera. I don't imagine *they'll* have any more to tell us."

"I know the shop," he replied. "We can go there now."

She placed a hand on his arm. "*We?*"

He blinked at her. "You know I have a vested interest in this."

"True . . . " she trailed off.

"So what are we waiting for?"

She frowned. "Nothing I suppose." She watched as he walked past. Really, she didn't mind the help, but she hadn't expected him to continue on after confronting his sister, and she was used to working alone.

With a heavy sigh, she retrieved the enchanted blade

she'd taken from Tomas. If it came to a fight with Rissine, she wanted the ability to nullify her sister's magic, even if it meant nullifying her own.

She could only hope Rissine hadn't been keeping up with her swordplay, though she sincerely doubted it.

CHAPTER EIGHT

Saida

Not long after getting dressed, Saida had been herded into a carriage. Curtains barred her view of the streets beyond. On her right sat one of Thera's cohorts, his shoulders half as broad as she was tall, and on her right, Thera. Across from them was the other thug, his heavy brow shading his gray eyes as he glowered. She hadn't seen Rissine again since their initial meeting.

"So," Thera began conversationally, "at which inn did you last see Elmerah?"

The thought of telling the truth made her sick, but what else could she do? Her only hope of escape was if Elmerah showed up. Her hands had been bound once more before leaving her temporary prison, and she still felt weak from whatever drugs were in the tea.

"The Crimson Jewel," she muttered, guilt making her throat tight. "It was not far from your shop."

"Very good," Thera said, patting her leg through the ruby gown.

The carriage rattled on across the cobblestones. Saida really had no idea if Elmerah would even return to the inn. If not, she might never see her again. Perhaps it was for the best, if it kept her away from vile women like Thera and Rissine. While Elmerah might not be the most charming sort, she was preferable to her present company.

The carriage continued on for what seemed like forever. Her captors remained silent. How far had she been taken from Thera's shop whilst unconscious? She couldn't imagine they'd moved her a great distance, lest their actions prove conspicuous.

"Have we passed it?" she asked finally. "It wasn't far from your shop." She turned to Thera.

Thera's smile sent a chill down her spine. "Do not fret, dear. You're too valuable to play bait. Now that we know where Elmerah is staying, someone else will go there to fetch her."

She started to stand, but the man on her right grabbed her bound wrists and pulled her back down, wrenching her arms painfully behind her.

"Where are you taking me!" she cried out. "Help!"

A meaty palm sealed her mouth. She struggled against the man now pinning her back to his chest, practically pulling her into his lap. Thera tried to grab her flailing feet and she managed to kick her in the face, giving Saida a brief moment of satisfaction. Then the man pinning her wrapped an arm around her throat and squeezed.

She continued to thrash, but her vision slowly went gray, then black.

BY THE TIME SAIDA REGAINED CONSCIOUSNESS, THE carriage had reached its destination, or so it seemed. She sat up from where she had been across one of the cushioned benches. The two men sat on the other bench, watching her.

Thera was gone, but she could hear voices outside.

"Are you positive it's her?" a male voice asked.

"Saida Fenmyar," Thera's voice assured. "She came in on one of our ships."

Saida's heart skipped a beat. They knew her full name? Had the pirates not just taken the first priestess they saw? What in the name of Arcale was going on?

The carriage door opened, revealing Thera and a man with long, honey blond hair. He wore thick burgundy tights, and a deep blue tunic embroidered with gold. His stockings above his buckled shoes were perfectly pressed, and jeweled rings glittered at his fingers. Behind him stood two guards dressed in the purple and white livery of the Empire.

Her jaw dropped as she leaned forward and looked up to the impossibly high walls of the castle. They were in the rear courtyard by the stables. She recognized it from her visit with her parents.

"Bring her out," the blond man instructed, not looking Saida in the eyes.

The thugs in the carriage moved toward her. One gripped her shoulders and forced her down the retractable carriage steps.

"Why are we at the castle?" she gasped, having regained her senses.

"This will be your home, for a time," Thera explained. "I

know not what the emperor wants with you. Perhaps he wants to make you his bride."

The blond man snorted. "I think *not*."

She looked a little closer at him. She'd only seen the emperor in passing, but remembered he had black hair and eerily pale eyes. He was most certainly not this man.

The blond man nodded to the guards behind him. "Take her to her chambers. Do not let her out of your sight. Keep her hands bound."

The guards stepped forward. Though one was young and one old, both were well muscled and had an air of sameness to them. Neither looked her in the eye. They each grabbed an arm and ushered her forward.

She struggled, twisting her upper body back to Thera. "You cannot just leave me here! We had a deal!"

Thera tsked. "Poor little pampered priestess. My heart *bleeds* for you."

The last thing she saw was the blond man placing a velvet coin pouch in Thera's hand, then she was forced past a tall hedge, blocking her view.

"Unhand me!" she growled, struggling against the two men now dragging her along. Her red dress tangled around her legs, scraping the toes of her boots across the stone walkway.

She knew once she was within the castle, there would be no escape. There were guards everywhere, not to mention she'd likely be locked in a room with her hands still bound.

She hated the tears slipping down her face. She had no idea what the emperor might want with her, but if he'd been willing to pay slavers to obtain her, she knew it wasn't good.

Alluin

BY THE TIME THEY MADE IT TO THE TEXTILE SHOP FROM the docks, the sun was high in the middle of the sky. Alluin would need to report to his uncle soon, to let him know what Vessa had done, but it would have to wait. He might have lost Saida, but if he could figure out why the slavers had taken her to begin with, the information might prove invaluable.

Elmerah stood beside him, features shadowed by her black hood, though passersby still gave her a wide berth as they eyed her height and the cutlass at her belt. "Are we sure this is the right place?"

"This is the place Vessa described," he replied. "I do not believe she was lying."

Her shoulders rose and fell with a sigh. "Alright, let us find this Thera. The sooner I can get to Rissine, the sooner I can leave this cursed city." She marched toward the shop, her head nearly brushing the brightly colored silks hung on display from the awning.

He followed, hoping they were not in for another fight . . . or at least not a fight with enchanted blades. Things would go more smoothly if Elmerah could use her magic unimpeded.

He shivered at his thoughts. A true, pure-blooded Shadowmarsh witch. The Shadowmarsh witches, a hereditary line possessing power over the elements, were the most feared among the Arthali. They were rumored to have been eradicated during the Great War, killed by their own people in exchange for orders of exile over death from the former emperor. He'd have to be more wary of her moving forward.

He jumped into motion as she swung open the door and

marched right inside. He pulled the door shut behind him as he entered, then glanced around the shop. More textiles were on display, along with spools of thread and a few other seamstress tools. A small counter stood before a door leading deeper into the building, likely where a storeroom, and perhaps the shop owner's living quarters, would be.

The door opened, revealing a young man with short red hair. Alluin placed him around eighteen, though the glint in the young man's eyes hinted at a certain cunning.

"Can I help you?" the young man asked, his attention on Elmerah.

As she straightened from observing a lower shelf of folded linens, the young man's eyes widened. It almost seemed for a moment as if he recognized her, then the moment passed.

Elmerah sauntered up to the counter, leaning her elbows on the surface to peer at the young man. "We're looking for an elf named Thera. We're told this is her shop."

The young man nodded. "Yes, this is her shop, but she's been away the past few weeks. Visiting relatives in Faerune."

Somehow, Alluin doubted that.

Moving nearly as fast as an elf, Elmerah grabbed the neck of the young man's billowy white shirt, twisting it taut. She leaned in, placing her face uncomfortably close. "Where is Rissine?" she growled.

The boy didn't so much as flinch. "Who wants to know?"

"Take a close look," Elmerah hissed, "then take a guess."

The boy observed her for several long moments. "I cannot tell you where she is, but I can set up a meeting with Thera. She'll decide whether or not you can meet with Rissine."

"I thought you said she was out of the city," Alluin interjected.

The boy shrugged, though his shirt was still twisted around his neck, and he was bent halfway over the counter. "Maybe yes, maybe no. It's not worth it to me to place myself in the middle of Arthali witches."

Elmerah let out an abrupt laugh, then gave the boy's shirt a tug, returning his attention to her. "Tell Thera to meet me at the Crimson Jewel at nightfall. She will show up alone, or we will run. I can guarantee you Rissine will *not* be pleased if we run."

The boy nodded sharply, and Elmerah released his shirt, then turned away.

His brow furrowed, Alluin followed her out the door. Once they were out in the street he asked, "How did you know he knew Rissine?"

She smiled coldly. "He seemed to recognize me at first. My sister and I look a lot alike. At least, we did when we were young."

He nodded. "Well in any case, we need to find my uncle before we return to the inn. I must tell him what Vessa has done, and he may provide us with a bit of protection when we meet Thera."

"Your uncle?" she asked as she started walking directly through the crowd, forcing them to move for her and not the other way around.

For someone who wanted to remain inconspicuous, Alluin thought, she didn't try very hard. He caught up to her side. "Yes, he is the head of our organization. He'll want to know what we've learned about Rissine's business as well."

"I don't like the idea of involving more people. I do not

want anyone to stand in the way of me . . . *speaking* with my sister."

"No one will stand in your way," he assured. "Our goal is to gather information, to predict the coming change in the tides. Thera nor Rissine will ever see anyone in our guild besides you and I."

After a moment's hesitation, Elmerah nodded. "I hope your uncle proves to be less of a thorn in my paw than you are."

He smirked. "Funny that you would view me as such, when I've been in two, nearly three brawls since I met you."

She chuckled. "That's what we call the Curse of the Arthali. You'll get used to it."

He wasn't sure he wanted to get used to it, but for now, like it or not, their fates were entwined.

Saida

SAIDA PROWLED AROUND THE SMALL CHAMBER, HER HANDS still bound. She'd been left alone, for what little good it did her. The chamber was high up in one of the castle's four towers. Even if she could manage to fit out the small window, the fall would surely kill her. The only other exit was the heavy wood and iron door, locked from the outside. Even if she managed to free her hands, there would be no breaking through the thick wood. The rest of the room was sparse, just a small bed, a washbasin, and a chamber pot.

She slumped onto the hard bed, then tensed at the sound of light footsteps outside the door. She crept her way off the bed, careful not to make the frame creak, then tip-toed toward the door, stationing herself against the adjacent wall. There was only one set of footsteps, and they seemed to belong to someone small-boned with lightweight shoes, not the boots of a guard. If she could manage to knock the person down, she might be able to escape and find a store-room to hide in until nightfall.

Her heart thudded in her chest as the footsteps halted outside the door. Whoever it was just stood there, not touching the lock.

She waited so long, she thought perhaps her dreary mind was playing tricks on her, and she hadn't really heard foot-steps at all. She slowly crouched, then pressed her cheek against the floor. Through the small space underneath the door she saw two feet wrapped in light leather, soft-soled boots, like what the Valeroot hunters wore. The smell of rotten fish hit her nostrils. She would have recoiled, except the feet shifted.

The person outside made a sniffing sound, as if . . . scenting her?

She scrambled away as they suddenly dropped to the floor. The loud sniffling continued as she pressed her back against the wall. Another set of footsteps, louder this time, echoed distantly.

The creature—she could only think of it as a creature—silenced for a moment, then stood and hurried away.

Saida let out a sigh of short-lived relief until the second pair of footsteps grew closer, close enough for her to realize it was two people, not one. She had a feeling this time the door would be opening, and there would be little hope of escape.

Sure enough, the footsteps stopped, and a key clinked in the lock. She scrambled away from the door and tried to stand casually, wanting to at least maintain a measure of dignity. What would her captors think if they found her panting and sweating on the floor like a fool? They obviously knew just who she was, and she refused to represent the Faerune elves poorly, even to those who held her prisoner.

The door opened, revealing a guard and . . . the emperor? While she'd only seen him in passing, she'd never mistake the man standing before her as anything less than the ruler of the Ulrian Empire. He wore a black tunic and thick tights in the style of the guards, though his garb was of much finer quality. The tunic boasted intricate embroidery echoed on the charcoal gray capelet. His jet-black hair was unadorned, though his fingers glittered with dark jewels.

The guard, a brown-haired man in his middle years, cleared his throat, and Saida realized she'd been gawking at the emperor.

"Saida Fenmyar," the emperor said, standing casually though he and the guard were the only thing blocking her from the slightly ajar door. "I must say, you've been rather difficult to track down."

She gave him her best steely glare. "Well perhaps next time you should hire more adept pirates to kidnap your quarry."

She'd meant it as an insult, but he merely chuckled. "I'll keep that in mind." He looked to the silent guard beside him. "Please unbind her hands. Lady Fenmyar is our guest."

She stood stunned as the guard moved behind her, then untied the knots on her wrists. She slowly moved her hands to her front so she could rub her aching wrists. "Why have you brought me here?" she demanded. "If I am a guest, and not a prisoner, why have you locked me in this room?" Her gaze shifted to the door, and the sliver of light beyond it.

Her hands were free now, and there were only two men standing in her way.

"I wouldn't try it, if I were you," the emperor purred. "The line between guest and prisoner can be quite thin. You wouldn't want to find yourself back on the wrong side of it."

"Emperor Dinoba—" she began.

"Call me Egrin," he interrupted.

She nodded. "Very well, Egrin. Please tell me why I've been brought here."

He smiled. It reminded her very much of Thera's wicked smile. It turned her insides to ice. Whatever she'd been brought here for, she wasn't going to like.

"I'm afraid I cannot tell you," Egrin explained. "It is a very sensitive matter. In fact, few in the castle even know you're here. It will only be another night or two though, and all will be revealed."

She glanced at the door again. All she could think was that he was holding her for ransom, but why? Egrin Dinoba had no shortage of riches. Perhaps a political move? Using her as leverage against the High Council of Faerune? She supposed it didn't matter, as she would not be sticking around to find out.

She shifted her weight, flinging out her foot into the nearest guard's groin. He doubled over with an *oof*. She gripped his shoulders and shoved him to the ground, then ran past him toward the door.

She reached it, flung it open, and started to go through, but she smacked into something solid. She bounced back from the impact, landing hard on her rump. She lifted trembling fingers to her bloody nose as she peered up at the empty doorway. What had she run into?

Footsteps walked up beside her. She turned wide eyes up

to the emperor. "It's a fun trick, isn't it? I told you it was a bad idea to try escaping. Try again, and you'll end up with more than a bloody nose."

Her eyes widened further. Her entire body had begun to tremble. "You have magic," she gasped.

He chuckled. "Say that to anyone else, and I'll have you beheaded." He walked past her through the doorway, then turned.

Still clutching her bloody nose, she stared at him. How could he have magic? The only humans who possessed that sort of magic were the Arthali, and some argued that with their long life-spans and above average speed, they weren't truly human at all.

"What are you?" she breathed.

"That, my dear, is a secret." He looked past her to his guard, who'd risen to his feet.

The guard hurried past her out of the room, producing a key from his belt.

Realizing she was still on the floor, she staggered to her feet.

"I'll send a healer to tend your nose," Egrin explained. "And I'll make sure you are fed. Attempt to escape again, and you'll find yourself starving in a dark hole."

With that, he turned and walked away. The guard slammed the door shut in her face, and seconds later, the lock clicked into place.

She stared at the door for a long while after that, the gears shifting in her mind. Her conclusion was not a pretty one. Egrin Dinoba had magic, which meant he was not entirely human. The Ulrian Empire had *always* been ruled by pure-blooded humans. If his people knew his secret it would be chaos. He would eventually be deposed, and perhaps executed for his treachery.

This only meant one thing to Saida. It meant she would never see her home again. She could not know the emperor's secret, and live to tell the tale.

CHAPTER NINE

Elmerah

E lmerah sat on top of the bar, dangling her feet over the edge. Two of the Woodfolk watched her warily, clutching their weapons. She'd been in the underground hideout for *ages*, waiting while Alluin met with his uncle.

Casting a glare at her guards dressed in the green and brown hues the Valeroot elves seemed to prefer, she summoned a small bit of magic internally, assuring herself that she hadn't overdone it back at the docks. Hopefully soon she wouldn't have to worry. It was like flexing a muscle. She'd get stronger the more she used it and not tire so quickly when she did. She summoned a little more magic, wishing she hadn't grown so lazy during her years in her swamp.

One of the guard's eyes widened beneath his mop of sandy blond hair, as if he could sense the trickle of power.

She had the urge to jump up and surprise him into pissing his pants, but she had a feeling she might end up with a dagger in her throat for her efforts. The other guard, slightly older than the first with a lump of scar tissue obscuring one eye, fiddled with a loose thread on his tunic, oblivious.

She looked at the guards. "Do these little meetings usually take this long?" Not being allowed into the meeting had her hackles up. She'd only known Alluin for a few days, and he'd not yet fully earned her trust. He probably never would, which said a lot more about her than it did about him.

The guards just stared at her.

She sighed and laid her back flat on top of the bar. The stone ceiling was a lot more interesting than her silent guards. They could have at least offered her a drink. She shifted her head to the side, eyeing the various bottles. Some contained liquids black as night, and others a pleasant lilac or amber, flickering in the lantern light. Her gaze settled on one particular bottle of pale purple liquid, sealed with a cork and wax. It had been ages since she'd sampled Valeroot wine. Now here she was, so close, yet unable to reach out and touch it lest her guards rat her out.

She turned her head the other way as the door leading to the house's basement creaked open, admitting Alluin and another elf.

"Get up," Alluin ordered, "we need to go meet Thera."

She glared at him, then rolled off the far end of the bar, crouching for a moment beside the bottles to absorb the impact. She rose. "I'm not the one who's delayed our return to the Jewel. There's no need for you to be grumbly with me."

Alluin sighed. "Two of our scouts returned while I was

meeting with my uncle. It seems a young Faerune elf has been taken into the castle."

Her brows raised as she stepped around the bar. "Saida? So she made it there after all?"

He shook his head. "Her hands were bound. She was delivered from a covered carriage by another Faerune elf, who was paid for her efforts."

A little tickle of rage worked its way through her. "It must have been Thera."

Alluin nodded. "We don't know why Saida was taken, but it must have something to do with the treaties with Faerune. I believe whatever the emperor is planning will soon be revealed."

One of the elven guards shifted uncomfortably at Alluin's revelations, likely because he was making them in front of an Arthali.

She glared at both of them, then headed toward the door. "Let's grab Thera while we have the chance. If she delivered Saida, she must know at least some of what's going on. We'll torture it out of her."

Alluin trotted to catch up with her as she opened the door. She headed up the dimly lit stairs with him close behind, and the two elven guards not far after. He said to her back, "Baeorn and Liam will accompany us. They'll remain out of sight, but will detain Thera should we lose sight of her."

Elmerah guessed Baeorn and Liam were her two elven guards, but she didn't bother to verify the information. She reached the top of the stairs and stalked through the rest of the house until she was outside. The sun had already made its descent toward the horizon, leaving just a sharp sliver of light to sting her eyes after so much time spent in dim lantern light.

Alluin emerged after her, followed by the other two elves. He peered up at the fading light. "We'll have to hurry to make it there by nightfall."

"Yes, so what are we standing around for?" She took off at a brisk pace toward the distant sound of growing evening chatter, and the thrill of the hunt.

Alluin

ALLUIN'S THOUGHTS RACED AS THEY MADE THEIR WAY back to the Crimson Jewel. If only he'd kept better track of Saida that day. He should never have let her go in the first place. Now his only link to Faerune might be lost, and the emperor was one step closer to enacting his plan.

If only he knew what that plan was.

Egrin Dinoba had been traveling a lot as of late. He'd met with the Dreilore in the East on numerous occasions, and had been sending slaves to work in their mines. Alluin could easily guess what Egrin might want with the Dreilore. They were an exceedingly long-lived race, with powers in metallurgy and alchemy. Their arcane machinery was understood by few, and their enchanted weapons were rivaled by none. Then there were the Nokken, not far removed from humans, but feared for their shape-changing abilities. The Nokken made excellent spies.

Elmerah slowed as they reached the Jewel, drawing him out of his thoughts. Baeorn and Liam had lagged behind. He trusted them to remain unseen unless they were needed.

Elmerah looked as if she might destroy the entire street with her mind.

"We should not begin this meeting with force," he cautioned. "If Thera is the last step before Rissine, she likely won't be swayed by threats, and if this is a trap, which it undoubtably is, we mustn't spring it too soon."

"I don't care about traps, and *everyone* is swayed by threats," Elmerah grumbled. "You just have to match the right threat to the right person."

"You really hate her, don't you?" he observed.

She smirked, though her gaze was still filled with ire as she stared at the inn. "Perhaps one day I'll tell you of my childhood, and you'll understand why I'd hoped to never see Rissine again, and why I'm more than willing to walk into a trap if it means I'll eventually be rid of her." Not waiting for a reply, she marched toward the inn.

He followed, sending out a small prayer to Arcale that she might control her temper. If Thera ran, they wouldn't find Rissine anytime soon, and with that loss went any hope of learning what the emperor planned before it actually happened.

Elmerah threw the door open hard enough to *thwack* against the exterior wall, startling several patrons who'd moved to enter behind her.

He shook his head, stepping around those who'd hesitated to go inside after her. A quick scan of the crowded common room showed that Thera had already arrived. Though she wore a deep purple hooded cloak, her white hair and pale skin gave away what she was. She seemed taller than Saida, and a few years older. Old enough to show no fear in the face of the agitated Arthali witch now looming over her.

He reached Elmerah's side and placed a hand on her

shoulder, pushing down until she sat in one of the vacant chairs across from Thera.

"I wasn't going to hit her," she whined, looking up at him.

Shaking his head, he sat, then laced his fingers beneath his chin as he peered at Thera.

"My associate said you wanted to meet with me?" she questioned.

"Yes," Elmerah replied. "And I think you know exactly what this is about, so let us skip the pretense. Where is Rissine?"

Thera smiled pleasantly. "I don't know who you mean."

Alluin watched as Elmerah's fingers flexed around the edge of the table.

"What will it take for you to tell us?" he interjected.

Thera tilted her head. "I still don't know what you mean."

This was getting them nowhere. He looked to Elmerah. If Thera wouldn't give them any information, they'd simply have to spring her trap so Baeorn and Liam could follow her. "Let's go. She obviously doesn't know Rissine." He widened his eyes a bit, urging Elmerah to catch on.

She turned a sneer to Thera. "Yes, let's."

Thera looked up at them as they stood. "Have a *pleasant* evening."

He leaned in against Elmerah's shoulder as they walked away. "It seems the trap will wait until we walk outside."

"Then let's have a drink," she suggested. "She'll have to leave eventually. I don't want your elves distracted by a brawl when Thera tries to slip away."

"Just try not to threaten anyone again. I'm sure there are other guilds about more than willing to pick a fight."

She swung down into a seat at an empty table, placing her back to the wall. "Don't worry, Alluin. I've already chosen my fight for this evening. I won't start any others." She raised a finger toward the barkeep.

He sat. He didn't see Baeorn and Liam anywhere, but knew they'd be watching. If Thera left ahead of them, they'd follow her.

The hunched old barkeep ambled up to their table and set down two tankards of Galterran ale. Alluin reached for his coin purse, but the barkeep held up one wizened hand. "Keep your gulls, just don't cause any trouble tonight." He glanced back at Thera, still sitting alone at her table, then lowered his voice, "And tell Rissine the militia locked up two of her men from last night." With that, he ambled away.

Her tankard in hand, Elmerah turned to him with a wry grin. "Perhaps Thera isn't our only lead on Rissine. I'll bet you our next drinks the barkeep is more likely to talk than Thera."

He sipped his ale, enjoying the herbal aftertaste specific to Galterran brews. "If the barkeep knows Rissine, this is likely an establishment frequented by her guild. It would explain why Vessa was here before. We *might* be in a bit over our heads." He flicked his gaze around, wondering how many of the other patrons belonged to Rissine, and how many knew just who Elmerah was. Her, they likely wanted alive. Him, not so much.

"She's moving," Elmerah muttered.

He glanced back toward Thera, and sure enough, she'd moved to the back of the establishment. A door in the back wall seemed to open of its own volition, admitting her.

"So much for following her," Elmerah grumbled.

"Something tells me we should have brought more men,"

he sighed, noticing several patrons, though not being obviously, had shifted toward the door, taking seats near the only escape route. He and Elmerah were very slowly and subtly being trapped. He glanced back at the barkeep, who watched his patrons warily, seeming to know something was about to happen, but not what.

"So," Elmerah began conversationally, "do we stay and fight, or do we go see what Thera is doing, and who she's with."

"That might be exactly what Thera wants," he debated.

Elmerah took a deep swig of her ale, then stood. "There's something you'll soon learn about me, Alluin. I'm quite the people pleaser."

He reached out to stop her, then a shrill scream cut through the air outside. Everyone within the establishment froze, even those who'd moved to block the door.

Another scream echoed.

A closer shout. "The Akkeri!"

Elmerah looked down at him, then toward those blocking the door, seeming to debate her next move.

Finally, Rissine's people made the choice for them. After a few murmurs, half of them opened the door and ran, while the others trotted back toward the door Thera had gone through.

More shouts and screams outside. Alluin couldn't quite believe the Akkeri would enter the Capital, but nothing else would cause such chaos.

Elmerah glanced down at him once more. "Feel free to run with the others if you please. I'm going after Thera." She charged across the suddenly empty room. Even the barkeep had disappeared.

The screams grew louder and nearer. It had to be a large

clan to have made it this far inland. They must have crawled up from the docks, as they'd never have made it past the city walls.

Thinking of Saida held prisoner in the castle, he made up his mind. He ran across the room just as Elmerah kicked the door down, her exposed cutlass sparking with yellow flame. She charged into an . . . *empty* room.

They both glanced around quickly and continued on to find an open door leading into the back alley. It swung back and forth on its hinges, muffling the screams and shouts sounding in short bursts.

Elmerah kicked the door with a grunt of rage, splintering free one of its hinges. Extinguishing her blade, she whirled on him. "Do you think your men followed her?"

He nodded. "If they hadn't, they'd be here with us."

She seemed to relax. "Good. We'll leave the tracking to them. Let's go out and see what all the fuss is about."

He blinked after her as she went through the now-crooked door. Of course she'd want to run toward the Akkeri and not away from them. He'd never entirely believed the legends saying Shadowmarsh witches were all half-mad, but he was beginning to believe them now.

Elmerah

EXITING THE ESTABLISHMENT, ELMERAH SHEATHED HER extinguished cutlass as she jogged down the back alley. She could hear the clang of steel on the parallel street, likely the militia fighting off the Akkeri. She'd be wise to stay away from the militia, but she at least wanted to catch a glimpse of what was happening. She'd seen the Akkeri a few times in her swamp, but they'd never given her any trouble.

She found an intersecting street and hurried down it, not bothering to see if Alluin followed. She wouldn't blame him for running away with all the others.

She neared the main street, then stood in shock at the sight before her.

Dozens of Akkeri, their sparse clothing still dripping with sea water, charged through the streets, slashing down militia men with gleaming scimitars. They appeared as corpses just beginning to rot, but with the pointed ears and silken hair of Faerune elves, their closest kin.

She glanced over her shoulder at approaching footsteps. "I suppose you're not a coward after all," she whispered as Alluin reached her.

"No, but I most certainly am a fool."

Though they stood far back in the shadows, one of the Akkeri whipped its head their way, spotting them, its cat-like eyes reflecting the moonlight.

Elmerah withdrew her cutlass, though she didn't charge it with magic, lest they draw the attention of more Akkeri.

The single Akkeri approached with predatory grace, ready to face down two opponents on its own. Without warning, it leapt, raising its scimitar to strike downward.

Just as quickly, Alluin threw one of his daggers. It landed in the Akkeri's throat with a meaty *thwap*, but the fiend kept coming, ramming Elmerah with its shoulder.

She stumbled against the building, wincing at a loud crunch in her jacket pocket. She raised her blade in time to meet the Akkeri's scimitar, then moved to parry another swipe. The thing was as swift as a Faerune elf. She could barely keep up with its attacks. It lifted its scimitar again, then faltered.

At first she didn't notice it in the near dark, but Alluin had flung another dagger, sending it through the creature's temple and into its brain. It slumped to the ground, dead.

Alluin knelt and retrieved his daggers, cleaning them on the creature's damp clothing. "We must go after the rest. With how fast they can move, many will die tonight if nothing is done."

She sheathed her cutlass. "Isn't that the responsibility of the militia?"

"Most of the militia are just human. They will die just as quickly as mothers and their children."

She glared at him. She didn't give a heap of dung about Galterra, but children, human or otherwise, didn't deserve to die at the end of an Akkeri blade.

"Fine," she hissed, then ran out into the street ahead of him. She could still see the last of the Akkeri running further into the city, leaving a trail of corpses in their wake. It was a large party. They'd kill many before the night was through.

"Do I smell lavender?" Alluin asked suddenly, looking her up and down.

She winced, then pulled the neck of the shattered bottle from her pocket.

His eyes widened. "You stole my uncle's Valeroot wine!"

More screams cut through the thin night air, echoed by the clang of steel and the groans of the dying.

She tossed the bottle neck aside, then removed a few large shards of wine-soaked glass from her pocket. "We better hurry before we're too late." Before he could argue, she took off at a run after the Akkeri, though she didn't miss him muttering, "Cursed Arthali," at her back.

With a smirk she continued running, keeping her gaze upward as she went. Hopefully most of the city's children would be safe in their beds, but she wasn't about to risk seeing any that had already fallen around her. It was better not to know.

Alluin caught up to her side, seemingly over the wine incident . . . for now. "It seems they may be heading for the castle."

Elmerah nodded. She'd thought the same thing, though she was unsure of their motivation or reasoning. Though the Akkeri seemed like monsters, she knew they were intelligent, and most could speak in the common tongue. Adept fighters as they were, they'd never make it past the castle guard. If they hoped to reach the emperor, they were fools.

Screams continued in the distance, though fewer seemed to be fighting the Akkeri now. The militia had probably grouped themselves around the castle, ready to protect what was *important*.

Her lungs began to burn with exertion, and sweat dripped down her brow, but she could see the tail end of the horde. Knowing the Akkeri disliked fire, she withdrew her cutlass and summoned it to her blade. It was a mistake to use up too much of her energy, especially when she was so close to finding Rissine, but there was no turning back now.

Alerted by the flicker of flame, three Akkeri halted their advance and turned around. They hesitated for a heartbeat, then charged. She whipped her blade through the air, sending a wave of flame powerful enough to knock them from their feet. They screeched in pain, but as their clothing was minimal and damp, the fire soon went out.

They scrambled to their feet and charged her with the speed of ice leopards. She whipped more flame from her cutlass into them as they neared, then Alluin was by her side, protecting her flank as she shoved her cutlass through a bony Akkeri chest, puncturing its heart. She tore the blade free, then sliced across the throat of the next. She turned just in time to see the third Akkeri fall dead at Alluin's feet.

He offered Elmerah a nod, then took off once more on the monsters' trail.

Elmerah gritted her teeth as she forced her feet back into a run. It would take all night to pick the Akkeri off three by three. How in Ilthune had this become *her* job?

More screams ahead. She snarled. She knew she couldn't possibly blame Rissine for this latest development, but she was adding it to her sister's long list of offenses regardless.

Saida

SAIDA LEANED OUT THE SMALL OPEN WINDOW, LISTENING to the screams. Her untouched plate of roasted lamb and silkroots still sat where it had been left by four guards. Apparently without the emperor around, she merited more caution.

She shivered, thinking about the emperor's magic. She'd never seen anything like it. She didn't think it was elemental power like Elmerah's, which meant he probably wasn't part Arthali, so what was he?

More screams tore through the night.

She hoped Elmerah was tucked away safely in a warm inn, far from whatever was going on. She also wished someone would have the decency to tell her what was going on.

She retreated from the window, finally thinking about testing her food. After her experience with Thera, she was wary of being drugged, though drugging her now would be useless. The emperor already had her exactly where he wanted her, and if he wanted her somewhere else, he had plenty of guards to make it happen.

She stopped by the plate of food left on the ground, since there were few other surfaces for it to be placed upon. The scent of cooling lamb and thistle jelly turned her empty stomach. After not eating since the previous morning, she would have preferred a dry hunk of bread.

She hiked up her ruby gown a bit, then sat on the floor, crossing her legs in front of her. She was glad she possessed excellent night vision, as she hadn't been provided with a lantern. She reached for the plate, then hesitated at a scuffing sound outside the door.

She shook her head, thinking it was just a rat, then she heard a long inhale, followed by the slight odor of fish.

Her mouth went dry. Perhaps if she remained perfectly still, whatever it was would go away.

After a moment, the thing outside her door moved, then another sharp inhale sounded at the base of the door. Was it sticking its face against the ground to better smell her? Or perhaps it was just smelling her dinner, but somehow, she doubted it.

She cleared her throat. She was behind a locked door. It couldn't get her. "Who's there?"

No reply, not that she'd expected one.

She jumped at the sound of a scream. It sounded like it

came from within the castle walls. Curse Egrin for placing her in a room with only a view of the back courtyard.

The thing outside seemed to lean against the door, settling in. At least it wasn't sniffing her anymore.

Seeing no other option, she started picking at her food. Maybe whatever was going on in the city would soon breach the castle walls and she'd be able to escape, but she doubted it. For now, she was stuck. She would simply have to keep up her strength and wait to see what fate Egrin would present.

CHAPTER TEN

Elmerah

E lmerah wiped black blood from her cutlass on the damp rags that served as clothing on a dead Akkeri. It seemed the worst of the attack was over, and the few remaining Akkeri had scattered. She and Alluin had chased them nearly to the castle. The massive, grey stone estate rose high above them atop a hill near the center of Galterra. Its four main towers stretched so high, they seemed to touch the crescent moon.

Alluin sheathed his wiped down daggers at his belt, joining her side to stare up at the castle. Blood dripped steadily from a gash in his forehead. His clothes were drenched in more of it, though she could not tell if it was from his own injuries, or from the Akkeri. "Odd to think Saida is being held prisoner there, so close, yet utterly unreachable," he muttered.

Elmerah nodded, her gaze still on the castle. The militia men who'd joined the fight were milling about around them, dealing the final blow to any Akkeri still breathing. None bothered either of them, though some had to have seen Elmerah's use of magic. She knew come sunrise, when fear of the Akkeri had passed, old hatreds would resume. She needed to be far from the castle when that happened.

"When will your men report back about Thera?" she asked. "That is, if they managed to follow her in the chaos."

"Liam will continue to follow her for as long as possible. Baeorn will report back at dawn."

She gazed up at the moon. Dawn was still aways off. "We should get some rest until then. I fear I will be useless without it." More than useless, actually. She'd drained far too much of her magic again. She really was terribly out of practice.

Alluin observed her weary state. "We can stay at the tunnel hideout. I don't think it wise to return to the Jewel."

She hesitated, then nodded. She'd be easy prey for Rissine in her current condition, though she did not enjoy the idea of staying underground with elves. "You better keep your hands to yourself," she grumbled. "I sleep with one eye open."

"And you'd better keep your hands off my uncle's wine," he quipped. "You still reek of lavender from the last bottle."

"You have my word," she agreed, though if she had another moment alone at the hideout bar, she'd at least steal a small sip.

He glanced around at the corpses, and the few militia men beginning to take notice of those still living. "We should go," he muttered, tugging his cowl a little further forward, obscuring his bleeding brow.

With a nod, Elmerah flipped her hood up. She had a few small cuts and gashes, but nothing serious. The Akkeri had feared her fire more than they'd feared Alluin's daggers. "I sincerely hope a warm meal awaits our arrival." There was a child crying somewhere not far off, and muttered voices of others who'd escaped the Akkeri attack with their lives.

They turned and walked away from the scene of the final battle in silence. By morning, funeral pyres would be erected to dispose of the corpses. The militia would tally how many were lost, and would take precautions to prevent such an attack from happening again. She would not be needed for any of that. She was only needed for the killing. Such was the Arthali way.

"Your magic," Alluin began after they'd been walking for some time.

"Yes? What about it?"

"The way you wield the elements is quite remarkable," he went on. "I was just wondering if all Arthali are so powerful."

She snorted. "I'm not as terribly powerful as you think, but no, not all Arthali have such skills. Most possess natural magics, but control over elements was a specific gift of the females of the Shadowmarsh clan. My mother had the same gifts, as did my grandmother on my mother's side."

"And your father?"

She sighed. "I wouldn't know."

He went silent after that, and she hoped to Arcale he wasn't pitying her. She had simply stated a fact, nothing more.

The next time he glanced at her, she glared, dissuading him from further conversation. She had no true family, just as she had no true friends, and she wasn't looking to change either one.

Alluin

IT WAS STILL DARK BY THE TIME THEY REACHED THE HOUSE disguising the underground tunnel, but dawn was not far off. Alluin could feel it in his tired bones, just as he could feel shifts in the weather and changes of tide. It was a gift all Woodfolk possessed, more subtle than the gifts of their Faerune kin.

Elmerah slumped against the wall near the front door as he glanced both ways, then knocked. He knew he was risking much in bringing Elmerah to the secret tunnel yet another time. Rissine would have many eyes out looking for her, and those eyes would surely report any other secrets they found. Yet, he saw no other choice. They needed a safe place to stay, and he'd not let his one link to Saida and Rissine go so easily. Whatever Rissine was planning was deeply entwined with the emperor's plans, and Elmerah was somehow a part of it all.

The door opened, revealing a young, female elven guard who nodded then stepped aside. Alluin led Elmerah through the house toward the basement, nodding at the other elves, and a few trusted humans, as he passed. He hoped his uncle was not around, as he had strictly forbade him from returning with Elmerah. However, a run-in was likely once the sun rose.

Hopefully they could both get a few hours of sleep before then.

He led the way through the basement, then down the second set of stairs into the opening of the underground tunnel. If Rissine wanted Elmerah, she'd have to go through two dozen elves trained to kill any who might threaten their operation.

If Elmerah was at all intimidated by the armed elves, she didn't show it, and instead sauntered into the underground room as if she'd been there hundreds of times before. He didn't miss the way she glanced longingly at the bar, but thought it best not to comment.

Sleep. They needed sleep.

One lone lantern hung from the ceiling, dim enough that he chose to leave it lit. The beds against one wall were empty.

He gestured to the neatly made beds. "Take your pick. Try to sleep as much as you can. I'd like to leave here as soon as Baeorn reports back."

"No hope of a meal then?" she asked.

He winced. He'd almost forgotten. He moved to rummage through the supplies near the bar while Elmerah removed her coat, then slumped onto the bed farthest from the main door, propping herself up against the wall with a lumpy pillow.

Cooking was out of the question at this late hour, but he managed to rustle up some strips of salted cod and dried kelp. He also came across a basket of recently gathered burrberries, only slightly soft from sitting around. With a roll of his eyes, he also grabbed a half-empty bottle of Vale-root wine, then returned to the beds and sat on the next mattress over.

They silently shared a meal, though *share* was a term Alluin would use loosely. Elmerah ate far more than her share of burrberries, and drank most of the wine.

Once she'd finished, she wiped her mouth on her sleeve. "You should see to that cut." She gestured to his forehead.

He dabbed at the congealing blood. He had a few deep cuts on his body as well, though he'd been reluctant to reveal

them, as Elmerah had come out of the battle virtually
unscathed.

"I'll take care of it," he assured.

She gave her lumpy pillow a few punches, then laid down
on her back.

He rose, ready to clean his wounds so he could get
to bed.

Elmerah was so quiet he thought she'd already drifted off,
but suddenly she asked, "Why do you think the Akkeri
attacked?"

"Who can say?" He sat back down. "They seemed to be
heading for the castle."

"But why?" she pressed. "They are intelligent creatures.
Why attack the castle with little chance of making it past
the militia? They should have known they'd be
slaughtered."

He was so tired, his skull felt full of cotton. "I cannot tell
you their motivation any more than I could say the motivation of an angry badger. In my opinion, the two are inter-
changeable."

She snorted. "An angry badger is motivated by the need
for food, shelter, and to protect its young."

"And what would you say motivates the Akkeri?"

She sighed as she looked up at him. "You really are quite
dense. They are not driven by survival, as tonight's attack
would suggest. I highly doubt they came in search of riches,
so that can only leave one thing."

"And what is that?"

"Revenge—" she hesitated. "Or to provide a distraction."

He sat back down on his bed. "A distraction for what?"

She shrugged, remaining comfortably sprawled. "Perhaps
the emperor motivated the attack. If the city is focused on

THE WITCH OF SHADOWMARSH

the Akkeri, they're not likely to notice treasonous acts taking place right under their noses."

"And here I thought you actually had a rational theory." He stood again to go tend his wounds.

"Mock all you want. If I'm right, you owe me ten bottles of Valeroot wine."

"And what do I get if you're wrong?"

She chuckled. "By the time you realize I'm wrong about anything, I'll be halfway back to my swamp with all the wine I can carry."

He turned away toward the bar, hiding his small smile, not because he thought she was joking, but because he believed her.

Elmerah

THE DAZZLING CRYSTALLINE SANDS WERE SOFT UNDER HER bare feet, butting up against the radiant blue waters. The sea was cold this time of year, but she didn't mind. She loved plucking tiny glittering shells from the surf.

Elmerah turned away from the sea, peering outward toward the impossibly tall trees, shrouded in a constant, dense mist. Most days, the trees' deep silver needles and the deep blue mountains far beyond made the mist take on a grayish hue. It was the reason for her homeland's name, Shadowmarsh.

She turned at the sound of footsteps in the sand, then smiled. Her older sister always came to check on her when she'd been gone too long. Already a head taller than Elmerah, Rissine took her small hand in hers. Their mother might have been busy conferring with the other Shadow-marsh witches on how to best push back the Ulrian Empire, but Elmerah didn't think much about it. Rissine was there to make sure she brushed her hair, and had a hot meal every evening.

She opened her free hand to reveal the tiny, glittering shells she'd gathered, showing them to Rissine.

Rissine's eyes lit up. "It must have taken you ages to separate them from all the sand."

Elmerah offered Rissine the shells. While she'd been coveting them only moments before, she realized she wanted her sister to have them. Rissine meant more than all the pretty shells in the world, and she was sure her older sister felt quite the same way about her.

SENSING A PRESENCE ABOVE HER, ELMERAH PLUNGED INTO wakefulness. Her eyes shot open, beholding an elder Vale-root elf looking down at her. Woodfolk were quite long-lived, not as long as the Dreilore, but longer than the Arthali. For one to be showing his age, he was likely over two hundred.

The elf narrowed his vibrant blue eyes. "I specifically ordered Alluin to never bring you here again."

She shimmied away from him to the other side of the small bed, then sat up. The bed next to hers was empty. She turned back to the angry old elf, bundled in a brown cloak. Alluin's uncle, she presumed. "If you'd take a step back, I will gladly leave and never return."

"You think I'd trust the word of an Arthali?" he hissed.

She didn't have time for this. "Hey, my people may be

known for their brutality, but *yours* are known for lies and trickery. You're in no place to insult me."

"I am in *my* home. I will insult whomever I please."

"Uncle!" Alluin's voice snapped as he hurried down the stairs then through the door left ajar by his uncle, or perhaps by the elven guard now peeking into the room after him.

With a final sneer at Elmerah, Alluin's uncle turned. "I hope you have at least learned something worthwhile."

Glancing at Elmerah, Alluin nodded. "Baeorn and Liam followed the Faerune elf Thera to the edge of the Spice Quarter. She entered a well-guarded estate, and last Baeorn saw, she had not emerged. Rissine may be inside as well."

Elmerah stood. She vaguely remembered where the Spice Quarter was stationed. She was sure she could make it there well before midday. She could confront Rissine, and put this whole cursed affair behind her . . . except she was once again drained of magic. At full power, she was perhaps a match for her sister, but as things stood, she would easily be overcome.

"What do I care for Rissine Volund?" the elder elf growled. "We are well aware of her . . . " he glanced at Elmerah, "*actions*."

She rolled her eyes, then reached for her black coat at the foot of the bed and slipped it on. "I already know all about Rissine's actions too, there's no need to be coy. And I imagine you *care* about Rissine a whole ship's worth of gold more than I do considering her involvement with the emperor you so despise."

The elder elf's jaw dropped. "*You*," he growled. "How much has my nephew told you?"

"I'm not blind," she growled right back, "and I don't know what you're so angry about. *You* weren't kidnapped from your home, carted across the ocean, and accosted by pirates."

His hands flew to his hips, a nimble motion showing no hint of his age. "No, I was only uprooted from my homeland to make way for cities that care nothing for the fate of the Woodfolk."

She rolled her eyes again. "You may be old, but I'll bet you all the jewels in Faerune you weren't alive when that happened."

"Enough," Alluin cut in. He glared at his uncle. "Rissine may be our only hope of learning what the emperor is up to before it's too late. Detaining us further could mean a bloody end to all our efforts."

The elder elf's face turned so beet red Elmerah thought his head might pop, but finally, he nodded. "Go. Learn what you can. We'll discuss your choice in *companions* later."

Alluin gave his uncle a curt nod, then turned to Elmerah. "Are you ready?"

She glanced at the angry old man, then to the guard still peeking in through the doorway, then back to Alluin. "Quite."

Though her stomach was pleading for another meal, she knew better than to ask for one there. Instead, she gave Alluin's uncle an exaggerated curtsy before proceeding past the guard and up the stairs.

She noticed a few wary glances as they proceeded through the house. They'd probably all heard every word with those pointy ears. Sucking her teeth in irritation, she followed Alluin out the front door to find Baeorn waiting for them. He was an older looking elf, though not quite as old as Alluin's uncle, and far more pleasant, though a deep gash of scar tissue obscured one eye.

He gave her a nod before falling into step beside Alluin. "What is our plan?"

Elmerah scurried after them, wondering the same question. Not that she'd necessarily follow any plan given, but she was slowly becoming more curious about Alluin's thoughts and true intentions. He *might* actually have a better plan than her, considering she usually led with her magic, and she was quite drained at the moment.

"We'll decide once we get there," Alluin replied.

She smirked. Brilliant, utterly brilliant. Looked like she'd be doing things her way after all.

She tugged her hood up over her loose hair as they left the back alley for a more populated stretch, then followed the elves silently, going over her options in her head. As they walked, she picked the last few shards of the broken wine bottle from her pocket, allowing them to tinkle across the cobblestones. She'd be much more careful with the new bottle she'd procured, though she knew it would be a struggle not to break it over Rissine's fat ugly head.

Saida

SAIDA PACED ACROSS THE BARE STONES NEAR THE DOOR, A note in her hand. Her smelly new friend had stayed outside the door most the night, not making a sound, though she could see a shadow underneath the door where it sat. At some point, she'd finally fallen asleep, and when she awoke, the creature was gone, and a note had been slid under the door.

She stopped pacing and looked down at the torn parchment in her hand.

Do not fight. I will follow.

SHE HAD NO IDEA WHAT IT MEANT.

She flinched at the sound of footsteps, three or four pairs this time. Was it just another meal on its way, or was she finally about to meet whatever fate lay in store for her? She lifted her ruby skirt and shoved the note down her stocking.

The footsteps stopped outside her door. She stared at it, barely breathing, then the lock clicked open, and the door swung outward.

Her heart fell at the sight of the emperor, dressed in deep blue with hints of gold today. The blue made his pale eyes and black hair stand out like ice chips framed by onyx. He stepped inside. "Your time has come, my dear. Those who want you have fulfilled their end of the bargain, and now I must hand you over." He looked her up and down. "*Pity.*"

Three guards entered the room and flooded around the emperor toward her. She recognized one from her previous meeting with the emperor, and the other two had been among those who'd brought her meal later that evening. They were probably the only souls who knew she was even in the castle. Well, other than Thera, her thugs, and the blond man who'd paid them.

"What happened last night?" she asked, taking another step back. "I heard screams."

"Merely a diversion," the emperor replied. "Now come, my dear, we mustn't be late."

She darted to the side before one of the guards could grab her arm. "Tell me where I'm going first."

The guards turned to follow her, but the emperor stepped past them, trapping her against the wall. Her heart thudding in her throat, she craned her neck up to look at him. If his magic could seal a doorway, what else could it do? He reached out a hand and stroked her cheek. "You are in no position to argue. Cooperate, and I won't hurt you."

Her palms grew damp with sweat. The emperor's nearness sent chills down her spine. What exactly was he?

Knowing there was no escape with him in the room, she hung her head. Perhaps she'd have better luck escaping whoever would have her next. In fact, she almost looked forward to the exchange. Anything to get her away from Egrin Dinoba, and his strange, pale gaze.

He smiled, and lowered his hand still hovering near her cheek. "There we go. It really is such a pity that you must leave us."

She tended to disagree.

The emperor stepped back. She held still while two of the guards stepped behind her and bound her hands. They pushed her forward to walk in front of the emperor into the hall.

She glanced both ways, knowing she couldn't run just yet, but unable to put the thought out of her mind. The hall in either direction was utterly quiet. She doubted she'd see another soul on their way out of the castle. Perhaps the entire tower was kept in privacy, a single spire reserved just for the emperor's darkest secrets.

Her knees felt weak as they reached the end of the short

hall, then traveled down a spiral staircase. Through one of the small windows they passed, she caught a glimpse of a covered carriage bearing the purple and white ice leopard insignia of the Empire.

Just as expected, they finished the journey through the barren castle halls and into the back courtyard without seeing a single other soul. Holding on to her bound wrists, the guard at her back guided her across the damp grass onto the stone walkway leading toward the imperial covered carriage. There was no coachman tending the two dappled mares, though there was someone waiting by the carriage door.

The long-haired blond man with jewels on his fingers leaned against the white carriage with his arms crossed. Saida thought the carriage a bit conspicuous for nefarious deeds, but she supposed the large cloth crest draped from the door would keep any of the militia from bothering them.

They reached the carriage, and two of the guards climbed atop the coachmen's box. One took the reins, and the other sat still with his hand atop the sword at his belt, eyes ahead.

The remaining guard gave Saida a nudge toward the carriage while the blond man held open the door. As she reached the steps, he gave a dramatic bow.

Refusing to acknowledge him, she climbed the steps into the carriage, careful not to trip on her long red gown. Once inside, the guard forced her down onto the rear bench, manhandling her more than necessary, then sat beside her. She felt sick as both the emperor and the blond man climbed in next, shutting and latching the carriage door behind them before sitting across from her and the guard.

The carriage lurched into motion, accompanied by the *clop clop* of horse hooves.

She tried to bite her tongue, but could remain silent no longer. "Please, just tell me where we are going," she pleaded, eyes on the emperor. "You've shown me that I cannot escape, so what is the harm in telling me?"

Egrin chuckled. "I want it to be a surprise. I have a feeling your reaction will supply me with entertainment for days to come."

The blond man waved him off. "Oh Egrin, give the poor girl a hint. Her heart might stop otherwise, then she'd be of no use to us."

Though curtains obscured her view of the courtyard, she marked the carriage's progress in her mind. It seemed they were circling the western end of the castle, likely heading toward the front gates.

Egrin rolled his eyes. "Now Daemon, why must you ruin all my fun?"

She turned her pleading gaze to Daemon, giving her best pathetic pout. Let them think she was a harmless, scared girl. As soon as she got away from Egrin, she could take care of the rest.

Egrin sighed. "Very well. You, my dear, are to be handed off to the Akkeri. They have paid a high price for you."

"The Akkeri?" she gasped, hunching over her suddenly knotted gut. "What could the Akkeri possibly want with me?" This wasn't possible. He had to be lying to scare her. The emperor had no contact with the Akkeri.

Egrin shrugged. "I do not know what they want, perhaps they wish to *eat* you. All I can be sure of is that to them, you are more valuable than all the coin in the Empire. More valuable than life itself, as it were."

She shook her head and looked to Daemon, hoping he would contradict the emperor's claims.

He shrugged. "My apologies, but it is true. Their leader requested you by name."

By name? "But the Akkeri are monsters! How would they know my name? I am no one special."

"You are the daughter of a member of the Faerune High Council," Daemon countered, "surely that means you're at least a bit special."

She looked to the guard beside her, but he showed no signs of surprise. Could he truly support an emperor who would bargain with the Akkeri?

A sudden thought dawned on her. "Last night . . . the screams. That was the Akkeri, wasn't it? *I'm more valuable than life itself to them.* You wanted them to attack, knowing they would be killed, but why?"

The corner of Egrin's thin lips quirked up. "Clever girl. It really is a pity we must give you away to those monsters. You could prove quite an asset otherwise."

She shook her head. Outside, she could hear the front gates creaking open while the carriage waited. "Why did you want them to attack?" she asked again.

Egrin leaned forward as the carriage started moving. "Because a city living in fear is willing to make allegiances they would otherwise rebel against. People will do most anything to save their own necks, and the scrawny little necks of their children. Especially when that threat can creep up from the ocean floor at any time."

Her jaw dropped. He'd sacrificed his own people just to make them afraid, and the Akkeri had sacrificed their lives for . . . *her*.

The emperor leaned back in his seat, seemingly satisfied with her reaction.

Her shoulders hunched. She was being sold off to monsters, but she was beginning to think the Akkeri couldn't possibly be as evil as the monster sitting right across from her.

CHAPTER ELEVEN

Elmerah

E lmerah took a deep whiff as they reached the spice district. She'd procured a steamed bun filled with burrberry jelly on the way there, but at the scent of the spices, her stomach groaned for more.

Or perhaps she was just distracting herself from the fact she was no closer to coming up with a plan for facing Rissine.

Ahead of her, Baeorn and Alluin halted.

"It's the house at the end of the street on the right," she heard Baeorn mutter as she sidled closer. "There will be a human man leaning next to the front entrance, a wide-brimmed wool hat atop his head as one would wear tending the fields. Another man is *resting* on the balcony above. Two more out back. I will find Liam, then return to hear your plans."

Alluin strolled toward the nearest spice cart as Baeorn disappeared into the slowly growing crowd.

Elmerah approached Alluin's side at the cart, pretending to look at deep red ground fire pepper, and large clumps of gray salt. The cart's proprietor, a young girl with white blonde hair in long braids, kept a casual eye on them.

"What do you think?" Alluin whispered, not looking at her.

"I'm not at my full strength," she muttered back, "but we cannot risk Thera relocating, and I do not want Rissine to find me first. I'd like to approach her on my terms."

"Liam and Baeorn will offer us a measure of protection, but three elves can only do so much."

She smirked, then wiped it away at the proprietor's questioning stare. "From what I've witnessed, three elves can do quite a lot."

"So you would like to approach? We can always wait and see if Thera or Rissine reveal themselves."

She shook her head. After the previous night's attack, she suspected something big was coming. There was no saying how long Rissine would even remain within the city. "No more waiting. We'll go for those guarding the back of the building, assuming it's out of sight from the street. We'll use stealth as far as we can. I do not believe Rissine wants me dead, so if the situation grows dire, *run*. Do not worry about leaving me behind."

He turned and meandered away from the spice cart.

She looked a moment longer, nodded to the girl, then followed.

"Why Elmerah," he whispered when she neared his broad back, "am I to believe you're actually worried for my safety?"

She snorted, startling a woman walking past. Once the

woman was out of hearing range, she replied, "Hardly, I just want to make sure there's someone left to rescue me."

He chuckled, then veered across the street. A crossroad came into view, marking the street's end, just as Baeorn had mentioned. Her eyes scanned down the row of houses. *There.* A man in a wide brimmed hat leaning near the closed door.

Pretending to peruse a stand piled high with fresh-baked bread under a gauzy cloth, she flicked her gaze once more to the building, spotting the second man atop the balcony.

Given the house's position, the rear end would be partially visible from the crossroad. It would be difficult to disable the men standing guard there without any passersby sounding an alarm.

She jumped as Baeorn appeared at her side, his large frame making him stand out despite the cowl covering his pointed ears. "I've spoken to Alluin. I will distract the men at the front. Liam will aid you at the rear."

She subtly nodded, then sauntered away. Alluin had already made it to the crossroad. Perhaps it would be best if she approached the rear of the house from the other direction.

She cut back across the street, weaving through the crowd. A few looked her up and down, then hurried away. It was all well and good for the elves to hide their ears. It was a little more difficult to hide her height and bronze skin. Anyone in the house who knew Rissine would have no trouble picking her sister out of the crowd.

At that thought, she pulled her hood a little lower over her brow, then darted onto the narrow dirt path between buildings, kicking up her black coat at the hem. A tall stone wall bordered the sides and rear of the house, obscuring her view of the other guards, however, it also kept the guards from seeing *her* . . . unless there was another high balcony like at the front.

She pressed her shoulder against the wall, just in case, then crept further along, occasionally glancing behind her to ensure no one followed.

She reached the end of the wall. By her estimations, Alluin should have been a few steps ahead of her. He would hopefully notice her once she entered the rear courtyard.

Saying a silent prayer to Arcale, or Ilthune, or whatever god would actually listen to an Arthali witch, she jumped, latching her hands atop the stone wall. Her breath heaved as she pulled herself upward, rolled across the top, then dropped down.

She crouched for a moment, crushing a patch of well-tended lettuce as she peered around. A short stone wall surrounding most of the large garden shielded her view of the house, just as it shielded her from those within.

She remained crouched for several heartbeats, but nothing moved. They hadn't seen her.

Keeping her head down, she crept to the garden's iron gate, then peeked out across the courtyard. The two men Baeorn had mentioned rested with their backs on either side of a heavy wood door mounted into the lower stones of the building. Halfway up, the stones transitioned to wood gray with age. There were several windows on both the lower and upper level, but nothing moved within.

She turned her gaze to the far wall just in time to see Alluin vault over it before ducking behind a large silver oak.

"What was that?" one of the men on guard hissed. "I think I saw something."

Elmerah peeked out as the man who'd spoken pushed away from the wall and walked across the courtyard, his loose crimson pants and hair nearly as red standing out amidst their green surroundings. Leaving him to Alluin, she crawled back away from the gate, then scurried to the other end of the garden nearer the house. She peeked over the low wall at the other man still near the door, paying little heed to his cohort's concerns.

She was tempted to take care of him quickly with magic, but she needed to save what little energy she had left for Rissine.

She was about to leap over the garden wall to charge the man, when he pushed off the wall with a yawn. After stretching his arms over his head, he opened the door and went inside.

Gritting her teeth, she looked back toward the red haired man, creeping near the tree Alluin was hiding behind. She jumped as elven hands whipped out, covering the man's face as he was dragged behind the tree. Within a heartbeat the other elf, Liam, vaulted over the wall and landed behind the tree. A few grunting noises ensued, then Alluin peeked out around the trunk of the massive oak.

Elmerah signaled to him, pointing to the door to show the other man had gone inside.

Alluin nodded, then pointed toward the second level of the house.

Her head whipped the other direction as she looked up, scanning the windows.

Hatred flared within her. Rissine stood framed by one of the central windows, looking out over the back courtyard. She didn't seem to be peering at anything in particular, just staring wistfully.

Elmerah's fingers flexed around the pommel of her cutlass as Rissine backed away from the window. At the only faint surge of magic summoned by her ire, she switched her grip to the enchanted short sword she'd procured from the thug at the docks further back on her belt. Touching the hilt instantly nullified her magic, just as it would Rissine's. She hated touching the thing, but it was likely her best chance against her sister.

She nearly jumped up and screamed as someone appeared crouched beside her.

With a hand held to her racing heart, she turned to Alluin. "Never sneak up on a woman plotting bloody revenge," she whispered.

"I'll try to remember that for the future." He shifted his stance to lean against the garden wall. "Liam is going around the side. He'll look for a place to climb up and enter through one of the windows. You and I will go through the back door. I'll create a distraction while you head upstairs and find Rissine. Hopefully by that point Liam will be able to assist you . . . " he looked her up and down. "Should you need it," he added.

She nodded. He moved to go, but she stopped him with a hand on his arm.

He looked a question at her.

"Alluin—" she hesitated, then deciding they might soon die, finished, "I just wanted to say thank you. I likely wouldn't have tracked down Rissine without your help."

"I'm doing this for my people too, you know. Rissine is my key to the emperor's plan."

She sighed. "I know, but you didn't have to include me, and now you're letting me have the first stab at Rissine, trusting I'll tell you whatever I learn. So thank you, I'm not used to being trusted."

"Well I'm not used to doing the trusting," he quipped, then hopped over the wall, racing toward the back door.

Cursing under her breath, she hurried after him.

He'd already entered the doorway by the time she arrived, and had left the second guard unconscious in the hall. He was buying her time, and she'd better not waste it.

Following the sound of another scuffle, she raced down the hall, her boots sounding a little too loudly across the floorboards. A shock of white blonde hair came speeding out of one of the rooms ahead.

For a moment she thought it was Saida, then the woman turned.

With a satisfied snarl, Elmerah launched a foot into Thera's face. She fell back with a screech, but Elmerah was already past her, heading for a set of stairs.

She raced up them, ready to draw the enchanted blade the moment Rissine revealed herself. She'd let her sister use up her energy launching attacks that would not hit, then she'd dispose of the blade and unleash her own magic. It would finally be time to see who was better.

She crested the stairs to find Liam hoisting himself in through a window, his sandy blond hair mussed from the climb. She didn't see any trees outside and had no idea how he'd managed the ascent, but she didn't bother questioning him.

"Watch the stairs," she hissed. "Give a shout if she tries to go down."

She stopped to listen for a moment as Liam moved past her. Fighting had broken out downstairs. Hopefully Baeorn had come in through the front to join Alluin, but she couldn't worry about that now. The real danger to them all was Rissine.

The upstairs portion of the house was smaller than the bottom floor. Just a long hall and several rooms. Rissine had to be in one of them, but she wasn't making a peep.

Elmerah walked first to the door she thought belonged to the window where she'd seen her sister. She withdrew the magic nullifying blade, then kicked it open.

It slammed back against the interior wall, but the room was otherwise perfectly still. Just a bed, a dresser, and a closet.

She took a moment to check under the bed and in the closet, then went to the next room, surprised Rissine was actually hiding . . . unless Rissine had immediately gone downstairs and escaped out the front while she and Alluin went in through the back.

She kicked the next door and went inside to look around. She had just turned to leave the empty room, when a shiver of electricity raised the tiny hairs on her arms. She whipped around, holding the enchanted blade in front of her body.

A bolt of lightning met with the blade, then dissipated, though it left Elmerah's hair alive with residual friction.

Rissine stood framed in a doorway that hadn't been there before. Elmerah knew she was not skilled in illusions, so it must have been a special feature built into the room.

"An enchanted blade?" Rissine questioned. The small bells and jewels at her hips jingled as she stepped forward, and rings glittered at her fingers.

Other than the new shiny baubles, Rissine looked just as Elmerah had imagined her. Thick black hair, a little more curly than hers, frothed around her face, falling well past her shoulders. The perfect olive skin of her bare arms showed the spiraling tattoos marking her as a Shadowmarsh witch.

Elmerah had been too young to obtain them before she'd left her homeland and, for that, she was glad.

Elmerah spun the blade in her hand, readjusting her grip to point the sharp end at her sister. "Why did you bring me here, Rissine?"

Rissine raised an eyebrow at her. "Not to fight you, dear sister. Though I suppose I cannot blame you for being angry about the pirates. I was simply too busy here to come myself."

She wasn't sure what was happening downstairs, but knew that prolonged commotion would draw the militia to investigate. She edged toward her sister. She had to make this quick.

"If you didn't want to fight me, why throw lightning at my back?"

Rissine laughed. "I had to make sure you're still the sister I remember, able to fend off *anything* I throw at you."

Elmerah sighed, then tightened her grip on her aimed blade. "What do you want? Why find me after all these years?"

Rissine prowled around her, heedless of the blade pointed at her throat.

Elmerah spun slowly, tracking her every move.

"There are about to be some big changes in the Empire," Rissine explained. "Egrin Dinoba has forged new treaties with the Dreilore and Nokken, betraying the old agreements with Faerune. Even the Akkeri have a place in this new world order. I've bargained for the Arthali exile to be lifted. We will have a new homeland soon on this large, rich continent."

Elmerah's jaw dropped. That wasn't what she'd been expecting, not in the slightest. "Why do you care about the

Arthali exile? You weren't much older than I when we left Shadowmarsh. We owe nothing to the Arthali."

"We owe it to ourselves!" Rissine hissed. "You may be content wasting your days in some swamp, but I've been here, slowly earning the respect I deserve. Soon I won't have to hide my heritage when I walk through the streets. We will build an empire of our own, and no one will dare ever spit on us again."

Elmerah shrugged. "I don't really mind the spit. Now I'm assuming the militia will be bursting in here at any moment, so tell me what any of this has to do with me. And what about Saida?"

"We're Shadowmarsh witches," Rissine replied like Elmerah had asked a very stupid question. "Who better to lead our people out of exile?"

Elmerah snorted. Her sister had clearly gone mad. "And what of Saida? Her name was on those contracts. Why *her*?"

Rissine shrugged. "The emperor wanted her. I did not ask questions. Perhaps it's part of his bargain with the Akkeri. They've long despised Faerune. Perhaps the priestess is why they attacked the city."

Revulsion made her shiver. Any man who would bargain with the Akkeri was mad, and if what Rissine said was true, that meant the emperor had planned the attack on his own people. She wanted nothing to do with any of it.

Without warning, she lunged forward, placing the enchanted blade against her sister's throat. "I want no part of your new empire. Give me your word you'll leave me be, and I might not slit your throat."

Rissine laughed, placing her throat more firmly against the blade. "There is no escaping for you. Things have already been set into motion, and you will not risk being on the wrong side of this war. The Faerune and Valeroot elves will have their peace no longer."

Elmerah stepped back at the sound of many footsteps, then Thera and two men dragged Alluin into the room. Thera's face was stained with blood from a broken nose, granting Elmerah a small measure of satisfaction.

Sensing Thera's intent, she darted behind her sister and held the blade to her throat. Her nostrils were hit with the scent of rich herbs and bitterroot, the latter a bad habit Rissine had picked up early on. The scent encased her in sudden nostalgia, which she quickly pushed away. "Let him go," she ordered.

Alluin struggled against the two men holding him as Thera withdrew a small jeweled dagger from the belt cinched at the waist of her white dress.

She pointed the dagger at Alluin. "I don't think you're in any position to give orders here." She looked to Rissine. "What would you like me to do?"

"I'd like you to not interrupt my family reunion you fool," Rissine growled, pulling against Elmerah's grip. "Get him out of here. Kill him for all I care. Elmerah will not harm me. She's always been full of bluster."

Clearly taken aback, Thera lowered her blade.

"Ugh!" Elmerah growled, "and you've always been a snake-tongued witch!" Tossing aside the enchanted sword, she shoved Rissine into Thera, toppling both women to land in a crumpled heap on the floor.

She withdrew her cutlass, summoning fire to her blade.

The two men holding Alluin let him go and stepped away, their hands held up in surrender.

"Go!" Elmerah shouted, shoving Alluin out the door just

as a bolt of lightning struck right where they'd been standing.

Rissine always had been the *gifted* sister. Elmerah couldn't summon lightning inside if she tried.

She and Alluin ran down the hall as another bolt chased after them, followed by thundering footsteps. They raced down the stairs to find Liam, only half conscious leaning against the wall.

Alluin and Elmerah each took an arm, dragging him toward the front of the house. If they could reach the street, Rissine would not be able to continue her attack.

They were almost there when Baeorn came running toward them. "I've barricaded the front, but the militia will soon break through. We must go out the back."

He took Liam's arm from Elmerah, allowing her to lead the way back through the house past expensive furniture and artwork. If only she hadn't tossed that cursed enchanted blade aside. Without it, she'd be weak to Rissine's next attack.

They reached the back hall to find the way blocked by Rissine, Thera, and the two men who'd captured Alluin.

"Militia men are out front," Elmerah snarled at her sister. "You better go let them in. You won't see your precious new world order if we all end up in the stocks."

Rissine glared at her for several heartbeats. "Fine, *go*. Take some time to think on what I've said, and do not try to run. *Next* time, the pirates will drug you and beat you within an inch of your life before taking you."

With that, she stepped aside.

Elmerah would have liked to get in one last insult, but from the sounds of it, the militia men were about to break down the door. With a glance back at Alluin, she hurried past Rissine into the hall, then let the elves go ahead of her.

She stole one final glance back at her sister, wondering at what point her best friend had fully warped into the twisted viper she'd become.

CHAPTER TWELVE

Saida

It felt like they'd been in the carriage for *days*. Saida's arms and back ached from remaining in the uncomfortable seated position with her wrists bound behind her back. Daemon and the emperor had spoken little since revealing Saida's fate. She longed to check the note in her stocking. Perhaps she would now understand what it meant, and why the creature had given it to her.

There were a few shouts outside, and the carriage ambled to a halt. Someone knocked on the door. The guard at her side leaned forward and opened it slightly.

She watched his every move, periodically glancing to the closed door on the other side of the carriage. If she could just get out into the streets, Egrin wouldn't be able to apprehend her without making a scene. He'd gone to great pains to ensure her capture remained a secret. Now, to try and lunge for the open door, or to use the distraction to open the closed one?

The guard leaned a little further out, arguing with someone outside. Daemon and Egrin both seemed bored with the entire event. Seeing this as the best opportunity she'd get, she took a deep breath, then lunged toward the partially open door, spotting just for a moment the two militia men outside before she was tossed back against the bench.

Daemon and Egrin still sat calmly across from her. Frantic, she tried to struggle against the ropes binding her hands, but her entire body was paralyzed. She tried to scream, but she couldn't *breathe*. Shooting stars crackling in her brain, she stared at the emperor. Had he—

He held a finger to his lips, which curved into a wicked grin.

She was quite sure he knew she couldn't call out if she wanted to. It felt like air was being forced into her lungs, expanding them painfully. She couldn't exhale. Her vision slowly went gray as the guard casually conversed with whoever was outside.

Daemon and Egrin watched her all the while, both clearly amused.

Finally, the door shut, and the carriage lurched back into motion.

The pressure filling her lungs and pinning her body eased, and she slumped against the bench with a long, aching exhale. Her pulse slowing, she took another ragged breath. She would have clutched at her burning throat if her hands weren't bound.

Distantly, she heard more shouts outside, and realized they were exiting the city gates. The militia men outside now made sense.

When her lungs had recovered, she asked, "We're leaving the city?"

Daemon smirked. "Clearly. We cannot hand you off to the Akkeri where anyone can see."

She straightened in her seat, still panting. If they didn't want anyone to see, they would likely not hand her off until dark. She still had time. For what, she did not know.

She stared at Egrin Dinoba, memorizing his face. He might possess frightening magics, but some day, no matter what, she would make him pay.

Alluin

"Your uncle doesn't want me back there," Elmerah argued.

They'd almost reached the hideout after barely escaping the militia men breaking down Rissine's door. Liam had regained consciousness, but had a deep wound on the back of his scalp. Alluin hadn't noticed it until the blood dripped down onto his tan shirt, and now feared his friend might have more injuries not as readily apparent as the bleeding.

"Alluin!" Elmerah hissed when he didn't reply. "He doesn't want me back there. I'll find somewhere else to recover." She stopped walking.

Releasing Liam momentarily, he turned and grabbed her wrist, then dragged her forward. "Trust me, if you tell my uncle what you told me, he'll let you stay."

"Or he'll just think I'm working with Rissine. He'll want to kill me before I can divulge his secrets."

Baeorn glanced at them both, then continued onward, helping Liam walk.

Elmerah tugged her wrist free of Alluin's grasp, then put her hands on her hips with a defiant look in her dark eyes.

Truly, Alluin was a little shocked she didn't want to see the Arthali restored to their former glory, but he believed her when she said she wanted nothing to do with it. Though it was true Ured didn't want Elmerah in the hideout, his uncle would soon understand just how valuable she could be to the elves.

He sighed. "I'll give you more Valeroot wine."

She crossed her arms and pouted. "I already have a new bottle in my pocket. If I go in there, your uncle will take it away from me."

He swiped his palm across his face, shaking his head. "Of course you do. We need to get you a coat with shallower pockets."

"I like my coat just fine."

He sighed again. "Elmerah, we don't have much choice right now. Your sister will be out looking for you, and now she may very well be looking for me too. We need a place to rest and come up with a plan. You thanked me before for trusting you. Now I need you to trust me."

She stared at him for several heartbeats. "Fine," she grumbled, "but your uncle better play nicely."

He forced a smile and nodded. His uncle Ured didn't understand the concept of playing nice, but he'd tell Elmerah whatever she wanted to hear if it would get them off the streets, far out of Rissine's reach.

They started walking forward again, past the scouts atop the roofs at either end of the long alley. They would have signaled had they been followed. For the time being, they were safe, but if what Rissine had said was true, soon *no one* would be safe.

He had to stop that from happening.

Reaching the house atop the hideout, Alluin knocked on the door. Moments later, an elf named Mariel opened it. Her coloring and hair were light enough to pass for a Faerune elf, though he knew she was pure Valeroot. She gave them both a nod, then welcomed them in, likely forewarned by Baeorn and Liam, who'd gone in ahead of them.

She shut and locked the door behind them, then remained on guard as they ventured further into the house. They didn't have a chance to venture underground before his uncle found them, Baeorn at his side.

"Uncle," Alluin began, hoping to keep Ured's temper under control until he could explain what happened.

His uncle held up a wizened hand. "Our scouts just returned from the city gates. Saida was removed from the castle and placed in a carriage bearing the emperor's insignia. The emperor and Daemon Saredoth are both with her."

"Where are they now?" Elmerah demanded, stepping forward.

Ured glared at her. "They left the city, headed down the Emperor's Path. If you hope to catch her, you must leave now."

"Uncle," Alluin began anew, "we found Rissine. The emperor has promised to lift the exile of the Arthali and grant them lands. He's planning on going to war. As we suspected, Faerune is likely the first target."

Ured nodded. "Baeorn told me what happened. He can fill me in on the rest."

"Stop delaying!" Elmerah snapped. "If she's already on the road, she may soon be lost to us."

She was right. He knew she was right, but could he leave his people in such danger, especially when Saida was likely lost to him already?

"We'll go through the tunnels," he breathed. He turned to Ured. "Uncle, may I?" He didn't say his full thoughts out loud, lest he anger his uncle further.

Ured nodded, catching his meaning. "You may bring her *there*, but if she speaks of it to anyone, both of you are dead."

That was all the permission he needed. He turned to Elmerah. "The tunnels are the fastest way out of the city. From there, I can procure us mounts."

He didn't give Elmerah time to complain about the tunnels, instead grabbing her wrist and pulling her along.

"Be careful if you see the emperor!" his uncle called after them. "I've long suspected he hides what he truly is!"

He barely heard his uncle's words. Everything was on the brink of falling apart. If the emperor set his plan in motion, the elves, both Faerune and Valeroot alike, would be the first to fall.

Elmerah

ELMERAH LIKED THE DARK, DAMP TUNNELS EVEN LESS ON her second venture through, given the sojourn was likely all for naught. She knew there was little chance of saving Saida. Rissine had all but won.

Still, if there was any chance of rescuing the girl who'd gotten trapped in her wicked sister's web, she would do it. In part, because Saida did not deserve to be sold off to monsters like the Akkeri, but also because she had been waiting a very long time to best her sister. She at least had to try.

She heaved a sigh of relief as they reached the final gate leading out to the cave. They'd spoken little on their journey, more focused on hurrying through the tunnels and unlocking gates with only the light of a sole lantern.

They exited to find the sun nearing the horizon. It would make sense for the exchange to happen under the cover of night. They were running out of time.

"We should run," she panted as they stepped into the dense woods. "If they have to stop and wait for the Akkeri, perhaps we'll catch them."

Alluin shook his head. "We won't catch them on foot. Come this way." He turned and walked further into the woods, opposite the direction of the Emperor's Path.

"Are you dense!" she hissed, kicking aside twigs and pine needles as she hurried after him. "You're going the wrong way."

He kept walking. "Remember what I said about trusting me? Please, do so."

She had the urge to tackle him and beat some sense into him, but deep down she didn't think he'd risked Saida's life on a whim. Perhaps he really did have a plan.

Once it was clear she would follow, Alluin started jogging. Though her tired limbs protested, she kept pace with him, carefully watching her footing for snarled roots.

She followed him deeper and deeper into the forest, farther than any sane man would go. Trolls could be found if you went too deep, along with Fossegrims and lesser wyrms. Yes, if you went deep enough into the forests of the West, you weren't likely to return.

Finally, when she thought her feet would carry her no more, a small settlement came into view.

She halted, her knees nearly buckling as she stared.

The log buildings were small and primitive, easily blending in with the dense trees. There was no sense of organization that she could see. The settlement literally seemed to be built *into* the forest. On one side, animal pens made of five rows of woven together branches contained the seemingly delicate animals within. They weren't quite horses, though they were similar, just with more slender bodies and necks, long wooly tan fur, and pairs of short, spiraling horns. She'd heard of the antlioch, but had never seen one up close.

"We don't have time to gawk," Alluin stated, tugging her forward, "and if you tell anyone of this place, my uncle will have both our heads."

He dragged her past a few buildings, and the elves that had emerged to stare at them. They seemed to recognize Alluin, but as soon as he passed, they aimed death stares at her.

Normally she'd gladly return a death stare, but there was something about the small settlement that made her instincts scream *danger*. They were running out of time anyway.

Alluin dropped her wrist and opened the gate to the nearest animal pen, then walked inside. He gestured to two of the creatures, both of which came at his command.

"They're very well trained," he explained hurriedly. "Just climb up and guide them with your legs, putting pressure on the opposite side from where you'd like to turn."

She stared up at the wooly beast before her. They were taller than horses too, and the horns sharp enough to pierce flesh.

She looked at Alluin hesitantly.

He hurried over, lacing his hands together and lowering them for her to step up. "We're running out of time," he urged.

He was right. She stepped into his palms, then swung her leg over the animal's back, nestling herself into the thick wool. It didn't startle or prance about like a horse might, and instead waited patiently for direction.

Alluin sprung off the fence and onto the second animal's back, giving it a little tap on its side with his foot. Elmerah's antlioch followed Alluin's out of the gate, then back in the direction they'd come.

"Well," Elmerah muttered, clutching the soft wool, "if I die today, at least I can say I rode an antlioch."

She gave her animal a tap and it picked up its pace, nearly toppling her from its back, her hood slipping off her head. Remembering Alluin's words, she righted herself, then put pressure on the antlioch's left flank. It turned the moment she commanded it.

With a nod of reassurance to her, Alluin clicked his tongue. His antlioch leapt forward, then sped off through the forest, quickly leaving her behind.

With a short prayer to Arcale, she entwined her hands in the creature's wool, leaned forward, and gave a more aggressive tap.

The antlioch bolted forward, deftly weaving through the trees. Cool wind that would only grow colder as night fell whipped through her long hair. She caught sight of Alluin's back through the shadowy trees, but as soon as she caught up with him, he clicked his tongue, urging his mount faster. It was all she could do to keep her head down and arms in, trusting the antlioch wouldn't run into any trees.

As she grew more comfortable, she lifted her head. The cool wind exhilarated her almost as much as the trees whipping by. Though it was nearly dark, they might just make it in time.

Saida

SAIDA'S GUARD DRAGGED HER OUT OF THE CARRIAGE AND onto the sand of the small inlet. Not expecting the carriage to be so close to the sand, she lost her footing, tangling her legs in her long ruby gown. The tall guard held her aloft by his grip on her arm, tugging her bound hands painfully behind her back.

Daemon stepped out of the carriage next, offering the guard a glare. "Now, now, don't damage our little princess. Save that for the Akkeri."

Still holding Saida aloft, the guard offered Daemon a bow of his head.

The emperor stepped out of the carriage onto the sand, heedless of his fine suede boots. He turned his pale gaze out toward the sea. "There," he pointed.

Pushing against the guard's grip to right herself, Saida peered out across the slowly darkening ocean. She wasn't even sure how the emperor had spotted the small ship so quickly. The wood planks were dark and the un-furled sail black, blending in with the coming night. Her elven eyes picked it out easily now that she'd spotted it, but a human should have had difficulty.

"They'll send a boat in to fetch you," Egrin explained as

he turned toward her, "I thank you for your contribution to building an even greater Empire."

She spit on his suede boots.

She expected a backhand, but no violent gesture came. Egrin only laughed. "It really is *such* a pity. Let us enjoy the evening while we can." He walked toward the distant surf.

The guard shoved her in the direction the emperor had gone and she stumbled forward. She had to do something. If she was brought to the Akkeri ship, there would be no escape.

As if sensing her thoughts, Damon stepped up beside her.

At least the emperor's back was to her. If she could knock down her guard, and slip away from Daemon, she might just—

"Do you think your parents know where you are?" Daemon asked suddenly.

She stopped walking. "What does that matter to you?"

He shrugged. "Simply curious what the Faerune elves would do if they knew we not only held you captive, but gave you to the Akkeri. They do not desire war, but would they throw out their ideals to avenge you?"

She blinked at him. She honestly did not know. Her parents loved her, that was true, but since the exile of the Arthali and Akkeri, they'd known peace. They would be reluctant to go against the Empire, even for such a grave offense. In the end though, she believed they would.

"How should I know?" she sighed.

She actually hoped her parents never found out what had happened to her. Faerune was likely an even match for the militia of the Capital, but still, many lives would be lost. She would not wish her kin to risk themselves, especially if she was already dead . . . which she likely would be before night's end.

Daemon smirked. "I think you do know. I think they would come running for you. They would fight, not knowing what allies Egrin has acquired, and they would *die*."

She stifled a shiver. "Yet, you have kept my capture a secret."

He shrugged and began walking again, causing her guard to shove her forward. "Yes, it is more important to let the people of Galterra believe more Akkeri attacks are imminent."

He said the last with an air of longing. Did he truly wish to go to war with Faerune?

Her moment of speculation ended abruptly at the sight of a small rowboat cresting the choppy waters halfway between the ship and the coast. Four Akkeri manned the boat, their pallid skin clear to her superior night vision. As she watched them, the last sliver of sunlight winked out of existence.

She shivered, knowing she might not see the sun again in this lifetime.

Egrin turned as they approached, aiming a wicked smile her way. Then suddenly, the smile faltered. Unable to turn around with the guard holding her arm, she craned her neck behind them.

The carriage was right where they'd left it, but the two extra guards were gone.

Daemon grabbed Saida's arm, tugging her toward him. "Go see where they went," he ordered the remaining guard.

He nodded, then turned and trotted toward the carriage, his hand on the sword at his belt.

Her heart in her throat, Saida watched as the guard

circled the carriage. He made it to the far side. There was a low grunt, low enough that she wasn't sure the emperor and Daemon would have heard it over the pounding surf. Moments ticked by, but the guard did not finish his walk around the carriage.

"Keep her here," the emperor ordered.

Saida's shoulders slumped. She did not understand what had happened to the guards, but she'd hoped Daemon would go next, to perhaps be eaten by a beast or snatched by a Fossegrim. With Egrin going, he'd surely best whatever awaited him.

Of course, she might be able to at least escape Daemon while Egrin was preoccupied. If she could make it across the Emperor's Path and into the forest beyond, she might be able to hide until morning.

Egrin reached the carriage, walking around it just as the guard had, only he reached the other side. His brow furrowed, he walked back around the front and opened the door. All three guards were piled up inside the dark interior. Whether unconscious or dead, she could not tell.

She glanced at Daemon, wondering if he could see the guards as well as she, but his gaze remained on the carriage. She turned back just in time to see Egrin narrowly avoiding a rock sailing through the darkness right for his head. With a snarl, he charged toward the lush vegetation likely concealing his attacker.

Sensing her chance, Saida tugged away from Daemon. She'd meant to aim her foot at his face, but she had too much momentum, and fell on her rump in the soft sand.

Daemon moved to grab her, but another rock sailed through the air from the opposite direction of the first, knocking him in the back of the skull.

In a wave of blond hair he fell beside her. Still somehow conscious, he scrambled to his feet, facing the direction from which the rock had come.

A male figure now stood further down the beach, his features obscured by a cowl and the night. Saida knew it was too strong a coincidence, but she almost thought it might be Alluin.

It took Daemon a moment to spot him in the darkness, then he drew his rapier and took on a defensive stance in front of her.

The other man charged, twin daggers drawn. He leapt at Daemon, who effortlessly parried the attack, moving as fast as any elf, though Saida had been quite sure he was human.

She scuttled back through the sand as the men continued to fight, falling back onto her bound hands painfully more than a few times.

"Help Elmerah!" the cloaked man grunted, his feet kicking up sand as he and Daemon fell into a rhythmic, deadly dance.

Her eyes widened. It *was* Alluin, and Elmerah was here too? Sudden panic hit her. That's who Egrin had gone after, and she wasn't aware of his magic.

She scurried further back in the sand, then used her shoulder to roll herself up to her feet. If only her hands weren't still bound, she could steal one of the immobile guard's weapons, but there was no time to try to cut the ropes. Elmerah needed her help.

Elmerah

ELMERAH SILENTLY RETREATED THROUGH THE THICK vegetation, slowly making her way toward the denser trees. She would attack the emperor—ye gods, she couldn't believe she was actually considering attacking the *emperor*—soon anyway, after she lured him further away.

She stopped behind a shrub with wide, waxy leaves found only near the coast.

The emperor continued to creep along, oddly without a weapon drawn. She'd witnessed him finding the three unconscious guards—or maybe they were dead, the rocks she and Alluin had hit them with had been rather large—so why would he come after her without a weapon in hand?

She took a step back, wincing as a twig snapped beneath her boot. They were far enough from the surf now that he'd likely heard it.

Sure enough, his gaze whipped in her direction, his eyes narrowed to peer through the growing darkness. She froze, unable to tell if he'd spotted her, or if he was simply looking for the source of the sound.

Seconds later, an enormous weight seemed to crush her chest. Her hands groped the empty air as her eyes darted frantically about. She couldn't breathe, yet nothing was touching her.

Through her panic, she heard footsteps crunching over the rocky earth. The emperor appeared before her. His pale eyes seemed to soak in the moonlight. She wanted to lash out at him, but her hands merely fluttered at her sides like dying butterflies.

"An Arthali witch?" he questioned, looking her up and down. "How . . . unexpected."

She sputtered, but couldn't form words. Was he somehow doing this to her?

Seeming to read her thoughts, he grinned. "Don't worry, you're not to die tonight. I need to ask you some questions first." His grin wiped away as something tackled him to the ground.

Suddenly she could breathe again. She hopped back from the tussle, realizing it was one of the Akkeri atop the emperor's back, smashing his face into the hard earth.

"Run!" the Akkeri hissed, looking right at her.

Though she was wildly confused, the creature didn't have to tell her twice. She turned and ran back toward the beach.

Her lungs burned horribly as she stumbled through the dark vegetation. If the emperor had magic . . . the thought was horrifying. He was so much more of a threat than she'd imagined.

She ran blindly as she neared the beach, almost colliding with Saida. She skidded to a halt, blinked at the elf in shock, then grabbed her by the shoulders and turned her around. "Get back to Alluin," she panted as they started running. "We need to get out of here."

Elmerah reached the beach right behind Saida to find Alluin still fighting with the bejeweled blond man, obviously a better swordsman than his appearance would suggest. She glanced out toward the sea at the sound of guttural shouts just in time to see the Akkeri leaping from their boat into the tide to reach the shore more quickly.

"Alluin!" Elmerah shouted. They needed to retreat to the forest, *now*.

Alluin parried an incoming swipe of the blond man's rapier, then jumped aside, rolling across the sand and coming up to his feet. He raised his fingers to his lips as he ran away, emitting a long, clear whistle.

The antlioch whinnied in reply, then both beasts came trotting out onto the beach.

As Alluin took a running leap onto his mount, the blond man, only a few paces away, thrust his rapier toward Alluin's back.

Elmerah's heart froze, then Alluin landed safely atop his antlioch and turned it away. Her attention was broken as the other beast charged right for her. It slowed as it reached her, and she leapt upon its back, barely able to cling to the wool and pull herself up. She turned around to grab Saida, but Alluin was already there, pulling her atop his mount to rest belly down across his lap, her bound hands sticking up awkwardly.

The blond man charged them again, heedless of their mounts, but they both urged the antlioch away from the surf and the charging Akkeri. They'd almost reached the abandoned carriage when Elmerah heard a shriek of fear. She saw a pale shape running through the darkness toward her, quickly realizing it was the Akkeri who'd saved her, running from the emperor.

Hoping she wouldn't regret her decision, she spun her antlioch around and charged right for them. She held out a hand as she reached the Akkeri. Their palms connected, and she used the antlioch's momentum to swing the Akkeri up onto its back behind her.

She then veered sharply to the left, taking off in the direction Alluin and Saida had gone. She leaned close to the antlioch's neck, waiting for the moment when the emperor's magic would hit her, but the moment never came. Maybe he couldn't catch a quickly moving target.

She exhaled a sigh of relief as her mount galloped across the Emperor's Path and into the woods. The Akkeri snaked its arms around her waist, making her squirm, but she didn't push the creature away. It had saved her life, after all.

She caught sight of Alluin's back and the other antlioch's rump ahead. The creatures were far faster and more nimble than any horse. The emperor would not be able to catch them, at least not *this* night.

She wrinkled her nose at the scent of old fish coming from the Akkeri. She couldn't understand why it had saved her, but it seemed to speak the common tongue—at least, it had known to tell her to run—so hopefully she would soon find out.

Alluin

ALLUIN EASED THE PRESSURE ON HIS MOUNT'S FLANKS AND patted its shoulder, signaling for it to slow. They'd gone far enough to not be found, and it was dangerous to run blindly through the deep woods, especially at night. It was the only reason the Valeroot settlement had gone unnoticed for so long. Not even hunters ventured into the deep woods. The prey there was reserved for trolls, wyrms, and other beasts.

Saida squirmed atop his lap, still belly down.

"My apologies," he said, holding her biceps while she slid off his lap to the ground. "I didn't see any other way to carry you without you falling off."

He couldn't tell in the darkness, but thought she grimaced before turning to Elmerah riding up behind her.

He narrowed his eyes in the darkness, realizing she had a second rider.

Elmerah's antlioch halted, and the witch atop it spat on

the ground. "How in Ilthune does Egrin Dinoba possess magic?"

Saida walked toward her. "I have no idea, but I experienced it myself. Now can someone please cut my ropes?" She extended her wrists behind her.

Alluin barely heard her. He was too busy staring at Elmerah's extra rider, a scrawny Akkeri hiding behind her back as if hoping for protection.

"It saved me," Elmerah explained at his look. "I couldn't just leave it behind." She swung her leg over her antlioch's back, then slid down. She withdrew her cutlass, then cut Saida's ropes.

As soon as she'd finished, Saida turned around and hugged her.

Elmerah stiffly accepted the gesture, awkwardly patting Saida's back until she let go.

"I'm not an it," the Akkeri muttered, its words hoarse and slurred. "I am male."

Elmerah glanced at the Akkeri. "My apologies. Now might I ask, why did you save me?"

Alluin glanced around the dark, still woods. "As much as I'd like to learn the answer to that question, we are not safe here. We should find shelter until morning."

Elmerah snorted. "Any shelter out here is likely filled with trolls, and I imagine the emperor will have the militia combing the woods for us by morning. We should venture further in."

"You're mad," Alluin argued. "We'll all die out here."

"I agree with Elmerah," Saida interrupted. "At least for tonight. I have much to tell you both." She turned her gaze up to the Akkeri still atop the antlioch. "And I think you have much to tell me as well. Are you the one who left the note?"

The Akkeri nodded.

Alluin had had about enough. They'd just attacked the emperor and his closest advisor, fled the Akkeri, and were now stuck in the deep woods late at night. Daemon might not be able to identify him by sight, but Elmerah and Saida were most definitely fugitives now, so they could not return to the city. At some point, he'd become honor-bound to help them both, and he had a feeling the Akkeri would soon be added to that list.

With that creature along, they could not return to the Valeroot settlement, nor to the tunnels. He could not risk *it* telling others of its kind about either location.

All this boiled down to one thing.

They were all *utterly* sunk.

CHAPTER THIRTEEN

Elmerah

The antlioch carried them deeper into the dark forest. Saida had volunteered to ride with the Akkeri, who'd introduced himself as Merwyn, leaving Elmerah to ride with Alluin. She was a bit uncomfortable straddling the antlioch behind him, but at least she didn't have to smell Merwyn any longer.

Though there were a million things to discuss, they rode in silence, not wanting to attract any monsters. Elmerah flinched every time the gentle steps of the antlioch disturbed tiny lizards and rodents to skitter across the dead pine needles and fallen twigs. If they could find a defendable area, perhaps they could survive until sunrise.

After that, she was not sure what she would do. Part of her still wanted to best Rissine at her own game, but mostly she just wanted to get away from her. If Rissine truly believed Egrin Dinoba would pardon the Arthali, she'd lost her mind. Treaties with the Nokken and Dreilore would be far more valuable to him. As far as she knew, the Nokken had never warred with the Arthali, but the Dreilore detested their race . . . along with *most* races, save their own. Long lives and fearsome magic tended to fuel egos and incite competition. The Dreilore would never support the Arthali ruling over a region of the Empire. It could only mean Rissine would be betrayed at some point, and all other Arthali with her. The thing she didn't understand was how Rissine couldn't see the fate in store for her.

"Stop," Alluin hissed.

The antlioch beneath her and Alluin halted, and moments later, so did the other. Elmerah peered through the darkness ahead for an explanation, then inhaled sharply and held her breath.

A massive wyrm, its black skin reflecting the scant moonlight, skulked across their path only twenty paces ahead. Completely blind, the wyrms of the deep forest used their four claws, tipped with razor sharp talons, to sense movement on the forest floor. The wyrm's forked tongue, darting from a face that was a mixture of reptilian and feline, provided the beast with a sense of smell.

Elmerah glanced at Merwyn behind Saida, cursing their luck. If the wind shifted while they waited, the wyrm would surely scent him.

Long moments ticked by as the wyrm crept onward, its body, as tall as six men lying head to toe, undulated with every step, rubbing sleek scales across tree trunks with a spine-chilling hiss.

The antlioch were utterly still, no doubt sensing the wyrm.

Elmerah let out her breath as the wyrm's twitching tail

disappeared from sight, though they waited several long moments more before moving again.

"We are blessed to have a Valeroot hunter in our midst," Merwyn muttered, his rasping voice entirely unpleasant to hear.

Elmerah could not see Alluin's face as he glanced at the Akkeri, but she imagined he was glaring. "And what do you know of Valeroot elves?"

Elmerah thought the twisting of the Akkeri's thin lips was perhaps a smirk. He asked, "And what do you know of the Akkeri?"

"I know you have killed many of my kind," Alluin grumbled. "Weakening us so that when the Empire formed, Valeroot was destroyed."

It was a history Elmerah knew well, though she felt little pity for Valeroot. At least the elves hadn't been exiled and subsequently hunted down like dogs.

Merwyn was silent after that, unable to argue with the accusation, though the war likely occurred long before he was born.

"Do you think we have ventured deep enough?" Saida whispered. "Will Egrin's militia truly search this far for us?"

"That depends," Alluin replied. "Just how important are you to the Akkeri? Why were you to be given to them?"

He glanced again at Merwyn. They'd learned Saida was to be given to the Akkeri in exchange for their attack, but not why the Akkeri would want a Faerune elf, and Saida in particular.

Merwyn kept his reflective gaze ahead, not answering.

"Merwyn," Saida muttered. "You must tell us why."

Merwyn sighed, cast another wary glance at their surroundings, then replied, "There is a myth about how the

Akkeri came into being. Some believe we were once Faerune elves, cursed by the goddess Ilthune to be her servants, sending our victims' souls to the underworld. Every sacrifice made is a testament to our goddess."

"Vile beasts," Alluin grumbled.

Ignoring Alluin, Merwyn continued, "Some believe that if we were to regain the favor of the sky god Arcale, our true forms would be restored to us. They believe our existence is cursed."

"That cannot be true," Saida whispered, her reflective eyes peering toward the path ahead. "The Akkeri have always existed, as far back as the histories can remind us. Your lost temples are as old as the walls of Faerune."

"I will not argue with you, priestess," Merwyn rasped. "I cannot say what is true, only what many of the Akkeri believe. They believe if the Konnungar, our ruler, weds a Moon Priestess, Arcale will favor us once more, and our curse will be lifted."

"A Moon Priestess?" Elmerah interrupted.

Saida looked like she might be ill, her pale face like a ghost's in the moonlight. "That is what I'm called. Most of the high priests and priestesses are born with gifts of magic, provided by Arcale. They are favored by the sun. Occasionally, children are born to these gifted pairs, but are not granted magics. We are called priests and priestesses of the moon, favored instead by Cindra, the goddess of fate and wishes."

"Cindra is the wife of Arcale," Merwyn explained, "and you are the only unwed Moon Priestess alive today."

That was news to Elmerah. She'd never even heard of Moon Priestesses before. "So your Konnungar wants to marry Saida because she was born without magic?"

"Born to a high priestess, and without magic," Merwyn corrected.

Elmerah snorted. What a smoldering dung heap of an explanation. Myths and legends, nothing more. "And why don't you believe in this curse lifting business?" she whispered.

Merwyn shrugged. "Who is to say I do not? All I can think, is that if we are to please the Sky God, we should help the Moon Priestess, not harm her."

"I'm not sure if you're all dense," Alluin interrupted, "or if you all really want to be eaten by trolls, but we should stop talking."

"What we should do is *not* go any further into the deep woods," Elmerah countered. "This should be far enough. Let us find high ground and take turns resting."

Though it was her idea, she shivered at the thought. At least atop the antlioch they could easily flee should more monsters happen upon them. Plus, it was as cold as the wild wastes of the North. She wasn't looking forward to spending the rest of the night without a fire.

"You're right," Alluin conceded.

"There's a crag off to the left," Saida added.

Elmerah could see no crag, but Alluin seemed to take her at her word. He shifted, pressing his right leg against the antlioch's side. The antlioch carrying Saida and Merwyn veered left and followed.

Soon the small crag came into view for Elmerah. It wasn't exactly higher ground, but it would provide protection to their backs, allowing them to look out for monsters in only one direction.

Reaching the crag, Elmerah dismounted, stretching her legs and stiff back. She was thankful now for the new coat she procured. If she'd stuck with the old cloak she'd stolen from the inn, she'd be freezing. Unfortunately, Saida only had a thin magenta traveling cloak atop her crimson gown, and Merwyn wore even less, though she was not sure if Akkeri actually felt the cold. They swam long distances in the ice cold ocean after all.

She watched as Alluin checked over both of the antlioch for injuries, then patted their sides in seeming dismissal. After the pats, the creatures set to grazing nearby. Elmerah hoped dearly they would not startle and run off, trapping them with a full day of foot travel through the deep forest.

Seemingly unfazed by the cold, or late hour, Alluin stalked about, patrolling the perimeter of their temporary camp.

Saida moved to the rocky escarpment, then sat with her back against the cracked stone. She pulled her knees to her chest and huddled beneath her light cloak.

With a wary glance at Merwyn standing silently nearby, Elmerah joined Saida, sitting by her side. She supposed it was finally time they offer each other full explanations.

"I can't believe you actually rescued me," Saida muttered. "Not that I'm not appreciative, but how did you even know where I was?"

"Alluin's scouts," Elmerah explained, tucking her knees up against her chest, her shoulder nearly touching Saida's. "We knew shortly after you had been taken to the castle too. We went to find Rissine for an explanation."

"Ah yes," Saida sighed. "I met Rissine briefly. I could see the family resemblance, and not in looks alone."

Elmerah scowled. "I am nothing like my sister."

Saida chuckled. "If you say so." She was silent for a

moment. "So," she began anew, "you were saying you went to find Rissine. Were you successful?"

Elmerah nodded. "Successful in finding her, at least. She told me why the emperor wanted you . . . well, she *speculated.*"

Saida rested her chin on her upward bent knees. "Yes, it seems you and I were both kidnapped with great intention, though I still do not understand your role in the emperor's plan."

"I don't have one," Elmerah sighed. "Before this evening, I don't think the emperor even knew of my existence. Rissine believes Egrin will pardon the Arthali and grant them new lands. She and I are all that remains of the Shadowmarsh line. She believes it our responsibility to lead our people to glory."

"I had suspected you were of that line," Saida admitted, "after seeing your lightning on the pirate ship."

Elmerah quirked an eyebrow at her. "Few would put that together."

"My people know much about the Arthali. It is important to remember the histories, and to be prepared should our enemies strike again."

Elmerah snorted. "The elves actually believe there is a chance of the Arthali returning?"

Saida tilted her head toward Elmerah, providing the full weight of her reflective gaze. "We are not the only ones, apparently. Rissine believes it too. Why do you not?"

Elmerah shifted her weight on the hard ground, then shifted again as a rock dug into her tailbone. "After the Arthali were exiled, the clans began warring amongst themselves. Rissine and I left Shadowmarsh when we were young. If we had stayed we would have been killed, just like our mother. It has been many years since that day, but I do not believe the clans will ever reconcile, and that is exactly what's needed for Rissine's plan to work. The Shadowmarsh clan used to rule over all, but she and I are only two witches. Other Arthali would sooner kill us, than follow us."

"Even if Rissine could provide them with new lands, and a pardon from the emperor, would they not band together then?"

She shook her head, running her fingers through a strand of black hair that had escaped her hood. She hoped not, but in truth, she did not know. The emperor's alliances with the Dreilore and Nokken were frightening, but both were also organized into well-ruled civilizations. The Arthali were wild and blood-thirsty, much like the Akkeri. No one in their right mind would ally themselves with either, yet, she didn't have the heart to say so out loud. She'd endured enough hatred already.

"All I know is that you and I should both run far away from the Capital."

Saida nodded. "Yes, I must warn my people, though I fear there may not be much time."

Elmerah felt for her. Though she'd lost her home long ago, she knew what it was like to have one's life destroyed by violence. She'd chosen to run, but suspected Saida would not.

No, the elf girl was more the type to go down with a sinking ship.

"We should get some rest while we can," Elmerah sighed. "Let Alluin take the first watch."

Saida obeyed by curling up on her side, her back pressed against the rock face, her tangled blonde hair draped across her chest.

Elmerah curled up next to her, though she knew sleep would not come easily. The urge to run far away had not left her, not after all these years.

In fact, it had only grown stronger.

Rissine

RISSINE SAT WITH A RIGID SPINE IN THE COVERED carriage. She wasn't sure why the emperor had summoned her, but it made her nervous. Had he heard about the militia men breaking down her door? It had taken every last drop of her control to not lash out when one of the men called her an Arthali dog. She'd added him to her list, memorizing every detail of his face.

When the time came, he would be one of many to pay.

The carriage halted, signaling they'd reached the Crimson Jewel. She was nervous about going *there* too, now that her sister quite likely knew it was she who controlled the establishment. All of the guilds knew as much, but none dared challenge her.

She pushed the carriage curtain aside to scan the dark street. It was late enough that things had gone quiet, though she knew there'd still be a few patrons inside.

It was no matter, she would be entering through the back, and so would the emperor, likely in disguise.

Her hands trembled slightly as she stroked the enchanted blade at her belt, letting the curtain fall back into place. Next time she faced her sister, she'd be better prepared.

She stepped out of the carriage, her loose white blouse

billowing around her in the gentle breeze. Her coachmen would wait for her outside. He knew to speak to no one but her.

Reaching the door, she sucked her teeth in irritation as she rapped her knuckles on the hard wood, staring at the glittering rings on her fingers. This was *her* establishment, but it was always like this where the emperor was involved. She was his loyal dog, and he could take over whenever he chose . . . at least for now.

The door opened just a crack, then a moment later, the rest of the way.

In the doorway stood Daemon Saredoth, his long blond hair combed perfectly straight and glossy. The vain bootlicker probably had the laundry girls in the castle press it with heated irons. A fresh bruise colored the skin around his left eye. "You're late."

"I came as soon as I could," she grumbled, pushing past him.

Just a few steps in, she froze, and her mouth went dry.

The emperor was sitting at the small meeting table as expected, but standing near him was a Dreilore lord. He was as tall as any pureblood Arthali, but his skin was deep gray with a blueish tinge. His pure white hair was laced with tiny jewels and silver clasps, standing out against the plain black tunic and tights he wore. She hardly noticed any of it though, as her gaze was affixed to his deep red eyes which seemed to glint with burning embers.

A throat cleared, and she managed to tear her attention away from the Dreilore. The emperor laced his fingers in front of his face. A black hood shadowed his features, though she personally would have recognized those pale eyes anywhere. Beside him sat a woman with wild, russet hair.

Her features were delicate, her honey brown eyes uptilted. Her skin where it showed through her deep green velvet vest was deeply tanned.

"This is Lord Orius," Egrin introduced, gesturing to the Dreilore, "and this is Cheta." He gestured to the woman.

Cheta's hair seemed to twitch, and Rissine had to stifle a gasp. It wasn't *all* hair. Atop her head were two ears like those of a fox. They'd been laid flat before, but one now stuck up, twitching as if she had an itch. She was one of the Nokken. A shape-changer.

"She wasn't followed," Cheta said.

Rissine blushed, realizing Cheta hadn't been itching, but turning her ear in the direction of the back alley, listening for anyone who might be near the door.

Daemon moved away from the door, then pulled a seat out for Rissine.

She sat. She didn't like that it put her closer to Cheta, but at least it put her further from Lord Orius. She knew the emperor had made treaties with both peoples, but seeing them at her inn was another thing entirely. She'd seen one of the Nokken when she was a child, but had never seen one of the Dreilore before. They tended to keep to the dark mines and castles of the Salisfait mountains in the Akenyth Province.

Egrin leaned forward toward Rissine as Daemon returned to his post near the door. "Something interesting happened this evening," he began conversationally. "You wouldn't happen to know anything about it, would you?"

She furrowed her brow. Was this not about her encounter with the militia after all? "This evening? I was at my home all day."

Egrin tilted his head. "Do you know of another Arthali

woman within the city? She had a taste of pure magic to her. Magic like *yours*."

She held her breath and counted to ten. What had Elmerah gone and done now? Rissine had wanted her sister for herself, not in the clutches of the emperor.

He waited, drumming his fingers across the tabletop. Cheta and Orius watched her silently.

She sighed under the weight of their heavy stares. There was no hiding Elmerah from him now, obviously. "What has she done?"

"She stole Saida Fenmyar before I could give her to the Akkeri."

Rissine groaned and hung her head. "That foolish woman."

"Yes," Egrin agreed, "quite foolish. This woman was accompanied by a man, likely an elf according to Daemon. They would not have been successful, had we not been caught off guard by a lone Akkeri. It attacked me while I held the Arthali woman immobile."

Rissine licked her dry lips. "An Akkeri? Why would an Akkeri help the elf girl escape its own people?"

Egrin raised a dark brow at her. "I was hoping you could tell me. Who is this Arthali woman? Your kin?"

Rissine nodded. Foolish Elmerah. If she would have stayed hidden, she could have protected her. "She's my sister, though I do not know why she'd risk herself to save the girl. The male elf you mentioned was with her earlier today. They paid me a visit, along with two more Valeroot elves."

The Dreilore pursed his lips at the mention of Valeroot elves. With lands bordering each other, the two races had long been enemies.

Egrin looked past her to Daemon at the door. "You will

see to the elves. Question every Valeroot elf in the city if you must." He turned to Rissine. "*You* will see to your sister. She and Saida are hiding with the others in the deep woods. I imagine, come morning, they will try to flee . . . if they survive that long. You will bring them both to me alive, or you will bring me their bodies. Hopefully the Akkeri will still be satisfied with the girl, even if she's no more than a mangled corpse."

Rissine's gut twisted at the thought. It had been ten years since she'd last seen her sister. She didn't bring her to the Capital to die.

She bowed her head. "It will be done."

"*Good*," Egrin snapped. "Now leave us. We have important business to discuss."

Rissine raised her head. "Business? Should I not be included in such talks?"

"You will be caught up later, once you find your sister."

Daemon appeared at her side. He pulled out her chair as she stood, then herded her toward the door.

She glanced back at the trio on her way out. The Nokken woman watched her with a smug smirk that made her blood boil. They were all now allies, yes, but apparently not equals.

As she left the inn, she once again stroked her enchanted blade.

Three more names had been added to her list.

CHAPTER FOURTEEN

Alluin

Alluin's shoulders slumped as the first rays of sunlight reached him. They were far from safe, but at least they'd made it through the night. He glanced back at Saida and Elmerah, lying close together for warmth. Merwyn was curled up like a cat against the cracked rocks, sound asleep. Alluin partially regretted not killing the creature in its sleep. It would hardly be justice for the atrocities of the Akkeri, but it would have been a start.

He turned back toward the ominous shadows of the deep woods. A single Akkeri was realistically the least of his worries. He needed to return to his uncle, to discuss what was coming, but first, they needed to get out of the woods. They'd been lucky thus far. Hopefully that luck would hold. The antlioch grazed nearby, ready to carry them back to civilization.

He startled as Saida appeared at his side, moving as silently as any skilled Valeroot hunter. "We should wake the others," she muttered, gazing out at their surroundings, her hair a messy web of tangles harboring a few pine needles. "I must warn my people of what is to come."

"You intend to return to Faerune?"

She nodded, the movement draping a pine needle into her line of sight. She quickly plucked it out, then began searching the rest of her hair. "I have no choice. I know it is a long journey, but I cannot risk re-entering the Capital, nor can I allow my people to remain ignorant." Finished with her hair, she turned to him. "I wish I could somehow repay you for all you've done."

"Warning Faerune is payment enough. I know how your kind view the Valeroot elves, but soon we will need to work together if any of us hope to survive."

She sighed. "Not all look down on the Valeroot elves. Even those who do will have to listen after what has happened to me. I intend to take Merwyn with me if he'll agree. I'd also like to ask Elmerah."

"Elmerah?" he questioned.

Saida shrugged. "I doubt she'll agree, but the emperor knows her face now. He'll be looking for us both."

They both turned at a rustling sound. Elmerah had finally woken. She sat up, stretching her arms over her head, her coat sleeves sliding down a bit from her wrists. Her hood had come down during the night by the look of her hair. Merwyn was still curled up like a cat, though his eyes were open, watching them.

Saida was right, Alluin thought. It wasn't safe for *any* of them to return to the city. At least he'd kept his cowl up during his tussle with Daemon Saredoth. The Valeroot elves might not yet be linked to Saida and Elmerah.

Elmerah stood as Saida approached. "No offense meant,

but I have absolutely no intention of journeying to Faerune."
She glanced at the Akkeri. "And I'd wager Merwyn feels the
same, if he has any sense of self-preservation," she looked
Merwyn up and down as he came to his feet, "which is
admittedly doubtful."

"But you cannot return to Galterra," Saida argued. "You
attacked the emperor. You'll surely be killed."

With a final glance at the surrounding trees, Alluin
joined the circle they'd formed.

"Trust me," Elmerah replied, running her fingers through
her tangled hair before brushing dirt from her coat. "I've no
intention of facing the emperor again." She wrapped her
arms tightly around herself. "Though I still want to punish
Rissine for kidnapping me."

"I'm sure my uncle will help hide you now," Alluin
offered. "You faced the emperor himself. Surely your loyalty
is proven."

Saida shook her head. "If you *really* want to punish
Rissine, help me stop the emperor. Come to Faerune."

Elmerah looked back and forth between the two of
them, finally settling on Alluin. "First, I am *loyal* to no one.
You and I simply have a common enemy in Rissine." She
turned to Saida. "Second, I don't think me coming to
Faerune will in any way stop the emperor. The elves would
sooner kill me than listen to me. Third," her gaze encom-
passed them both, "you're both utter fools if you think you'll
be stopping this war. The emperor himself bribed the Akkeri
to attack his people. He's signing secret treaties with the
Dreilore and Nokken, and who knows who else? If what
Rissine said is true, even the Arthali will be returning to this
continent. While I'd like my revenge, I think I'd like even
more to be as far from all this as possible."

"So you'll flee?" Alluin questioned. "Even with all you now know?"

She snorted. "Are you daft? It's *because* of all I now know that I must flee. Both of your plans will only result in me getting killed. There's nothing I can do to change that."

Saida held a pale hand to her chest, seemingly shocked by Elmerah's behavior. "But there is so much at stake."

Elmerah glared at her. "There is so much at stake for the Faerune elves," she turned to Alluin, "and your people as well. I don't know if either of you've noticed, but my people are living in exile. You are asking me to fight a battle that is not my own."

Alluin scowled. Could she truly be so callous? "So you care nothing for the innocent lives soon to be lost? The lives that have *already* been lost?"

She matched his glare. "Every single one of those people would either spit on me or run the other way. Why should I care for them?"

He crossed his arms. "If you care as little as you say, why did you fight the Akkeri? Why risk your life for the people you so despise?"

"Children don't deserve to die that way," she grumbled.

Ah, so she had a heart yet. Alluin's eyes narrowed. "Children will die in this coming war. Elf, human, and Arthali alike."

With an irritated grunt, Elmerah walked past him toward the antlioch. "Be that as it may, there is nothing I can do." She turned to face him. "Putting down a raiding party of Akkeri is one thing. That was within my power. But a war of this magnitude? Fighting the Dreilore?" She shook her head. "We have already lost."

She turned back to the nearest antlioch and less-than-gracefully pulled herself atop its back. "Now, let's get out of this cursed forest so we can all get on with our lives."

His face hot with anger, Alluin walked across the small clearing and pulled himself up onto the other antlioch. He offered his hand to Saida as she approached. She took it, hiked up the skirt of her ruby red dress, and gracefully mounted the antlioch behind him. No matter what Elmerah said, he'd do what he could to stop this war. He would not abandon his people, and neither would Saida. In fact, he was quite sure even Merwyn would do his part to stop the war. If Elmerah wanted to flee, he would not stop her.

Apparently he had misjudged her from the start. Not waiting around while Merwyn climbed atop the antlioch behind Elmerah, he guided his antlioch in the direction of the coast. His scowl deepened as Elmerah's antlioch caught up, bringing with it the pungent fishy smell of Merwyn.

Alluin shook his head. Neither of them mattered. Once they were near the relative safety of civilization, he would turn north toward the Capital, and Saida and Merwyn would need to turn south to begin their long journey toward Faerune. Which way Elmerah would turn . . . he did not know, nor did he care.

"Troll!" Elmerah hissed, drawing him out of his reverie.

He couldn't believe she'd seen it before him, but sure enough, far ahead of them loomed the imposing figure of a troll, its gangly body, covered in algae and moss, blending in with the tree trunks. Fortunately its back was turned, and it didn't seem to notice them as it lifted a long-fingered hand to scratch its meaty, fur-clad rump.

The antlioch halted at silent instruction from their riders.

Alluin gestured to his left, realizing they were far off

enough that the troll might not notice the light steps of the antlioch. They could simply go around it and continue on their way.

The sound of breaking branches far to the right drew his attention a moment later. Another troll revealed itself. It was an older male, its craggy skin like boiled leather. The furs draping its body left little to the imagination. Its drooping, bald head was turned in the direction of the other troll.

Alluin gestured left again. The antlioch began to move. If the trolls spotted them from this distance, they should be able to outrun them.

He cursed under his breath as another troll came into view, blocking their course. They'd ridden right up into the middle of their party, but the dumb creatures hadn't noticed yet.

He patted the antlioch's side for it to stop, then glanced over his shoulder past Saida. They would need to go back the way they came and find another way around.

Spotting no other trolls, he met Saida's wide eyed gaze. Not wide-eyed because of the trolls, he realized, but because she was holding in a—

Achoo!

As one, three giant heads snapped their way.

"Go!" Alluin hissed.

Both antlioch turned the way they'd come and leapt forward, racing through the trees. Thundering footsteps followed, shaking the earth and sending birds fluttering up from the branches above. Saida wrapped her arms tightly around his waist, pressing herself against his back.

He glanced toward Elmerah and Merwyn, only to witness a massive log sailing right past Elmerah's head.

One of the trolls let out a grunt—a grunt far too close

for Alluin's liking—then a fist-sized rock flew so close to his head it disturbed his hair with its momentum.

"Cursed Ilthune," Elmerah hissed.

Alluin glanced at her again, shocked to see her toss Merwyn off her antlioch's back, and right toward Saida. Merwyn screeched, then held on, managing to straddle the beast behind her.

Elmerah withdrew her cutlass as her antlioch skidded in the dirt, then turned toward the oncoming trolls. "Keep going!" she shouted.

Thunder boomed in the sky. His antlioch raced onward. He knew he should keep going. He should get Saida to safety. *Oh cursed Ilthune.* "Hang on to the antlioch!" he shouted.

Saida instantly removed her arms from his waist, and he vaulted from his seat, landing hard on the forest floor before tucking into a roll, then coming up to his feet again.

He charged back toward the trolls as a light mist coated his face, and lightning cut across the sky above.

Elmerah

Stupid, disgusting trolls, Elmerah thought, raising her cutlass toward the sky. She hadn't wanted to stop, but one of her party would have soon been struck dead by a flying rock or log. She stood better chances of survival facing the trolls head on.

The antlioch pranced nervously beneath her as she faced the three trolls, now looking upward with small, red-rimmed eyes at the sound of thunder.

She held tight to the grip of her cutlass. She was about to use all her blasted magic again, leaving her defenseless when she needed it the most.

A bolt of lightning met her blade, raising the tiny hairs on her neck. In one smooth motion, she flung the bolt at the central troll, the older male.

The ugly creature shrieked, then stumbled backward, knocking into a tree with a deafening *crack*.

Not taking time to assess the damage, she flung another bolt at one troll, than another at the third. Smoke curled from their wounds, bringing with it a sickly sweet odor. While she knew she was being unwise, the unbeatable thrill of electric magic zinged through her. *This* was what she was meant to do, not hide in a swamp. The sky grew increasingly dark with her small summoned storm, bringing with it moisture to coat the earth. She tossed another bolt at the two standing trolls, striking one in the neck. She hesitated before flinging the next, then finally hurled it square in the chest of the other.

The sizzling trolls shrieked in pain, but it wasn't enough. The two still standing set their sights on her and charged.

She called more power, knowing it might be the last thing she did. If she fainted in this wretched forest, she'd likely be eaten alive, but if she didn't fend off the trolls, she would die anyway.

The air crackled around her. Holding tight to the antlioch's wool with her free hand, she sent two more bolts, charged with everything she could muster, into the trolls charging her. The bolts knocked them back, sending them crashing against tree trunks. One slammed into the third troll trying to climb to its feet. She just needed to disable them long enough for her to flee without risking a rock to the back of her skull.

She sent a lesser bolt toward the trolls, inhaled sharply, then realized she'd gone too far. Her body went weak, and she toppled from the antlioch's back.

Arms caught her, and she was cradled against someone's chest, then the world went black.

Alluin

ALLUIN STARED AT THE TROLLS FOR SEVERAL HEARTBEATS, cradling Elmerah like a child. A very tall, somewhat heavy child who possessed magic the likes of which he'd never seen. The remnants of it were still crackling overhead.

As the patter of rain increased, one of the trolls groaned.

Knowing he should be as far away as possible when the creature roused, he beckoned the nervous antlioch near, then hoisted Elmerah across its back on her belly. It wouldn't be the most comfortable position for her should she wake, but it was the easiest way for him to keep her on the antlioch's back. He retrieved her fallen cutlass, threading it through his belt, then climbed up behind her, moving his knees beneath her limp body.

With a final glance at the trolls, he urged the antlioch to trot. If Saida and Merwyn had continued running, they would be difficult to find, but he had a feeling they would have stopped and waited not far off.

He looked down at Elmerah's back as they rode, wondering why she'd turned to face the trolls. Though it was true the beasts would have soon overcome them, he was surprised she didn't take the slim chance that others would die and she would survive.

She was undoubtedly the most confusing woman he'd ever met.

Elmerah groaned, then started squirming.

"Stay down for a moment," he instructed, raising his voice over the patter of rain. "I want to make sure we're far from the trolls before we stop to reseat ourselves."

"Says the man without a mouth-full of antlioch wool," Elmerah's muffled voice replied, hitching with every bounce of the antlioch's gait. "The trolls survived?"

"At least one did. I didn't stay around long enough to check for heartbeats in the other two. Your magic is—"

"Pathetic, I know," she grumbled. "It used to not drain me so dramatically, but I'm out of practice."

"Pathetic was not the word I was going to use," he muttered.

They continued trotting, but there was no sign of Saida or Merwyn. He didn't want to take the time to dismount and track them, lest the trolls rouse themselves and catch up. Hopefully they hadn't changed course.

They rode on in silence, far enough that he doubted the trolls would follow, even if they were able, then he finally allowed the antlioch to slow.

Elmerah pushed up from her belly and tried to wriggle her left leg onto the other side of the antlioch's back, but she paused her movements halfway through, seemingly dizzy.

She started to sway, so he wrapped an arm around her waist and pulled her the rest of the way to a seated position in front of him.

"You can let go of me now," she grumbled, clinging to the antlioch's wool.

"Can I? You seem ready to fall on your face."

She didn't argue, indicating to him that her condition was more serious than she was letting on.

He kept his arm around her waist, and eventually she slumped her back against his chest.

"Does your magic drain you like this every time?" he questioned.

"No, just the lightning. It's more difficult to summon and control than fire, though as you've seen, it's far more effective."

"You know, such powers could protect many in the coming war."

She snorted. "I'll be drained now for days. I'm truly not much use to anyone. Never have been."

"Then why does your sister want you so badly?"

She sighed. "Rissine is far more sentimental than I."

"So you really intend to just leave?" he pressed, unable to let the subject drop.

"This isn't my home," she grumbled. "You cannot expect me to feel the same way about the people here as you. Now can we please stop talking about this? If we'd actually had a morning meal, I'd be losing it right about now."

"Fine," he sighed. He'd spotted Saida and Merwyn ahead anyway. As he'd suspected they'd stopped to wait for them. Both were dismounted, standing silently beside the antlioch.

Saida's head whipped in their direction as they neared. Her eyes wide, she hurried toward them.

"Are you well?" she asked, looking up at Elmerah.

"Hmph," Elmerah replied, going limp against his chest.

He gave her a light shake, but she did not reply.

"She's unconscious," Saida scolded, reaching up toward Elmerah. "What happened?"

He leaned Elmerah's torso toward Saida, who grasped her beneath the armpits and dragged her from the antlioch's back. Once she had Elmerah down, she couldn't quite hold her, and they both slowly toppled to the forest floor.

Merwyn hurried forward to join them, helping Saida roll Elmerah off her. Saida stared at Elmerah's unconscious face.

"She used her magic to disable the trolls," Alluin explained, sliding off the antlioch. "Though we must keep moving in case one of them wakes up. They are excellent trackers. Not to mention the other things this deep in the woods."

Saida nodded, her attention mostly on Elmerah as she checked the pulse at her neck, then felt her forehead, for what little good it would do. "Her heartbeat is strong, and no fever. I imagine she's just exhausted. She was a bit like this when we escaped our kidnappers, though she did not faint."

"We must keep moving," he said again. "Perhaps she'd be more comfortable if you ride with her." He flicked his gaze to Merwyn, not enjoying the notion of riding with the smelly Akkeri, but he knew Elmerah was displeased with him. She'd not appreciate waking up in his arms once more.

"No," Saida argued. "You're as tall as she is. You can better hold her aloft."

He looked at the Arthali witch sprawled on the forest floor. It was hard to believe such powerful magic came from such a crude, blustering woman.

"Alright," he sighed, crouching to lift her. "She'll have to go back on her belly though. It's easier to hold her steady that way."

Saida nodded. "Perhaps we can get her back to the—"

she cut herself off, glancing at Merwyn. "The place where you took us before. She needs proper rest and care."

Alluin thought it over. The hideout would be the best place for her . . . "But she doesn't want to go back to the Capital," he argued.

Saida placed her hands on her hips. "She just risked her life to save us, now she needs us to return the favor. She'll be defenseless until she regains her strength."

"Fine," he grumbled, though he hated the idea for more reasons than one. While he didn't want to deal with Elmerah's whining once she awoke, he also knew bringing her back with him would put her in danger. It was one thing if she went willingly, ready to risk her life to save others, but it was quite another if she had no choice in the matter. If the emperor captured her, it would be entirely his fault.

"Help me get her back up," he instructed. He took hold of one limp arm, while Saida took the other. They hoisted her, then with her feet dragging between them, they walked her toward the antlioch. When they reached it, he had to take Elmerah by the waist and lift her, as Saida was not tall enough to be of much help. Once he had her situated, he climbed up behind her, while Saida and Merwyn mounted the other antlioch.

Alluin glanced at the Akkeri, then to Saida. "You know we cannot bring *him* there."

"I know," she sighed as their antlioch began walking. "Merwyn and I will accompany you as far as we can, then you'll have to take Elmerah the rest of the way on your own."

"You'll need supplies," he argued, his own mouth quite dry, and his belly painfully empty. "If you can wait a day before departing for Faerune, I can bring them to you."

"It would be appreciated," Saida agreed. "I fear my chances of making it to Faerune are slim enough as it is."

He could not argue. Chances were slim for them all. He only hoped Saida could reach Faerune to warn them before it was too late. They were the only possible ally the Valeroot elves had left.

Merwyn cleared his throat, drawing Alluin's attention past Saida. The Akkeri's chin drooped. His eyes darted about.

"If you have something to say, then say it," Alluin ordered.

"I know of the tunnel into the city," Merwyn admitted, "and of the Valeroot settlement."

Alluin's mouth went dry, and this time, not just from thirst. "W-what did you say?"

Merwyn avoided eye contact. "I have been in these woods a long time. Explored much. I followed Saida from the start."

"You couldn't have come through the tunnels," Alluin balked, having to grab Elmerah before she slipped from the antlioch's back. He'd been so distracted, he'd forgotten to brace her.

Merwyn shook his misshapen head. "No, not through the tunnels, but not hard to tell where they ended. The water flows through. I follow the water."

He must have meant the stream flowing through the cave system. "So you figured out where the tunnel ended, but how did you enter the Capital unseen?"

"I'm small," he explained, "like a child. With my face covered, no one questions a child."

Alluin shook his head in disbelief. Or, not quite disbelief. The Akkeri had managed to follow Saida into the emperor's castle. For someone so adept, entering the city gates would be easy.

"So you know about the tunnel, and the settlement," he breathed. "Yet they have both still remained a secret."

Merwyn shrugged, still looking down. "Why would I tell? I have no reason to tell. No reason to harm the friends of Saida."

Alluin shook his head and turned forward. The Akkeri were age-old enemies of both Valeroot and Faerune elves, and now one knew of the hidden settlement. Yet, it hadn't brought others of its kind down upon them.

"We will head straight for the settlement," he breathed. He glanced at Saida. "It will be faster for you to resupply directly, and you can take one of the fed and rested antlioch to speed you on your journey."

She smiled softly. "Thank you."

"Don't thank me yet," he muttered. "My uncle may very well have us all killed upon arrival, but I suppose it is a risk we must take."

Merwyn seemed to wilt like a flower, trying to make himself as small as possible. It was odd seeing one of the normally blood-thirsty Akkeri acting so cowed, but Alluin supposed anyone would act in such a way when cut off from their kind. With the emperor's new treaties, they were all just one step away from becoming like Merwyn. Cut off from their kind, and waiting for the final blow to fall.

CHAPTER FIFTEEN

Elmerah

Elmerah awoke in a hut full of elves. Something cold and wet was on her forehead, and a heavy blanket covered her body.

Unsure of where she was, she kept her eyes closed to mere slits, and shifted her hand beneath the blankets to her belt beneath her opened coat. Her cutlass was gone.

The four elves present, two males and two females, had their backs to her. Two other beds against the opposite wall were empty.

"We cannot let her go on her own," one of the female elves whispered. "She'll never make it."

"Protecting our own kind is more important than warning Faerune," one of the men argued. "We cannot spare any of our scouts for such a long journey, not when tensions are so high."

"Perhaps we should just turn her in," the other female elf

whispered. "She's the reason our kind are being questioned, after all. Just give the emperor what he wants, and perhaps he'll leave us alone."

Elmerah shot up in bed, tossing aside her blankets before grabbing a broomstick and holding it before her like a quarterstaff. A soggy wash cloth plopped from her head to the hard-packed earth floor. "You won't be giving me to the emperor," she growled.

All four elves turned startled expressions toward her.

The hide flaps serving as the hut's door parted, revealing Alluin. "Ah, you're up. We have much to discuss."

She hurried over to him, broomstick still clutched against her chest. "Yes, we do. Your friends are talking about delivering me to the emperor."

Alluin sighed. "No," he said, giving each of them a cold look, "I imagine they are discussing Saida. All Valeroot elves in the Capital are being questioned by the militia on the whereabouts of a young Faerune priestess. A reward is being offered, as well harsh punishment for concealing her."

Elmerah raised an eyebrow at him. "Is no one looking for a beautiful Arthali witch?"

He shook his head. "No, they are only asking about Saida."

She glowered. "I faced the emperor and lived, and I don't even get a bounty?"

He glanced at the four elves, now watching them quietly. "Perhaps we should discuss this outside."

He held open the hide flaps for her, and she ventured out ahead of him. The soft purple and pink hues of dusk waited for her. Just how long had she been asleep?

Alluin joined her, then gestured for her to accompany him across the settlement toward the antlioch pens.

He leaned in toward her shoulder as they walked. "Are you planning on doing some cleaning?"

At first she didn't realize what he meant, then she cringed at the broomstick in her hands. She stopped walking and tossed it aside. "Someone stole my cutlass."

He glanced at the broom sitting forlornly in the grass, then reached beneath his brown cloak to his opposite side, pulling her cutlass from his belt. With a smirk, he handed it to her, hilt first, but the smirk soon melted away. Something was wrong. He was *worried*.

She accepted the weapon and resheathed it at her belt, feeling better as soon as she was armed. She wasn't sure how long she'd been out, but was quite sure it was still the same day judging by her condition—she was hungry, but not starved, and the state of her bladder wasn't overly . . . *pressing*.

Alluin continued to watch her.

She didn't see Saida anywhere, so . . . "Are you not going to tell me what has happened since you brought me here? Where is Saida? Why do those elves want to turn her in to the emperor?"

"Saida and Merwyn are both here," he assured. "They are gathering enough supplies to see them to Faerune. They will warn Saida's people of what is to come."

Elmerah nodded. It was as she expected, though she was surprised Alluin had brought Merwyn to the settlement. "Will you be *gifting* me with supplies as well? Or is my journey home not as important?"

He shook his head, his gaze distant. "You truly intend to leave, after all we have learned? What about Rissine?"

She fidgeted. Cursed Rissine. "I don't imagine my sister will live for long whether I leave or not. She truly believes the emperor will pardon the Arthali, but I think it more likely he will use Rissine until her value is gone, then he will have her killed for knowing too much."

"And you do not wish to save her?"

She narrowed her eyes at him. "Haven't you been following along? I *hate* my sister."

"But you do not wish her dead. If you stayed—"

She lifted her hand. "Why are you so determined to have me stay? Don't tell me you've fallen in love with me."

He snorted half-heartedly. "Hardly."

"You're not doing yourself any favors with that attitude," she grumbled, glancing around the small settlement. A few elves cast them wary glances as they walked by, but none outwardly gawked at her presence.

Alluin sighed, then glanced over his shoulder before leaning in close. "The emperor has terrifying magic," he whispered, "and so do you. You may be one of the few people in the empire capable of besting him."

She furrowed her brow. "He nearly *killed* me. My magic does little good if I can't move or breathe. And since when did we begin plotting to kill the emperor?"

He shook his head. "We're not. Not yet, but I'd be a fool if I didn't consider the possibility. He's allied himself with the Dreilore and Nokken. He bribed the Akkeri to attack the Capital, giving him an excellent reason for the new alliances. He can announce them to the city, and his people will cheer because their emperor is ensuring their protection from Faerune."

"From Faerune?" she balked.

He nodded. "I believe that is his plan, to blame the elves for the Akkeri attacks. The rumors are already beginning to spread. The emperor seeks a Faerune priestess. He wishes to beg her to uphold her people's treaties before it is too late, and he will pay a very large amount of coin to find her."

Her jaw dropped. "He wants them to believe Faerune is planning an attack?"

Alluin nodded. "I believe so. It is only rumor currently, there's no saying where it came from. But you have to agree, the theory fits."

"Perhaps it does," she agreed, "but to what end? He could justify the new treaties simply based on the Akkeri attacks. Why blame Faerune?"

He shook his head. "I do not know. Perhaps he wants to justify breaking the treaty by approaching the Dreilore. His people might question why he did not beseech Faerune for peace instead."

Her shoulders slumped. If Alluin was right, it would mean all out war with Faerune. They were a mighty civilization, but when faced with the Empire *and* the Dreilore, they would surely crumble. Then there were the Nokken, less powerful, but highly capable as spies. In fact, some of them might have been in place in Faerune already.

She shook her head. "This is not my problem, not my war. I do not belong here."

"You say that," he began, "but I saw you turn around to face the trolls. You knew you might die, but you risked yourself to save three people you've only known a matter of days. I know there is good in you."

She stared at him, fighting the slight trembling in her hands. Others had thought there was good in her too, and now they were dead. She would not make the same mistakes twice. "You know nothing about me, please do not pretend otherwise."

Spotting Saida and Merwyn emerging from a hut, she

turned away, not wanting to contemplate their fate. Both carried heavy leather sacks across their backs, and had water skins slung across their shoulders. They both seemed so small and defenseless. Yes, they could fight, but neither would likely make it to Faerune alive, let alone in time to warn the elves. If Alluin was right, the emperor could declare war on Faerune at any moment.

"I'm glad to see you awake," Saida said upon reaching them. She tugged her new forest green tunic straight over thick suede leggings. "I didn't want to leave without saying goodbye, but time is short."

Elmerah took in Merwyn's hunched frame, his eyes, as usual, on his feet. The few elves milling about glared whenever they glanced his way, absentmindedly stroking the daggers at their belts.

"You'd better protect her," Elmerah ordered.

Merwyn's head finally lifted. "I will protect her with my life."

She nodded, "Good." She turned to Saida. "And good luck. If you're ever in the swamps of Outer Crag . . . "

Saida smiled. "I find that unlikely, though if you're ever in Faerune . . . "

Elmerah couldn't help her smile. "Also *unlikely*."

Saida laughed, then turned to Alluin. "My thanks to you. I *will* convince Faerune the Valeroot elves are our only true allies. We will not let your people fall victim to the emperor's machinations."

Elmerah didn't bother stating that is was too late. If Saida wanted to try and save everyone, who was she to stop her?

"I've equipped your antlioch with a few weapons," Alluin

explained, his gaze on Saida. "A bow for hunting game, and a few daggers for protection. I hope that you will not require the latter."

Seemingly at a sudden loss for words, Saida hugged him, then quickly pulled away and turned to Elmerah with tears glittering in her eyes.

"No, no," Elmerah held up her hands. "No tears."

Ignoring her defensive stance, Saida barreled forward and hugged her.

With a heavy sigh, Elmerah returned the hug. While she felt sympathy for the girl's plight, she could not afford to become overly emotional. Saida's fate was not her problem. She had absolutely no business meddling in the affairs of emperors and elves.

Alluin

ALLUIN WATCHED AS SAIDA AND MERWYN CLIMBED ATOP an antlioch already bearing extra supplies, then rode away through the forest.

He let out a heavy sigh, wondering if they'd make it to Faerune. It was a long journey, and there would be many dangers along the way. Saida had promised to keep to the border of the deep woods near the Emperor's Path. That would put her in some danger of running into the militia men searching for her, but she'd more easily evade them than some of the creatures dwelling in the deep woods.

There was nothing more he could do for her regardless. He couldn't go with her. His people needed him.

"Well," Elmerah began, fidgeting at his side. "I should be off too. I don't suppose you can spare a messenger for a small task?"

He turned toward her. "What task?"

"I want to send a message to Rissine, telling her I've left the city, and to not look for me."

"You truly believe that will do any good?"

Elmerah nodded. "Yes, it will make her look for me *outside* the city, when really, I'll be buying my way onto a ship at the docks."

He turned away. "I will not argue further about you leaving, but I also cannot spare a messenger for such a task. They'll risk being questioned by the militia."

She walked around his shoulder so he had to look at her. "Consider it a thank you for saving your life. You know those trolls would have bludgeoned us all if I hadn't intervened."

"Fine," he grumbled. "Compose your letter and I'll deliver it to her house in the Spice Quarter." He walked past her toward one of the central huts where he knew he could find a quill, parchment, and ink.

"You?" she balked, hurrying after him. "I don't see why you'd need to deliver it yourself. You might be recognized."

He reached the hut, then pushed aside the hide flap to enter. "I need to go into the city regardless. If my people are being questioned, I must ensure none of them are thrown into the stocks."

She followed him inside, then took a seat in front of a small desk made from rough hewn wood. She stared up at him. "You really believe you can make a difference in what is to come? You're only one elf."

He met her unwavering, dark gaze. He knew there was

only so much he could do. War would come whether he liked it or not, but . . . "Even just saving a single innocent life makes a difference. In your short time here, you've already made more of a difference than most will their entire lives." He turned away and opened a trunk, then set a sheet of parchment and a quill in front of her. Next he uncapped a small vial of ink and set it beside the quill. "Try not to make any errors, we only have a few sheets of parchment left."

She stared at him a moment longer, then picked up the quill and started writing.

"Your penmanship is abhorrent," he commented, leaning over her shoulder. He couldn't help himself, her writing was little more than a jumble of cross-hatched straight lines.

She glared at him until he backed away, then continued writing.

Once she was finished she blew on the parchment to dry the ink, then rolled it tightly. With a heavy sigh, she stood and placed it in his waiting hand. "Are you sure you want to be the one to deliver it?"

"Worried about my well-being?"

"No, just worried the letter won't make it to Rissine when you're caught halfway there by the militia." She walked past him out of the hut.

He followed. "I imagine you'll want to use the tunnels to re-enter the city?"

She turned back to him. "Yes, if you don't mind, though I wouldn't pass up a meal first."

His stomach growled at the thought of food. He hadn't had a chance to eat since they'd reached the settlement, what with the other elves worked up over the emperor's search.

He was ready to lead the way to a hot meal, when a familiar form caught his eye.

Noticing the direction of his gaze, Elmerah spotted her too. "Is that—"

He didn't hear the rest of her sentence as he stormed toward his sister, emerging from a hut. Half her face was purple and blue with fresh bruises, and her right arm was bandaged.

"What are you doing here, Vessa?" he hissed upon reaching her. She'd made quite clear whose side she was on.

She glared at him, her green eyes made even more vibrant in contrast to the dark bruises. "I'm trying to stay alive. Thera found me before I could leave the city."

Well that explained the bruises. "You knew the risk you were taking in getting involved with Rissine."

Vessa snorted. "What does it matter now? None of us can be seen in the city with the emperor on this new rampage."

"It's that bad?"

She nodded. "There isn't an elf left who hasn't been questioned. Why does he care so much about one Faerune priestess?"

Elmerah finally joined them as he replied, "Perhaps I would tell you if you wouldn't just use the information to return to Rissine's good graces."

Vessa sneered, then turned her gaze to Elmerah. "I see *you're* still alive too. Pity. If you keep venturing around with Alluin, I'm sure he can change that for you."

Elmerah snorted, then turned to Alluin. "Food?"

"Yes," he answered, still glaring at his sister.

"Don't look at me like that," Vessa growled. "You know I'd never sacrifice anyone *here*."

"Oh?" Elmerah chimed in. "So you only sell elves you *don't* know?"

Vessa's glare darted between the two of them, until she finally huffed in exasperation. "You two should stick together. You're perfect for each other." She stormed past them toward the antlioch pens.

"Food?" Elmerah asked again, looking at Alluin.

He rolled his eyes and continued onward. He wasn't sure which woman was worse. His morally corrupt sister, or the hungry witch eyeing him like he might soon become the meal if he didn't feed her.

Elmerah

THAT EVENING FOUND ELMERAH MAKING WHAT SHE hoped would be her *final* journey through the secret tunnels. Despite Alluin's displeasure with her, he'd supplied her with a small satchel full of goods, enough to last her for a couple days on a ship. She'd be able to resupply once said ship docked somewhere else, then she could buy proper passage back to Outer Crag with the remaining coin in her pouch. She only wished she'd be able to stay in her small hut in the swamp once she arrived, but she knew Rissine would send more pirates for her. She'd have to gather her belongings and go somewhere far away.

She nearly ran into Alluin's back as he paused to unlock the final gate. They both went through, and soon enough the door leading into the hideout came into view, with one lone elf standing guard. She cringed when she realized it was

Baeorn. One more person to call her a coward for running away.

Alluin greeted him with a silent nod and no explanation as to why they were there.

Baeorn looked to Elmerah. "Be careful in the city. The emperor's bounty may be for the Faerune priestess, but the guilds are looking for an Arthali witch."

"That would be Rissine's doing," she grumbled.

Alluin laughed bitterly. "I thought you *wanted* a bounty on you."

She glared at him, then walked through the door as Baeorn held it open.

She endured the glares of many elves on the other side, as if blaming *her* for the questioning they'd suffered. She gritted her teeth and kept quiet until she and Alluin reached the door leading out into the alley.

He stepped outside with her into the cool night air, shutting the door behind them. "I'll stay here for tonight. I'll deliver your note first thing in the morning."

She nodded. "You have my thanks."

They stared at each other for several long moments, but did not speak.

She inhaled sharply, then straightened her satchel over her black coat and pulled her hood up. "Well, I suppose I'm off to find an inn near the docks."

He reached out and gently grasped her arm. "I wouldn't forgive myself if I didn't ask you one more time to reconsider. You could save a great many lives."

She bit her lip. There was that cursed *guilt* again. She couldn't quite make herself meet his eyes. "This is not my battle."

His hand dropped from her arm. "Then I wish you luck

on your journey." He abruptly turned and went back into the hideout, leaving her alone on the quiet narrow street.

She stared at the door for several long moments before skulking away.

She could not get out of bloody Galterra soon enough.

CHAPTER SIXTEEN

Alluin

T he next day, Alluin found himself making his way
through the city. He stuck to the larger crowds,
knowing that even with his face hidden deep in his cowl,
some might recognize him as an elf. If one of the militia men
tried to question him . . . well, he wasn't sure he could keep
his temper to himself.

He hurried through the crowd, everyone moving more
quickly than normal at the threat of rain. He shouldn't have
stayed in the city this long at all, but his scouts had caught
word the emperor intended to make an announcement. He'd
left Elmerah's note with one of the guards outside of
Rissine's house, then he'd made his way to the main square.
He wanted to hear Egrin's announcement with his own two
ears, even if it meant being trapped within city walls no
longer tolerant of his kind.

He reached the large, grassy square, surrounded by
guards dressed in the emperor's purple and white livery. All

men stood at attention, hands resting upon the short swords at their right hips, and sword breakers at their left.

He stood back, careful to remain unnoticed. A glossy white carriage similar to the one they'd encountered near the coast had already arrived, though the emperor was yet to reveal himself.

The crowd muttered all around him, wondering why the emperor would brave the city on a soon-to-be rainy day. Normally, they would only see him on festival days, or on rare occasions where the lower classes were allowed in small groups into the castle.

The carriage door opened, and out stepped Daemon Saredoth, his straight blond hair almost as glossy as his pompous buckled shoes. Next emerged the emperor, his navy ensemble, though fine, no match for Daemon's . . . sparkliness. The crowd muttered excitedly, then fell utterly silent as a third man stepped out from the shadows within the carriage. No, not a man. A Dreilore lord. His pure white hair, interwoven with twinkling jewels, was a shock against his black clothing. His skin mimicked the color of the stormy sky above, and his eyes were like pyres filled with embers.

Crushing certainty twisted Alluin's stomach. He'd been right, right about everything. The emperor was about to announce his new alliance with the Dreilore, and the Nokken would likely not be far behind. The Faerune elves would be blamed, and perhaps even Valeroot, though they were disorganized, and didn't even have a home besides Galterra.

The emperor stepped up upon a wooden dais in the center of the square, leaving Daemon and the Dreilore to stand off to either side behind him.

Egrin surveyed the crowd, then spoke. "It is with great pity!" he called out, "I must inform you our great empire has been betrayed by those we've trusted most. I've learned it was Faerune who sent the Akkeri here, mere scouting parties to precede the main attack."

The crowd erupted in a series of murmurs and gasps.

Alluin found himself stepping forward without thinking. He had to hear what would be said next.

The emperor looked back at the Dreilore lord, then gestured for him to step forward.

The crowd fell silent again as they all stared at the Dreilore.

"Fear not, good people!" the Dreilore called out, speaking the common tongue with perfect pronunciation. One might think he'd grown up in Galterra, if such a thought weren't so utterly ridiculous. "The Dreilore of Salis-fait are here to offer you aid. We will cut off the Faerune threat at its head. You will not know the sharp end of elven blades. Together with the Empire, the Dreilore will protect you now, and in the times to come."

The crowd was so silent, Alluin was able to hear the first raindrop fall. Then another, and another. Though the emperor had not accused the Valeroot elves, it did not matter. To commoners, all elves would now be viewed as enemies, the far distant kin of the Akkeri who'd burnt their homes and murdered their children, and closer relatives to Faerune, the latest alleged threat.

He slowly backed away into the crowd. He didn't need to hear any more. They were all as good as dead.

Elmerah

Elmerah stood in the shadows of an alley near the docks as the first raindrop fell. She felt wary being out in the open, but it was a risk she had to take. The Galterra docks were the only place where ships large enough to cross the Murutane Sea could come to port. All she'd need to do was wait until one of the ships waiting for cargo was nearly loaded, then sneak onboard. If Rissine had received her letter, she'd be looking for her in the deep woods. The city was actually a perfect place to hide until her ship departed, despite the guilds keeping an eye out for her.

"I thought I'd find you here," a woman's voice said from behind her, making her flinch.

She turned to see Rissine approach. An emerald coat hugged her curves and provided a hood deep enough to obscure her features. Surprisingly, she was alone.

"Cursed elf couldn't even deliver a letter," Elmerah scoffed, turning her attention back toward the docks. If Rissine planned on attacking her, she would have done it while her back was still turned.

"Oh I received your letter," Rissine replied as she came to stand beside her. "I also received orders from the emperor to search the deep woods for you, but I knew you'd be here."

Elmerah kept her glare affixed to the distant sea. "Oh? And how did you know that?"

"Because a ship is the wisest way to run, and if there's anything you're good at, it's running."

Elmerah crossed her arms. "You left Shadowmarsh too."

Rissine sighed. "You know that's not what I'm talking about."

She finally turned toward her. "You wanted to gain allies

to bring down the Empire, and now here you are, working for the emperor himself. I was right to run from you."

Rissine shook her head. "You were never able to see the bigger picture. If we work with the emperor long enough to gain lands of our own, we can rebuild. You think the Dreilore will continue to support Egrin once they have another option? Not a chance. And once Faerune is destroyed, Egrin will have no other allies to come to his aid."

Elmerah's jaw dropped. She knew her sister had a grand ego, but this was ridiculous. "You actually think you can gather enough Arthali to pose a threat to the Empire? Aren't you forgetting what happened to our clan? Why, we are perhaps the only two Shadowmarsh witches left?" She shivered, forcing away the image of her mother's broken and bloody body. She'd been betrayed by her own people, her *kin*. Elmerah shook her head slightly. If she would have stayed, she would have been next.

"That was the Empire's fault," Rissine growled, closing the small space between them.

Elmerah took a step back, but soon hit the wall of the building she'd been hiding near, preventing her from moving further.

Rissine shivered, like a raven settling its feathers into place. "You know the Arthali attacked us to save themselves from the Empire. It was the deal to secure exile instead of utter obliteration."

Elmerah sighed. She knew the reasons all too well. The former emperor, Soren Dinoba, had let the Arthali live on one condition: destroy the most powerful clan amongst them. Arthali would no longer be killed on sight, but they were never to band together again.

"This is all ancient history," Elmerah grumbled. "Disbanded, the Arthali are weak, even if some magics still exist amongst the other clans. Your plan will ultimately fail."

Rissine turned her gaze out toward the sea and the dark clouds moving inland. The raindrops began pattering more heavily around them. If the coming storm worsened, Elmerah wouldn't be escaping on a ship any time soon.

"I now know the emperor intends to betray me eventually," Rissine breathed. "He has named Lord Orius his ally, claiming the Dreilore will protect the Empire from Faerune. I know not yet what part the Nokken will play."

Elmerah sucked her teeth. It seemed Alluin had been correct in many of his assumptions. "Protect them from Faerune?"

Rissine nodded. "Egrin is blaming the Akkeri attacks on Faerune. He claims the elves broke the treaty, and will soon attack the Empire."

The rain, now pounding steadily, slowly seeped through Elmerah's coat, chilling her to the bone. She wondered if Saida knew just what was coming for her people. "Why tell me all of this now?"

"Egrin's plan has been set in motion. Faerune will be destroyed. He may be going back on his deal with me, but there is still an opportunity to be had. Even with the Dreilore, war with Faerune will weaken the Empire. Egrin will be focused on the South, leaving an opening for us to *take* the lands promised to me in the North. I will remain his ally as long as it is beneficial."

Elmerah clenched her jaw. Men on the docks were still loading two of the larger ships, but the sky was growing darker. They'd not likely depart until the storm had passed.

"You're a fool, Rissine. The Arthali will not follow you.

You'll be conquering these new lands on your own, and once Egrin is done with Faerune, he'll come for *you*."

"So you'll stand idly by while your elf friends are massacred? You know it will not just be Faerune. The Valeroot elves will be the first to go. The Dreilore have hated them for centuries."

She clenched her fists. All as Alluin had predicted, but it was not her problem. It was his choice to fight a losing battle. If he was wise, he'd run far from the Empire's borders.

Rissine stared at her.

"*What?*" she growled.

Rissine shook her head. "You *truly* care for no one but yourself."

A brief surge of angry magic washed through her, then quieted. "You are in no position to judge me, *slaver*."

Rissine shrugged. "Perhaps not. Perhaps I care little for the elves or humans, but I do care for you, and our people. At least I have something to stand for. I'd hoped you would feel the same."

"Well I don't," she snapped. "As soon as the storm passes, I will board a ship, and then another, and perhaps another. I'll go so far from the Empire you'll never find me again. Perhaps I'll find a place where no one has even heard of the Arthali, because only then will I know peace."

Rissine watched her for several moments, then her shoulders slumped. "In that case, you are not deserving of the Volund name, nor of the pride that comes with being part of the Shadowmarsh clan."

Elmerah spat on the wooden boards beneath her feet to hide the tears burning at the back of her eyes. "Our name is worthless, and our clan is dead. Perhaps once Egrin runs a sword through your heart, you'll finally understand that."

She walked out toward the docks as her sister silently watched her go. She'd find another dark alley to wait out the storm. Alluin and Rissine could worry about the emperor and his Dreilore dogs. This was not her home. Her home had been lost long ago, the day she left Shadowmarsh and never looked back.

Saida

THE RHYTHMIC SWAY OF THE ANTLIOCH MIGHT HAVE PUT Saida to sleep if it weren't for the icy rain making its way through the tree canopy above. She and Merwyn had done as Alluin asked, keeping to the border of the deep woods while heading roughly south. Once they were well out of reach of Egrin's scouts, they would take to the road, speeding their journey to Faerune. What would happen once they arrived was anyone's guess. She'd have her hands full protecting Merwyn from the guards at the crystal gates.

"Why are you willing to do this?" she sighed. "I know you don't believe that marrying me off will lift your curse, but why go as far as to help me?"

Merwyn was silent for a moment. She was about to look back to see if he'd fallen asleep, when he finally spoke. "The Akkeri are violent and cruel. I was born small, and always looked down upon. When we came to the Empire, I saw a chance for escape. Then, I saw another small, weak creature soon to suffer a fate worse than mine. I think, if my curse is ever to be lifted, I must gratify myself to Arcale through noble deeds, not through forced marriage."

Her face burned. "I take it I'm that small, weak creature you spotted?"

"My apologies," Merwyn muttered.

"No, no, I'm not offended. For a Faerune elf, I'm nothing impressive. But you're saying you snuck into the castle, and later faced the emperor himself just to help me? Not that I'm not grateful, but I feel I still don't fully understand your intentions."

Merwyn sighed. "I do not fit with the Akkeri. I am not a warrior. I had hoped if I helped Faerune, Faerune would help me."

"Ah," she replied, "now that makes more sense." Unfortunately, Faerune was not likely to help him, though she was reluctant to say so out loud. She would help him if she could, but the High Council rarely listened to her at the best of times.

Thunder crackled overhead, making her wince. They could not risk seeking shelter at one of the many inns along the Emperor's Path, not with the militia likely scouring the area for her. It was going to be a very wet, uncomfortable night.

"What do you think your people will do now that they've lost me?" she questioned.

"The emperor failed on his bargain," Merwyn answered. "The Akkeri will either attack him, or try to recapture you. No saying which way they will go."

She shivered at the thought. She'd come so close to being taken by the Akkeri. If it weren't for Elmerah and Alluin . . . she sighed. She felt she'd somehow failed them in leaving, though she was doing just as Alluin wished. Still, it felt wrong to leave when the Valeroot elves were in danger. Yet, she saw no other choice. Like Merwyn had said, she was small and weak. She had none of the magics possessed by most of her kind.

"What do you think the Emperor really wants?" she questioned abruptly. "Why work with the Dreilore, and why target Faerune? I asked Elmerah once, and she said it was either power or revenge, but as far as I know, the emperor has no vendetta against Faerune, and he already possesses great power."

"Maybe he wants more magic," Merwyn suggested.

Her spiraling thoughts halted. She wiped a damp strand of hair from her face. "What do you mean?"

"Dreilore have magical metals. Metals only found deep in the Salisfait mines. Faerune elves have gems. Moonstone to harness the power of Cindra. The emperor has magic. Maybe he wants more."

The rain seemed to fall harder, though maybe it was just her imagination. "But only the Faerune elves can harness the magic of the sun and moon. To Egrin Dinoba, our precious gems would be little more than baubles to adorn his fingers."

"Maybe the emperor is different."

She took a deep, shaky breath. The emperor was, in fact, *different*. She'd never heard of magic like his. Besides what was possessed by the Arthali, most magic was more subtle. The Faerune elves could call upon the goddess Cindra to bless their crops. They could make the flowers grow, and make long-dried streams run crystal clear. The Dreilore, on the other hand, used their magics for crafting. They were known for their arcane weapons and alchemy. Both races were particularly long-lived as well, likely evidence of their magic, but none could suffocate a person with their thoughts.

"You're right," she muttered finally. "He *is* different. I fear we may never know what he truly wants until he *takes* it."

Another rumble of thunder sounded overhead, seeming to echo her words. The rain began to gush, soaking her cloak and tunic, the loud pattering drowning further conversation.

She supposed it was just as well. They should focus on their surroundings, and the danger surely lurking ahead.

Alluin

ALLUIN FLED THE CITY WITH A STORM LICKING AT HIS heels. He needed to check in with his scouts. If the Dreilore intended to *protect* the Capital, that meant they'd be slithering out of the dark Salisfait peaks to invade Galterra. While most humans feared the deep woods, the powerful Dreilore would not. They could easily find the Valeroot settlement, and Alluin had no illusions as to what would happen if they did.

The rain increased as he ran, keeping to the shadows of back streets and alleyways. He wouldn't bother with the main gates—the elves were all still being questioned about Saida's whereabouts—and instead hurried toward the secret hideout. He would use the tunnels to escape, and might not return any time soon.

He slowed as he reached the narrow street leading to the hideout. He didn't see the usual scouts atop any of the

nearby roofs, but that didn't mean much. The Valeroot elves
were experts at remaining unseen.

Still . . . something about the emptiness of the street
made him nervous. The pounding of rain was almost deafening, blocking out any other sound.

He crept forward, hands near the twin daggers at his
belt. He continuously glanced from side to side, searching
for the scouts, but none revealed themselves.

He reached the front door to the hideout, then pressed
his ear against the damp door. *Silence.* It still might not
mean much. Most of the elves had likely fled to the
settlement.

Normally he would be expected to knock so the guard
inside could admit him, but the hairs had all risen at the
back of his neck, and he smelled something sharp and tangy
mingling with the smell of rain. *Blood.*

He withdrew his right dagger, then opened the door left-
handed.

The scent of blood increased, turning his stomach. He
knew without a doubt something terrible had happened.
Part of him wanted to turn and run, but deep down he knew
he had to see for himself who had been lost, and if anyone
remained to be saved.

He stepped lightly into the dark entry room, lit only by
the open door. His eyes slowly adjusted to the darkness,
revealing the first of the bodies. Baeorn. He'd likely been the
elf on guard when the attack occurred.

Though Baeorn's tunic was stained with dark blood,
Alluin still knelt and checked his pulse. His body was cool,
but not yet icy, indicating the attack was fairly recent. He
choked back tears. How could it be? He himself had slept in
the hideout the previous night. When he'd departed that

morning, everyone had been alive and well. He must have just missed the attack.

He stood, sadly leaving Baeorn's body behind to investigate further. He noted a few more corpses, but did not venture close enough to identify them. There would be time for that after he made sure whoever had attacked was gone. He felt almost as if he were floating through the house, a mere ghost with no connection to the dead, except . . . they were all like family to him. He knew he'd experience the impact of this atrocity later, but for now . . .

He moved deeper into the house. It became almost too dark to see, then he reached the stairs leading down to the basement, still illuminated by two small sconces flickering in the darkness. Another elven guard lay crumpled at the base of the stairs in a puddle of blood.

Reaching the bottom, he once again checked for a pulse, though he knew he wouldn't find one. The body was cool to the touch. The door ahead was slightly ajar.

With trembling, bloody fingers, he opened the door, then reeled back at what he saw.

This was where the majority of the massacre had taken place. The elves from the upper floor had tried to flee, but they hadn't been fast enough. Whoever had killed them had cut them down before they could even reach the door leading to the tunnels.

Alluin forced himself down the stairs. A few lanterns lit the small space, their flickering light reflecting off puddles of blood. The first wave of emotion hit him as he spotted the last person he wanted to see. His Uncle Ured was sprawled in the center of the floor in front of the other bodies, as if he'd been trying to protect them. A short sword lay near his outstretched hand, the blade clean. Ured had been a skilled fighter, with nearly two hundred years of experience, yet he hadn't managed to inflict any damage before meeting his demise.

Forcing his gaze away from the bodies, he examined the rest of the room, hoping for some hint of what had transpired, and why.

Even as he searched for what would not be found, he realized he already knew the answer. Humans would not be able to cut down so many elves so quickly. Not even the Akkeri would have made it this deep into the hideout. There was only one answer to what had happened. He'd feared the rest of the Dreilore might *soon* arrive in the Capital, when in truth, they already had.

CHAPTER SEVENTEEN

Elmerah

E lmerah wrapped her arms tightly around herself as she skulked through the pouring rain. The storm had only grown worse as evening fell, trapping her in Galterra for another night. Hopefully it would clear up by morning, and she could sneak onto a ship.

She debated seeking Alluin's help for a night's shelter, but their last parting had been uncomfortable enough. She didn't need to see the quiet judgment in his eyes the next morning. She'd be better off at an inn. Now that she didn't have to worry about Rissine, she'd likely be safe. What were the chances she'd run into any militia men on the lookout for her this late in the evening, with a storm flooding the streets?

She stopped below a carved wooden sign swinging violently with gusts of cold wind. She could barely make out a carving of a female elf fetching water from a well, surrounding the words *The Elven Maiden*. Though candlelight bled through the windowpanes, the place seemed utterly deserted. While she might not enjoy whatever meal she found inside, at least she would not risk being seen by the wrong people.

Running a hand across her forehead and back over her dripping wet hair, she pushed the rickety door open and stepped inside. The door slammed shut behind her with a particularly violent gust of wind. As suspected, most of the round wooden tables were clean, and their surrounding chairs empty, save two in the back corner. The two male Valeroot elves sitting there gave her wary glances, then huddled back together to speak in hushed tones.

Elmerah removed her coat and wrung it out, leaving a puddle of water on the floor. She scanned the rough wooden bar at the back of the room, then stepped forward and peeked down a dark hallway. No barkeep was to be seen.

She cleared her throat, garnering the attention of the two elves. "Am I mistaken in believing this is an inn?"

The elves stared at her. One was slightly older, but had similar features to the younger one. She placed them as father and son.

"Who wants to know?" the father elf asked.

She wrung water from her hair. "A lowly traveler, obviously. I'd rather not sleep in the sopping wet streets."

He stared at her for several long moments, then waved her off. "Take a room if you like. Eat what you please. We'll be leaving soon regardless." They turned away and continued their quiet discussion.

She frowned. She wasn't about to pass up a free meal and lodgings, but . . . "Why are you leaving?"

The elves turned their gazes up to her as she approached their table, leaving tiny puddles of water in her wake.

"Have you truly not heard?" the younger elf blurted, inciting a sharp glare from his father.

"Heard what?" she pressed.

Cowed by his father's continued glare, the younger elf turned his gaze down to the table.

She took another step forward to loom over them. Either they hadn't yet realized she was Arthali, or they simply didn't care. "Look, I'm far worse off than you in this city. If you think I'll go running off to the militia, you're dead wrong. They'd sooner arrest me—" she hesitated. "*Or* just execute me before they'd listen to a single word I had to say."

The older elf let out a heavy sigh. "I suppose you're right. The elves were first, but the few Arthali in the city will likely be next." He tilted his head to meet her gaze. "This morning the emperor announced he'll be letting the Dreilore into the Capital to protect us from Faerune, then, not hours later, we caught word that some of our kind were massacred. My son and I are leaving before the same fate befalls us."

She swallowed the sudden lump in her throat and stepped back. Valeroot elves massacred? Could it be? "*Names,*" she demanded. "Give me names. Who has been killed?"

The father elf's brow furrowed. "We don't know names, girl, and we'll not be staying in the city long enough to find out. Our lives are not worth the risk. The Dreilore will be knocking at our door next."

Her arms broke out in goosebumps at the second mention of Dreilore. Due to interbreeding, few races had true magic anymore, but the Faerune elves and Dreilore had remained mostly pure, and their hatred for each other was as old as time itself.

"Why would you run instead of sailing?" she questioned,

debating her own options. "Surely sailing far away from this continent is the wisest option."

The father elf snorted. "Akkeri ships were spotted just as the storm rolled in. None of the ships will be leaving port until that threat has been assessed."

Her heart plummeted. The Dreilore were closing in on one side, and the Akkeri on the other, all on the orders of Egrin Dinoba. Did he truly wish for his own people to be slaughtered? Did he even care?

She took a shaky breath as she realized the appearance of the Akkeri was likely no coincidence. Ordering the monsters to lurk nearby would force those who hoped to leave the Capital through the city gates, where guards could observe any who passed.

The elves had turned back to their conversation, but it didn't matter. She wouldn't be staying there that night.

Without another word, she turned away from the pair, donned her wet coat, and headed for the door. She went outside, grimacing as she found the rain had increased.

Not that it mattered. She was drenched to the bone regardless.

Her soggy boots carried her over the slick cobblestones back toward the eastern end of the Capital. If she couldn't catch a ship, her first order of business would be to get out of the city. She should have just gone with Saida in the first place. She could have snuck onto a ship in Faerune instead, far from the Akkeri threat.

Movement caught her eye and she whipped around, drawing her cutlass with a metallic hiss.

The dark form that had approached her back hesitated, then lifted hands in surrender.

"Alluin?" she balked, her cutlass still raised. Something

was wrong with him. The skin around his eyes seemed swollen, his face pale in the moonlight. His long brown hair was soaked, and his ear tips were bare to the elements.

Slowly, he lowered his hands. "I'd hoped the storm would delay your departure. I figured I'd find you somewhere near the docks." His tone was bland, contrasting sharply with his bedraggled appearance.

She lowered her cutlass. "*Why?*" she demanded, then everything fell into place. She shook her head. "The elves who were killed. They were your kin, weren't they?"

Alluin nodded. "Cut down by the Dreilore like dogs."

A shiver trickled down her spine. Egrin's grand scheme had begun.

She grabbed Alluin's arm, then hurried him toward the deep shadows of the nearest awning. She didn't want to be out in the open with the Dreilore about, even with dense clouds mostly obscuring the moonlight.

Once they were leaning against the wall of a small shop, temporarily out of the rain, she turned back to Alluin, but he wouldn't look at her.

"Your uncle . . . " she began, unsure of what to say.

Alluin stared out at the raindrops bouncing off the street. "Dead, along with many others. Those at the settlement are safe, for now, though I've instructed them to flee. They are not safe anywhere near Galterra."

She reached out to touch his arm, then let her hand drop. She knew what she was thinking was insensitive, but she had to ask, "Why would Egrin want them dead? I know they were sneaking people in and out of the city, and spying on the emperor, but why not just arrest them?"

Alluin flinched, though his gaze remained distant. "We weren't just spying. We were planning a revolution. My uncle Ured had every intention of overthrowing the Empire."

Her jaw agape, she slumped against the wall. "How? How could he have hoped to accomplish such a feat?"

Alluin finally turned toward her. "Do you know how many Valeroot elves live in the smaller villages surrounding the Capital? And how many beyond that?"

She shook her head. If she had to guess, she'd say humans within the Empire outnumbered elves thirty to one. That was, of course, excluding Faerune, an empire unto itself. "I do not know, but not enough to overrun Galterra."

He wiped away the water dripping down his brow. "Overrun? Perhaps not, but there are more ways than one to overthrow an empire."

She stared out at the dark street, now grateful for the rain, as it prevented anyone nearby from overhearing their treasonous conversation. "I still don't understand. Even if you managed to eliminate Egrin, and any other possible claimants to the throne, the people of the Ulrian Empire would never follow elves . . . no offense meant."

"No, but they would follow a legitimate claimant to the throne, one more sympathetic toward the *lesser* races, and one with a deep hatred of the Dreilore."

Turning her gaze back toward him, she frowned. "Such a person does not exist."

"Isara Saredoth exists."

Her frown deepened. "Saredoth, as in Daemon Saredoth, Egrin's closest advisor?"

Alluin smiled, though it was more of a snarl. "Yes, she is Daemon's sister, and both are cousins to Egrin."

She'd been away from the Empire for a long time, and hadn't kept up with politics. She didn't even know of

Daemon's existence until she met him. "You're going to have to give me a little more to go on. I'm not well versed in politics."

He sidled closer to her. "Isara Saredoth once lived in the castle with her brother. She left when Egrin took the throne after his father's death. She's a scholar, and wanted to learn more of other cultures. Her father was the same way, but he was killed by the Dreilore."

Elmerah nodded, the pieces slowly falling into place. Someone of royal blood, but with sympathies for other races, and a reason to hate the Dreilore. "But where is she now, and how would you ever hope to put her on the throne?"

"She's in Faerune," he explained, "one of the few humans who actually lives within the crystal walls. The High Council would surely stand behind her if she were to become Empress, as would the Valeroot elves. Many humans would too, since she will be the only remaining legitimate heir."

Elmerah's eyebrows raised. "Oh will she now?"

"Yes, just as soon as Egrin and Daemon are dead."

She cringed, wishing he hadn't told her any of this. Just knowing this information could get her executed . . . of course, she'd personally attacked the emperor. Her head was bound for the chopping block either way.

"Why are you telling me all of this?" she sighed.

He gripped her arm, startling her. "Half my kin have been slaughtered. I've sent Liam and Vessa to rally the other elves further from the Empire, but alone, I stand little chance of eliminating both Daemon and Egrin."

She jerked away from him. "I ask again, why are you telling me this?"

He closed the space between them, his green eyes intent.

"Elmerah, I've seen your magic. You are more powerful than any elf, perhaps even more powerful than the Dreilore. If anyone can help me, it's you."

"And why would I help you?" she hissed, leaning away from him. "Why should I risk my life for the elves?"

He grabbed her arm again, more gently this time. "Because I saw you risk your life to rescue Saida, then again to protect us all from the trolls. You care more than you're willing to admit."

She tugged away half-heartedly. Risking herself for someone like Saida was one thing. Fighting for those who looked down upon her, who would sooner see her dead . . . She shook her head. "The elves might not detest the Arthali as much as the humans, but that doesn't mean placing Isara Saredoth on the throne will make any difference for me."

"What if we make lifting the Arthali exile part of the bargain for putting her on the throne?"

She shivered. "Most of the Arthali are monsters. Only a fool would invite them back into the Empire."

He let out a harsh huff of breath. "Then what do you want, Elmerah? Name it, and it will be yours."

"To be left alone."

He waited, clearly not satisfied with her answer.

"Fine," she growled. "I want to no longer be looked upon as an insect. I want to visit any city and be able to walk openly through the streets with my hair blowing in the wind, and not worry about who might try to harm me. I want to know the carefree feeling I had in my homeland, before my mother was murdered."

His shoulders slumped. "I cannot give you any of that, but I can give you the gratitude of all elves on the continent.

The humans and other races may still look down upon you, but to the elves, you will be treasured."

She blinked at him. He wanted her to risk her life to gain the respect of a few elves? It was absurd, and yet . . . the look in his eyes tore at her heart. He'd just had half his kin murdered. Could she truly turn him away? "I'll hear your plan," she decided, "but I reserve the option of fleeing at any time, and if I choose to go, *you* have to help me find a ship."

He smiled, though it was tainted with a seemingly fathomless pit of sadness. "Was it really the adoration of elves that did it for you?"

She snorted. "Hardly. It was actually the unspoken promise of all the Valeroot wine I can drink."

His smile seemed a little more *real* this time. "There may not be much left at the settlement, but I'm sure we can manage to scrape up at least a bottle or two."

She gestured out toward the rain. "Lead the way. I'm more than ready to get out of this festering rathole of a city."

With a nod, he turned and stalked off into the rain ahead of her.

She followed closely behind, watching his back more than anything else. He'd just had half his kin slaughtered. Such an unbearable loss.

She knew the feeling all too well.

Alluin

THOUGH THE RAIN HAD CLEANSED THE BLOOD FROM Alluin's skin and clothing, he found it could not cleanse his mind as he led Elmerah back toward the hideout. He'd piled the bodies up in the basement, and would set them aflame once he and Elmerah were prepared to escape through the tunnels. It was the best he could do for them. Proper burials were not to be had.

His uncle Ured's face flashed though his mind, his skin speckled with blood. He'd devoted his entire long life to keeping the clans together. Though Valeroot was gone, the Valeroot elves lived on. Scattered, but united. Alluin was determined to finish what his uncle Ured had started, despite all odds.

He pushed his sopping hair out of his face as he glanced over his shoulder to make sure Elmerah still followed. He was surprised she'd offered to hear his full plan, but he'd of course left out a few important details. Namely, that Isara Saredoth had not yet been approached about taking the throne, and she might not be too keen on the idea since it entailed her brother's murder.

Still, he had hope. Isara had spent the past several years in Faerune, obviously preferring the elves to her own kind. His uncle suspected she would fight for them . . . especially when she learned the Dreilore were coming. He could only hope she'd learn the latter while there was still time.

Elmerah caught up to his side, and he carefully wiped the emotions from his face.

"Will we be using the tunnels to exit the city?"

"Yes," he muttered. "The streets may seem empty, but the militia will be watching the gates. There is no other way out, save taking a boat from the docks."

"Are the tunnels where . . . "

"Yes."

"Oh," she replied, then did not speak further.

They walked on in silence, save for the thundering rain.

The streets were beginning to pool with water, rushing to lower areas in wide streams.

Elmerah hopped over one particularly large puddle, though her boots had to be soaked through by now.

"I was hoping you could help me burn them," he said suddenly.

She stumbled, then continued walking with her gaze on him.

"We won't be able to stay to make sure they burn completely," he explained, "so a large amount of fire at once would be best."

Surprisingly, she nodded. "I can do that."

They did not speak again until they reached the closed door of the hideout.

Elmerah stared at the door as if it might bite. "Are we sure there are no lingering Dreilore around?"

He leaned his ear against the door and listened. All seemed quiet inside, though it was difficult to tell with the pounding rain. "I don't see why they'd come back," he replied, removing his ear from the door. "Egrin's message was delivered. That was the only reason for sending them."

He opened the door and went inside.

Elmerah followed, shutting the door behind them, leaving the room in near perfect darkness.

He fumbled along the wall until he reached a shelf where he knew a lantern rested. Retrieving it, he walked back to where he thought Elmerah was, then extended it. "If you don't mind?"

Her hands groped his until she had a firm grasp on the lantern. A moment later, a small flame flared within.

Elmerah let out a low curse at the puddles of blood on

the floorboards, most smeared from dragging the bodies to the space below.

"We should move quickly," he urged.

"It will do you no good," a thickly accented female voice said from the darkness ahead.

Alluin stepped back, his hands on the blades at his belt.

A female Dreilore stepped into the light. Her long, pure white hair flowed loosely to her waist atop fitted leather clothing. A thin, curved sword rested at her hip, sheathed in black. Her irises flickered like hot embers.

He did not know if this woman had been among those who'd slaughtered his family and friends, but hot rage coursed through him regardless.

The Dreilore looked past him to Elmerah. "You must be the Arthali woman Egrin seeks. Where is the elven priestess?"

Elmerah set the lantern on a shelf by the door, then stepped forward. "Perhaps she's in the underworld. Would you like me to send you there to find her?"

The Dreilore smirked, then drew her long blade. "It makes no matter to me. I must only deliver your head."

Elmerah withdrew her cutlass, already flickering with flame. "Come and get it then. We haven't got all night."

Alluin stepped aside and drew his blades as the Dreilore charged. He'd never fought one of their kind before, but was astonished by the woman's speed.

Her long, deadly blade arced down toward Elmerah, who parried the blow with an explosion of orange sparks.

Alluin lunged at the Dreilore's back, knowing the attack would only serve to distract her, but hoping to buy Elmerah time.

The Dreilore spun on him, blocking his thrust with her

sword before spinning away. There was a brief moment of stillness, then she attacked Elmerah again.

Elmerah whipped a wave of flame at her before that long, thin sword could slice toward her again. The Dreilore stumbled back, then glared. "Not *just* Arthali then? I was told there was only one Shadowmarsh witch in the Capital."

Elmerah sneered. "The emperor lied. Care to rethink your allegiance?"

Instead of answering, the Dreilore charged again. She seemed to have forgotten Alluin, which was just as well since it gave him ample time to fling a knife toward her.

Not even turning to look, she whipped her blade backward and flicked the blade aside with a sharp *clang*. Elmerah lunged with her flaming blade, throwing the Dreilore off balance.

Alluin readied another dagger, then reconsidered as the Dreilore's blade began to glow a sickly green color. It must have been composed of the legendary magic metals of Salisfait. The Dreilore slashed the glowing blade at Elmerah, who parried the strike, but her flame went out on contact.

The Dreilore laughed. "Silly Arthali, your magics are no match for the greatness of Salisfait."

Ignoring the insult, Elmerah stabbed at the Dreilore with her extinguished blade, then used the momentum to hook the nearby lantern with her foot, flinging it at the Dreilore's face. The Dreilore lowered her blade as she protected her face with her free hand. Alluin stilled his breath, then flung another dagger, knowing this might be his only chance to actually land a hit.

The lantern shattered on the ground. The last thing he saw was the Dreilore raising her weapon, then staggering back, clutching the blade planted in the side of her neck with her free hand.

Within a heartbeat, Elmerah's blade relit, providing a measure of light. The Dreilore was still standing.

The seemingly glowing embers of the Dreilore's eyes intensified as she turned toward Alluin. Dropping her hand from a wound that would have killed a human, she lifted her blade toward him, then staggered again.

At first Alluin wasn't sure what had happened, then he noticed the blade of Elmerah's cutlass, still flickering with flame, as it erupted through the center of the Dreilore's tight leather clothing.

Elmerah tugged the blade free from the woman's back with a spray of blood, then shoved it in again, piercing the Dreilore's heart. She withdrew the blade again, bathing them in momentary darkness as the flame passed through the Dreilore's body.

Finally, the light in the Dreilore's eyes darkened, and she slumped to the ground. Elmerah held her flaming blade above the monster, prepared to stab her again if need be.

Alluin's eyes met Elmerah's across the fresh corpse.

"I'd never hoped to face one of the Dreilore," she remarked, "but she really wasn't as scary as they're made out to be."

The Dreilore's body lurched.

Muttering a curse, Elmerah stabbed her again with her flaming cutlass, flickering the light in the room before she withdrew it. "Bloody hard to kill though."

"Indeed," he commented, kneeling beside the now still corpse. He snatched his knife from its neck, all the while feeling like the Dreilore might reach out and grab him.

Elmerah fetched another lantern and lit it, then set it

where she'd placed the first one as she cleaned her blade on the edge of a cloak hanging on the wall near the door. The action made his gut twist, imagining the cloak belonged to a fellow elf, but he supposed the cloak's owner would not be coming back for it.

He tried not to speculate on just who the cloak's owner might be. There would be time to think on that later, when they were far away from any Dreilore.

"We should hurry," he muttered, peering down at the monster at his feet. He wondered if she'd been the one to kill his uncle. There had likely been many more present, judging by the carnage, but he'd probably never learn their names, or be able to seek vengeance.

Finished cleaning her blade, Elmerah sheathed it, then gestured for him to lead the way.

He had to force himself to move on. He did not relish the idea of seeing his uncle's body again, but there was no other choice. He fetched the lantern and moved deeper into the house. He maintained a blade in his free hand, wary of any more lurking Dreilore. He would have liked to know why the female had returned, but there was no asking her now.

They passed through the basement, and into the hidden area below where he'd piled the bodies.

Elmerah gasped as she entered the space.

He supposed it was quite the sight, but he refused to look too closely. He'd seen all he needed to see for a thousand nightmares. He only realized he'd stopped moving when Elmerah's hand alighted on his shoulder.

He turned toward her.

"We should douse them in the stronger liquors. That should ensure they burn completely."

He nodded, glad she had the wherewithal to give them a proper burial, as he wasn't thinking clearly.

Elmerah walked behind the bar and gathered several bottles in her arms. She returned to him, handed him two of the bottles, then uncorked one of the remaining bottles braced in the curve of her arm. She emptied the bottle atop the bodies, then uncorked the next.

With a shaky breath, Alluin joined her, saturating the corpses in various liquors. It began to seem almost demeaning to the dead as they continued their work, then Elmerah opened a bottle of her coveted Valeroot wine and poured it atop all the rest. The liquid wasn't as flammable as some of the more potent liquors, but he appreciated the sentiment.

He found that was his final thought as Elmerah lit the bodies with her magic, and they hurried away through the tunnels. There might have been people in the world that would kill elves simply because of what they were, but there were also those who would fight beside them.

He would need to gather many more to their cause before long, but for that night, someone like Elmerah, as crass as she might be, was more than enough.

CHAPTER EIGHTEEN

Saida

Saida huddled against a tree, trying to keep her map out of the rain that had come in during the night. Merwyn watched over the antlioch nearby. He didn't seem to mind the rain, but then again, his race was capable of swimming long distances through the ocean. They were used to being . . . *wet*.

Pushing a strand of damp hair behind her pointed ear, she turned her attention back to the map. She knew Faerune was south, but she'd only traveled the distance in a caravan of well-protected, covered carriages. She was ashamed to admit she hadn't paid much attention to the route taken. She'd left that up to the coachmen, and the numerous guards sent to protect the members of the High Council making the journey.

Leaving the antlioch to graze, Merwyn approached. While she wasn't sure she believed in the Akkeri's curse, she had to admit he looked quite a bit like a Faerune elf, only smaller, withered away like a partially desiccated corpse. He'd fortunately been granted a dark brown cloak at the Valeroot settlement to cover his ragged clothing. Even with the cloak though, it would be difficult to hide what he was in the light of day. There would be no inns in their future, unless he snuck in through the window after nightfall.

Of course, she had no intention of being alone in a room with him, his good deeds aside.

"I'm not sure which path would be best," she admitted. They'd gone far enough that they were likely safer out of the woods, but the main path diverged in several directions, and the map did not make it clear which one would be best. They were all just solid lines, with no hint as to what monsters might lurk.

Merwyn turned to look out toward the path from within the cover of the trees boughs. "We stay near the sea. If a path leads us too far west, there is only so far it can go. Too far east, we may end up in the Pinewater Wilds or Dracawyn Province."

She lowered her map. "You seem to know something about geography. Odd for an Akkeri."

Merwyn nodded. "Yes, Akkeri keep to the sea." He grinned, showing blackened teeth. "But we can still read maps."

She laughed. "Yes, likely far better than I." She folded her damp map, then stuck it in her borrowed satchel. "The western path it is. Following the sea might make for a slightly longer journey, but at least we won't end up somewhere else entirely."

The rain had finally lessened, letting a sliver of early morning sunlight through.

Saida walked toward the antlioch, wondering if Elmerah

had managed to make it onto a ship, or if she'd gotten caught up in the storm.

Elmerah

ELMERAH GROANED AS SHE AWOKE. AFTER BURNING Alluin's kin, a particularly gruesome task, they'd stayed the rest of the night at the Valeroot settlement. The rest of the elves had departed, which was wise. The Dreilore would not fear the deep woods. Since they'd found the hideout, they'd eventually find the settlement.

While she didn't mind not seeing any other elves, she wished they'd left behind an antlioch or two. She was not sure where they'd go next, but wherever it was, it would take *ages* to travel on foot.

A sliver of light cut across the small hut's interior as Alluin opened the hide flap and peeked in. "Are you awake?"

"No," she groaned, turning over on the straw mattress that did little to pad her body from the hard ground.

Alluin entered the hut, then let the flap fall shut behind him. "We should discuss our next move while there's still time. There's no saying when the Dreilore will find this camp."

She sat up and glared at him. "You believe they'll find this place soon?"

"The Dreilore are excellent trackers. Many elves ventured between here and the tunnel."

She frowned, then climbed off the mat to her feet. "When you put it that way, let's get out of here."

Alluin nodded. "My thoughts exactly."

She took a moment to actually *look* at him, noting his puffy eyes and slumped shoulders. She decided not to comment, as she wasn't sure what to say. She knew how it felt to have one's kin slaughtered, but when it happened to her . . . there was nothing anyone could have said to make her feel better, nothing to be done to make it hurt less. She wouldn't have heard the words even if someone had tried.

And so, instead of offering comfort, she stretched her arms over her head and yawned. "You wouldn't happen to have any more hidden encampments, would you? Perhaps something a little farther away from the Capital?"

He nodded. "Yes, there are many more settlements, but we must first plan our next step."

She sat back down on her mat and pulled her boots toward her. "That next step being the death of Daemon and the emperor?"

"As much as I'd like that to be our primary goal, we must first reach Isara. She must be ready to take the throne before someone else can step in."

Done lacing up her boots, she raised a brow at him. "So we're going to Faerune?"

He shook his head. "We're going to find Saida. If anyone can reach Isara, it will be her."

Elmerah stood. "And why couldn't you have sent word with Saida *before* she left? It seems you missed an opportunity there."

He turned to lead the way out of the hut. "As far as the Faerune High Council is concerned, they are allied with the emperor." He turned toward her as he held open the hide flap. "What do you think would happen if Faerune discovered the Valeroot elves intended to kill their ally?"

She walked through, wincing at the raindrops that met

her on the outside. "You believe they would attack your people to protect the emperor?"

He stood beside her, peering out into the misty forest. "They would at the very least inform the emperor of our plan. To do otherwise would be treason."

Elmerah scowled. She'd always hated politics. "And they will not do so now?"

He shook his head. "Not once the Dreilore begin their march. Faerune will have to believe us then, or risk utter obliteration."

She followed him as he moved into one of the other huts and began gathering supplies. "You believe the Dreilore can conquer Faerune?"

He stuffed a few small rolls of hard bread into a satchel. It seemed the departing elves had left them very little. She was glad to still have the original satchel Alluin had given her, though she'd tossed out the bread after it got soaked through in the rain.

Finished, he secured the buckles on his satchel. "Defeat them? Perhaps not. Severely weaken them, especially if the emperor sends additional human soldiers? Most certainly."

Her stomach growling, she followed him back out of the hut. "But why? Why weaken Faerune? What does the emperor hope to gain in destroying a previously beneficial treaty."

Alluin shrugged as he led the way out of the settlement. "Who can say? All we know is that he's doing it. There is no other reason to blame Faerune for the Akkeri attacks, or to call in the Dreilore."

Seeing little other choice, she followed him through the dense woods, regretting her decision to stay and hear his plan. Perhaps there was still a chance of catching a ship and sailing far away from Galterra. "Maybe there's something in Faerune he wants. Something he's willing to kill for."

"Whatever it is," Alluin muttered, "it will be his undoing."

She sincerely doubted his claims. The emperor possessed a fortress, powerful magic, and an army of Dreilore. While she had no clue what Egrin Dinoba wanted, only a fool would try to keep it from him.

She was starting to realize that she herself . . . was a *fool*.

Saida

SAIDA HUNCHED HER BACK, HER HOOD PULLED LOW OVER her features. Merwyn sat behind her on the antlioch in much the same position. Unfortunately, the antlioch was more conspicuous than either of its riders. The settlement they rode through was small, but it was still risky taking the main path down the center. It seemed the best way around though, with farms taking up the land to the east, and to the west, a rocky escarpment leading down to the coast.

None of the townsfolk going about their midday tasks paid them much mind except to point at the antlioch, muttering amongst themselves. They were likely used to all manner of travelers passing through their village on their way to and from the Capital.

The thundering of hooves warned her just a moment before someone on horseback came charging up behind her. The antlioch skittered to the side as the rider swung down from his skinny brown horse.

Clinging to the antlioch's wool, Saida stared at the rider in horror, but soon realized he'd barely even noticed her.

He rushed forward to meet a woman who'd spotted him. "We have to go," he urged, clinging to the woman's offered hands.

Her plump face turned red. "Go? Whatever do you mean?"

The man panted to catch his breath before he could reply, "I was heading toward the textile shop to sell our wool when I caught word that the emperor would make an announcement." His bony shoulders slumped. "Faerune is responsible for the Akkeri attacks. Next it will be the elves themselves who will cut down our kin."

"That's absurd!" Saida blurted, then slapped her hand over her mouth.

The man and woman turned toward her and Merwyn, just as a few of the townsfolk approached.

"It's one of them!" the man hissed, backing away. "A scouting party! Get them!"

"Go!" Merwyn rasped in her ear.

He didn't have to ask her twice. She kicked the antlioch's side, inciting it to take off with a graceful leap. She leaned forward and clung to its wooly neck, hearing the shouts of villagers not far behind.

She stole a peek back to find the mob chasing them on foot, splintered wooden beams, farming tools, and other crude weapons raised. They were no match for the speed of the antlioch, however, and soon fell behind. The beast carried Saida and Merwyn far away into the woods beyond the village.

When their mount finally slowed, they were deep within the trees far from the path. Saida slid from the antlioch's back, then hunched over, hands on knees as her fear faded. "What were they talking about?" she panted. "Why would they think Faerune would attack?"

Merwyn dismounted beside her, less riled than she. "This was what Alluin suspected, was it not? The emperor wanted a reason to attack Faerune. Now he has it."

She looked up at him. "But to say Faerune is responsible for the Akkeri attacks? The Akkeri have long been our enemies."

If he was hurt by the statement, he didn't show it. "It is clever. The people will think, *why would he lie?* An emperor would never attack those he is sworn to protect. Faerune is far away with little contact, easy to blame."

She wrapped her arms around her cramped stomach, then slowly dropped to her knees. Tiny rocks pressed through the fabric of her suede leggings "This is worse than we thought. There is no way we'll make it to Faerune in time to warn them."

Merwyn approached and placed one mottled hand on her shoulder. "We must try."

Still panting, she nodded. He was right. They at least had to try. Her breath hitched at the distant sound of voices. "The villagers?" she gasped.

Merwyn shook his head, then tilted his ear upward to listen. "They do not speak the common tongue," he whispered after a moment.

Saida pushed through her panic enough to actually listen to the voices. He was right. They spoke a language she'd heard once or twice from the scholars of Faerune.

Her body began to tremble. "They are speaking Akenyth," she rasped, "the language of the Dreilore."

Merwyn silently gestured for her to stand, then helped her onto the antlioch. The distant voices grew nearer.

Merwyn climbed onto the antlioch behind her, then whispered into her ear. "Toward the coast, out of the woods. Do not run unless they spot us."

She nodded to herself, barely noticing the stench of fish that came with his breath. *Dreilore* so near the Capital. When Alluin first mentioned the Dreilore, she thought him crazy, but it seemed he'd predicted much.

The antlioch crept onward through the trees, heading toward the distant coast. She wasn't sure why Merwyn had instructed her to go that way, except that it would place them on the other side of the Emperor's Path from the Dreilore. Of course . . . there could easily be more of them near the road.

Spotting something white near the distant trees, she quickly patted the antlioch's side, making it halt. Her breath hitching in and out, she narrowed her gaze. It was white *hair*. Since the person's back was turned, she could not tell for sure if he was one of the Dreilore, or if he was even a he—though she thought so—but the long white hair was a defining characteristic of their race. Only those of noble standing grew it past their shoulders. Lesser Dreilore were forced to keep their hair short.

Her heart thudded in her chest as she stared at the distant form, waiting to see what direction he'd move, but he just stood there, peering in the direction of the coast.

Merwyn tapped her shoulder, then pointed past her face to the left.

Her eyes darted in that direction and she nearly fell off the antlioch. Approaching the lone Dreilore was Egrin Dinoba himself. She no longer heard the distant voices, and couldn't help but wonder if Egrin had come from that direction.

Saida felt unable to move as she watched the emperor approach the Dreilore through the trees. The Dreilore turned, then offered Egrin a small bow. Tiny white jewels in the Dreilore's hair caught the sunlight.

The pair began conversing, but they were too far off for her to make out what was said.

Merwyn tapped her shoulder again, then gestured to the right, indicating they should try and quietly flee.

She knew he was right, but something stopped her. Egrin Dinoba, the man framing her people for the Akkeri attacks, was *right there*. If he were to disappear, Faerune might be saved from the war that was surely approaching. She'd never killed anyone before. She had no idea how she'd actually best him . . .

She turned around to meet Merwyn's waiting gaze, then mouthed *you must run*.

Merwyn's sea-blue eyes widened, then he shook his misshapen head.

Saida turned her gaze back toward the emperor, then gasped. Both he and the Dreilore were *gone*. She glanced all around, but saw no signs of them.

She turned back to Merwyn. "If Egrin disappears," she whispered, "I can delay the war. I can buy my people time to prepare."

He shook his head again. "If you get yourself killed, there will be no one left to warn them. We must make for Faerune. We cannot sacrifice your life for this."

"The Dreilore are here. War has been all but declared. A warning means nothing if it comes too late."

She slid down from the antlioch, narrowly avoiding

Merwyn as he reached for her. Clutching her borrowed belt knife to ensure it was still there, she hurried away through the trees. If Merwyn knew what was good for him, he'd take the antlioch and run far away. She needed to find the emperor. If he was simply meeting with the Dreilore and intended to part ways soon, this might be the most vulnerable he'd *ever* be. She gritted her teeth as she remembered the bow on the antlioch, but it was too late to return for it now, lest she lose Egrin's trail.

Her back stiffened, then she turned around and glared at Merwyn atop the antlioch. He pointed to the creature's back, clearly implying she should get back on.

She shook her head sharply, then thought better of moving on without the bow. She hurriedly crept back to the antlioch's side, unstrapped the bow from their supply sacks, then just as quickly hurried onward. The emperor could already be heading back toward a horse waiting to carry him to the safety of his castle.

Merwyn dismounted the antlioch and scurried up behind her. "These woods may be filled with Dreilore. You do not stand a chance of reaching the emperor," he whispered.

He was right. She knew he was right. "I have to *try*," she hissed.

"Then let me help you," he sighed. "I'm a far better sneak than you."

Finally, she turned fully toward him. He *had* managed to sneak his way past countless guards into the castle. She knew she'd never manage the same. If *anyone* stood a chance of sneaking up on Egrin Dinoba, it was Merwyn.

"You might be killed," she breathed. "I cannot ask you to do this."

"Let us keep our distance from him and watch," he whispered. "He may remain with the Dreilore, eliminating any chance of success regardless."

She thought about it for several long moments, then nodded. They could lose a few hours to watch Egrin and see if an opportunity to end his wretched life presented itself. If he remained well-guarded, they would continue on toward Faerune. It was a compromise both she and Merwyn could live with . . . hopefully.

Elmerah

ELMERAH KICKED A ROCK IN HER PATH. ALLUIN WALKED ahead silently. Without mounts, it would take three wretched days of travel to reach the next Valeroot settlement. At this rate, they'd never catch Saida to send message to Isara . . . not that she cared, she assured herself. Alluin's plan was far-fetched at best. To overthrow an entire empire was absurd.

And yet, here she was, still following him.

"What if we can't catch up with her?" she called out. "She and Merwyn have the antlioch after all. They're likely halfway to Faerune by now."

"Then we'll travel all the way to Faerune," he replied, not so much as glancing back at her. "This plan cannot move forward until we know Isara will take the throne. Once that has been ensured, we will kill Daemon and Egrin."

"So we'll just travel halfway across the bloody continent, then turn back around and murder two of the most well-protected men in existence, is that all?"

He finally stopped walking and faced her.

At the look of desperation in his eyes, she suddenly wished she hadn't spoken at all.

"Don't you think I realize how foolish this all is?" He tossed his hands up in the air. "To enact *years* of planning all at once?" He shook his head, lowering his hands. "This is the only way, Elmerah. The only way to stop what has been put into motion. I can't just stand idly by while my people are slaughtered. I cannot just run and hide."

She winced. Running and hiding was exactly what she wanted to do. She'd been placed in a similar position once before, when her sixteen year old sister had wanted to rally the Arthali to attack the Empire, even after their mother had been murdered.

"I know what to do," she breathed, resignation making her knees feel weak.

He eyed her steadily. The wind picked up, blowing about his rich brown hair, making him seem a bit wild, a bit *crazed*. "If you still want to run," he said finally. "I cannot stop you."

She shook her head. "I think, perhaps, I've run enough for one lifetime. I know someone who never runs away from anything, and she may be the only person who can bring your mad plan to fruition. I feel if I don't give in to this now, it will be too late." Her instincts screamed at her to shut up. She did *not* want to do this.

He blinked at her, clearly stunned. "Who? Who can possibly help us?"

She was either going to help him, or she wasn't. She had to make a choice. She gritted her teeth. "My sister. Her ultimate plan is to overthrow the Empire. You are not the only one with a mad plan in the Capital."

His jaw dropped. "But she's working *with* him. She's

sending slaves to the Salisfait mines, and who knows where else."

Elmerah nodded. "All to gain lands for the Arthali. She wants to strengthen our people once more, and while the emperor is busy conquering new realms, she will strike at his back like the viper she is."

He shook his head. "I do not understand. What is it you think Rissine could do for us?"

Her shoulders rose and fell with a heavy sigh. She couldn't believe she was actually saying this. "You want the emperor dead to save the elves. Rissine wants to use the emperor to restore the Arthali, at which point she'll want him dead too. She may be an evil witch, but her goals are not far from yours."

He nodded, seeming to catch on. "And if Rissine supports our cause, she'll be partially responsible for placing Isara on the throne. It could put her in an excellent position to strengthen the Arthali."

"Yes," she breathed, her chest tight, "and Isara would be allied with an army of Arthali. My people would be restored and your new empire strengthened."

"You don't sound terribly excited about the prospect," he observed.

She met his eyes solidly. "Your kin were murdered by the Dreilore, enemies you would gladly slay if given the chance. My mother was murdered by her own people, the people I would have to agree to rally alongside Rissine if we want her help."

His expression softened. "And you would be willing to do that?"

She bit her lip. She had *hated* the Arthali since the day she found her mother dead. They'd killed the Shadowmarsh witches to save their own necks. If she and Rissine hadn't been out on a small fishing boat at the time, they would have been killed too.

She opened her mouth, then closed it. She didn't want to do this. If she never saw another Arthali as long as she lived, it would be too soon. "I think that if the emperor is to be stopped, this is the only way. If we can convince Rissine to help us now, the rest can be figured out later, once Egrin Dinoba is dead."

He reached out and took her hand. "I don't know how to thank you."

Birds chirped in the trees around them, grateful for a bit of sunlight on such a dark day. Elmerah wished she could feel the same. "Don't thank me yet. I still need to speak with Rissine."

He nodded. "And I still need to find Saida to tell her of Isara."

They eyed each other across their joined hands.

Elmerah sighed. "I suppose this means we must say goodbye, for now. I'll find Rissine, and you'll find Saida."

"But how will I find you again after that?"

Elmerah smirked. "Don't worry, if Rissine agrees to this mad plan, I'll have an entire guild at my disposal. Come anywhere near Galterra, and I'll find *you*."

He smiled. "You know, you are a far different type of person than I'd originally surmised."

She snorted, then pulled her hand free of his. "I get that a lot. Now you better be on your way if you stand any chance of catching Saida."

He started to turn away, then hesitated. "How will you get back into the city?"

She shrugged. "I'll figure it out when I get there."

"Perhaps you *are* the sort of person I'd originally surmised," he chuckled.

"I'll take that as a compliment," she said with a grin.

With a final long look at her, he turned away, then took off at a jog.

She almost debated taking the opportunity to forget her new promise and run, but instead, she turned back in the direction of the Capital. She'd have a long day's walk to once again reach the gates, and an even longer night finding her sister on the other side.

CHAPTER NINETEEN

Saida

Saida leaned her back against a tree as she gnawed on a hard piece of bread. They'd heard and seen more signs of Dreilore throughout the day, but the emperor was nowhere to be found. It was as if he'd disappeared into thin air, leaving a seemingly large, but scattered, contingent of Dreilore in the woods. Fortunately, it seemed she and Merwyn had eventually left the Dreilore behind, as they hadn't heard them speaking in several hours.

Merwyn stood in front of the antlioch, stroking its forehead. While he wasn't one to gloat, Saida suspected he was quite pleased to have gotten his way. With no signs of the emperor, they might as well head straight for Faerune.

Stuffing the last bite of bread into her mouth, she began to approach Merwyn, then halted at a *thwish* sound sailing toward them, making the hairs on her arms stand on end. An arrow landed with a thunk in Merwyn's back, toppling him toward the startled antlioch.

Saida screamed, and the antlioch ran.

"Quiet *girl*," a man's voice hissed.

She turned in horror to find the male Dreilore she'd seen speaking to the emperor. He had a second arrow nocked, its tip aiming straight for her heart.

A panicked whimper escaped her lips. She wanted to check on Merwyn, but could not tear her gaze from the Dreilore before her. His eyes seemed to burn like smoldering coals as a cruel smile curved his smooth, bluish gray lips.

Looking her up and down, he lowered his bow. "I thought you'd be halfway to Faerune by now."

"Who are you?" she rasped, raising a trembling hand to her heart. "Why would you harm Merwyn?"

He raised a white eyebrow at her. He was tall, taller than Elmerah or Alluin, making her feel tiny and helpless. "A Faerune priestess calling one of the Akerri by name? How . . . odd. Truly, I thought I was saving you from the beast. As for who I am, you may call me Lord Orius. I am the high commander of the Dreilore."

Her entire body began to tremble. This Dreilore obviously knew who she was. She knew the emperor wanted to give her to the Akkeri, but to trouble the Dreilore's high commander with such a task? "What do you want?" she demanded, her voice not coming out as strong as she'd hoped.

Returning his arrow to a quiver slung across his chest, Lord Orius stepped forward. "Why, I want you, of course. The emperor has my people searching for you high and low. It is beneath us, and I would like it over with."

She glanced at Merwyn, lying still in the moss and soggy pine needles, then back to Orius. She needed to run, but she could not leave Merwyn behind, not if there was a chance he yet lived. "Why do you follow Egrin Dinoba? Your kind detest humans."

Orius took a step closer. *Too* close. If he tried to grab her, she might not be able to evade him. "Yes, perhaps we do, but not as much as we despise the Faerune elves worshipping the Sky God in their crystalline towers."

She shivered at the thought of the Dreilore tumbling the crystal walls of Faerune with this . . . *creature* leading the way. "Just as we despise the Dreilore," she said boldly, "worshipping their demons in the dark tunnels of Salisfait."

She heard a faint snuffle, and flicked her eyes to the side, spotting the antlioch slowly approaching. The stupid loyal creature was going to get itself killed. She turned her eyes back to Orius, hoping he hadn't noticed the direction of her gaze.

He smiled at her smugly, giving nothing away. "Let us hope you live long enough to meet our *demons*, brazen elf. The rest of my contingent will be here soon to take you to the emperor. I have more important places to be."

She winced, realizing why he hadn't yet attacked. He was waiting for his inferiors to come and do it for him. If she didn't run soon, it would be too late. She glanced again at Merwyn, then gasped. He was gone.

Her gasp came too late for Orius as Merwyn, his body sprawled on the ground, stabbed his dagger into the back of the Dreilore's calf.

Orius cried out in pain, then stumbled as he whirled on Merwyn who breathed raggedly, the arrow still protruding from his back.

Saida staggered back, then lifted her fingers to her lips, letting out a long whistle like she'd heard Alluin do once before. The antlioch charged forward from its hiding spot in response.

Not having time to draw a weapon, Saida lunged at Orius, ramming her shoulder into his side just as he was thrusting the bottom edge of his longbow toward Merwyn's skull. Put off balance by his injured leg, he staggered sideways, then braced himself against a tree.

Leaving her back vulnerable to the Dreilore, Saida grabbed Merwyn under his armpits and helped him onto the antlioch as it reached them. Holding onto a clump of wool, she smacked the antlioch's rump, then used the momentum of its startled leap to pull herself up behind Merwyn.

An arrow whizzed right past her eartip as they sped away into the woods. Though Merwyn had been conscious when she'd helped him atop the antlioch, his body now suddenly sagged. She grabbed his spindly body the best she could with an arrow jammed in his back. His blood began soaking the arms of her green tunic, and it was all she could do to keep him from toppling off the bounding antlioch.

"Please don't die," she gasped through her tears. She could hear shouts in the distance, back in the direction of where they'd left Orius. Her stomach clenched at the thought of him coming after her.

If he hadn't fully despised Faerune elves before, he most surely did now.

Elmerah

IT WAS NEAR DARK BY THE TIME ELMERAH REACHED THE farms leading up to the city walls. She had her hood up, but the farmers all still eyed her askance as they penned their live-stock for the night. She'd been hoping to hide in a cart going into the Capital, but it was far too late for that now. None of the farmers would be moving any goods until morning, and she couldn't wait that long. If she did, she might lose her nerve.

An elderly farmer near the road gave her a judgmental glare. "We don't want any trouble, you hear?" His voice was like rough pebbles crunching under one's boots.

"Then I'd move far from the Empire," she hissed. "A lone witch will soon be the least of your troubles."

The farmer continued to glare at her as she passed, clearly not taking her warning to heart.

She sighed, continuing on. Here she was, on her way to save the entire Empire, and they were glaring at her like she was a villain. She continued the rest of the way with her head down until the city gates came into sight.

Once she was close enough, she sidled off the road to devise a plan. The imposing iron portcullis was open, but few traversed the expansive stone bridge over the waterway spanning the outer walls, likely put off by the bevy of guards questioning any who ventured in or out. Torches blazed within the massive arched walkway, making it impossible to hide one's face.

Elmerah stepped further aside as a red-faced man rode up on horseback, then dismounted as he headed toward the gates.

She hurried to his side, halting his progress. "You wouldn't happen to be a guild member, would you?"

His horse's reins in hand, he stood back and blinked at her. "I am but a simple farmer, here to warn the emperor that the Faerune scouts have arrived. I saw one in my village with one of the Akkeri."

"Oh?" she questioned, her eyebrows raised. "What did you do?"

The man snorted. "We chased them, but they escaped, else we would have put them down."

Her shoulders relaxed. Saida wasn't being very careful if she was passing directly through villages, but at least she and Merwyn had escaped. Unfortunately this man's tale would only verify the emperor's claims that Faerune was responsible for the Akkeri attacks.

While she thought things over, the man backed away from her, then continued toward the gates.

She let him go. He was no use to her if he didn't know anyone in the guilds.

"I heard you asking about the guilds?" an oily voice said from behind her.

She turned to see a lanky man in a black cloak. His blond hair was slicked back from his face with sweat . . . or perhaps with filth. The overwhelming scent of bitterroot covered any other possible odors.

She tugged her hood a little further forward. "Who wants to know?"

He grinned, showing blackened teeth. "Someone who can help you find who you're looking for." He held out a bony hand, obviously expecting a few gulls in exchange for his information.

She resisted the urge to reach for the coin pouch hanging from the back of her belt. It had grown perilously light, and she wasn't sure she wanted to risk her remaining coin on him.

"I need to get into the city," she whispered, leaning far closer than she wished.

He chuckled, encasing her in another pungent wave of

bitterroot. "That will cost you considerably more coin."

She eyed him steadily. "Coin that you will receive once I'm in the city."

The man grinned again. He'd probably spend any coin she gave him on bitterroot and potent Faerune liquor, but it wasn't her problem. If he could get her into the city without alerting the guards, she'd pay.

"We'll need to speak to the guard to the right," he whispered. "You'll walk with me. Keep your head down and he won't ask questions."

"He's a guild member?"

He shook his head. "No, but his pockets are fat with guild coin."

She tapped her fingers on her leg as she quickly thought things over. It would have to do. "Let's go then, and if you betray me, you'll be dead long before the guards can act."

He smiled again. "Don't worry *witch*. I'm not stupid."

Apparently the hood and coming darkness hadn't done much to conceal what she was, but that the man was still willing to help an Arthali witch meant he perhaps knew Rissine. "Let's go."

He nodded, then moved to her left side. She lowered her chin as they approached the stone walkway leading over the canal, passing a few farmers and other folk moving in the opposite direction, heading to their homes after a day at the market.

Elmerah let her hand brush the hilt of her cutlass where it rested between the side-slit in her coat as they walked, assuring herself that if the man betrayed her, she was capable of escape. She had enough magic in her currently to at least give the guards pause.

They reached the guard with *fat pockets*. He had fat everything else too. Probably buying too many steamed buns with his dirty coin.

Seeming to recognize her greasy companion, as promised, the guard waved them onward.

Elmerah heaved a sigh of relief as they entered the archway leading into the Capital. Once they were well out of danger, she'd question the greasy man about Rissine's whereabouts. Maybe if he learned she was Rissine's sister he wouldn't demand his coin, but it was unlikely.

"Hey!" someone called after them.

Her shoulders tensed. To fight or flee? She settled on glancing back to make sure the guard was actually speaking to her.

Sure enough, he was looking right at her, not the guard they'd passed, but an older man with graying hair. She turned to her other side to find the greasy man was gone. "Son of a Dreilore wench," she grumbled. She turned and waited for the guard to approach her. Running now would only incite a chase.

The guard itched his graying beard as he reached her. "Where are your papers?" he sighed, clearly bored. "I didn't see you present any when you walked through."

"I did too," she argued. "Do you truly think one of your men would let me pass if I had not?"

He seemed to finally look at her as his heavy brow furrowed. "Remove your hood," he demanded.

Cursed Ilthune, she thought, *now everyone would know the Arthali fugitive had re-entered the city.*

"She's with me," a pleasant voice said from behind her.

She turned to gawk at Thera as she approached, an ugly bruised nose marring her otherwise perfect face. Had Thera known she would be re-entering the city and wanted revenge for the nose? She turned back to the guard, expecting him to arrest Thera right then and there for being a Faerune elf, but the guard simply bowed his head and backed away.

Thera laced her arm through Elmerah's, then tugged her further from the gates. "Act natural," she muttered. "We don't want to draw any more attention than we already have."

Elmerah matched Thera's pace, then narrowed her eyes at her, taking in her fine silk gown and burgundy linen cloak. "Shouldn't you be fleeing the Capital with all the other elves?"

Thera smirked. "Now why would I do that when I have the emperor's protection? The gate guards know not to question me. As for everyone else, well," she glanced to one side, prompting Elmerah to spot a man dressed in black, watching them from an alleyway, then to the right, where a lethal looking woman stroked a dagger at her belt, "most know not to bother me," she finished.

Elmerah rolled her eyes, allowing Thera to pull her further into the city past inns and stables. It seemed much of the panic from the previous day had died down, as the few city dwellers she spotted went about their regular business.

"Where's Rissine?" she asked finally.

"Have you reconsidered her offer?" Thera questioned.

"That's between me and her."

Thera chuckled. "You two are quite alike."

"Now, now," Elmerah cautioned, "let's not start throwing insults. I'll have to start comparing *you* to ugly wyrms and trolls."

Thera laughed again, then turned down a narrow street,

forcing Elmerah to follow by their joined arms.

Leaning against a stone wall further down was the greasy man. Spotting them, he approached. "I'll take that coin now," he said to Elmerah.

"I think not," Thera interjected.

The greasy man looked to her. "I helped her into the city, elf."

Footsteps sounded behind them, and the greasy man looked up. *Way* up.

Elmerah glanced at the presence at their backs. He was a mountain of a man, his skin like faded leather. She turned back to see the greasy man backing away, hands raised.

"Consider it a favor," the greasy man muttered, then turned and ran down an intersecting street.

Thera continued walking. "As I said, *most* know not to bother me. Those who do not know—tend to learn quickly."

Elmerah resisted the urge to glance again at the massive man following them. She wasn't sure if his continued presence was for their protection, or to keep her from running, but she had no interest in finding out.

"Where are we going?" she questioned, wondering if they'd meet Rissine at the Crimson Jewel, or at the docks.

"I'll take you somewhere to wait for Rissine. We cannot go to the Jewel, unless you want to risk the emperor becoming aware of your presence." She glanced at her with a smirk. "I assume that is something we'd like to avoid for now?"

"For*ever*," she corrected.

Thera laughed. There was something a bit off about her, something Elmerah didn't like. A bit like the greasy man, but greasy on the *inside*. Rissine had obviously lost her sense of judgment if she trusted the exiled Faerune elf.

"You didn't answer my question," she pressed as they turned down another street. They were keeping to less populated areas where few would make notice of them in the growing darkness.

"Somewhere safe," Thera assured. "You will wait there while I fetch Rissine."

Elmerah stopped walking and tugged her arm free of Thera's. "Oh, so I'm just to wait in some undisclosed location while you plan the ambush?"

Thera crossed her silk-clad arms. "I'm not sure what you're talking about. I simply thought it best for you to wait in hiding, considering you're a fugitive. If you run into the wrong people, they will attempt to kill you on sight."

"Fine," Elmerah hissed. "I'll *hide*, but if anyone shows up besides Rissine I'll burn down whatever building you put me in."

Thera replied with a nod and a smile. "Duly noted."

Elmerah walked past Thera's offered arm, continuing in the direction they'd been going.

Thera hurried to catch up. At some point the mountain man had left them, but Elmerah had little doubt he'd reappear if trouble cropped up. It didn't matter. She'd burn *him* down too.

The night was pitch black around them by the time they reached a small wooden shack on the outskirts of the slums. If the goal was to not be seen by any of the emperor's militia, they'd achieved it. The slums were run by a different kind of law.

Thera withdrew a key from her belt-pouch then unlocked the shack's door.

Elmerah waited for her to go inside first and light a lantern. Once there was light, she peeked her head in to ensure the shack was empty, save Thera. Once she felt confident there would be no ambush, she walked inside.

Thera offered her the lantern. "There's not much in the way of supplies here, but hopefully you will not have to wait long."

Elmerah took the lantern in her left hand, then patted her mostly-empty satchel with her right. "I'll be fine."

Thera nodded, the shiftiness of her pale eyes making Elmerah uneasy. Was she nervous to be harboring a fugitive, or was there more to it?

With a fake smile, Thera turned and left the shack, shutting the door behind her.

Elmerah watched her go, quickly deciding there was no way she would remain waiting in the shack. She'd find a hiding place outside where she could watch for Thera's return.

Saida

SAIDA CROUCHED IN THE DARKNESS, BINDING MERWYN'S wound with strips of her cloak. She'd managed to remove the arrow, but he'd lost a lot of blood. Somehow he was still conscious. She never actually thought she'd be grateful for the hardiness of the Akkeri.

"You must leave me," Merwyn rasped as she tugged her final knot tight, his slurred words now even more difficult to decipher.

She lifted her belt knife from the ground, then severed the excess fabric from the makeshift bandage. "Don't be silly.

We'll take you back to the Valeroot settlement. Alluin will find someone to care for you."

Merwyn tried to shake his head, then winced. "You have lost enough time already. You must go to Faerune."

She glanced around the dark woods, still wary of Dreilore though they'd ridden far from the place they were attacked. She turned back to Merwyn. "I will not leave you." Truly, she wanted to. After her experience with Lord Orius, she wanted to run straight to Faerune and never look back, but . . . Merwyn had saved her life. She could not just leave him to die, despite his urging.

She stood and guided the antlioch near, then crouched to help Merwyn stand. He had little strength left, and was hardly more than dead weight as she hoisted him atop the antlioch. It was fortunate he was even smaller than she, else she never would have managed.

Once he was in place, she climbed up behind him, her tired, blood-soaked limbs protesting every movement. She settled into the thick wool of the antlioch with one arm around Merwyn's ribcage, then urged the beast onward, back toward the Capital. While most would feel uneasy in the darkness, she was incredibly grateful for it. She knew Dreilore could see in the night better than humans, but their night vision could not compare to that of a Faerune elf. She would hopefully spot any adversaries long before they would spot her.

Merwyn did not offer any further protests as they rode, only occasional grunts of pain. If she did not get his wounds properly tended soon, she feared he would perish. If only the settlement wasn't so far away.

"We are," Merwyn rasped, "dooming Faerune."

She held on to him, ignoring his pungent smell and

congealing blood. "Faerune will have to protect itself for now. My kin will not fall so easily."

What she didn't say was that she was foolish to ever think she could make it on her own in the first place. She was a failure of a priestess, and as Merwyn had proven, a failure of a friend for putting him in danger. Just as she'd thought when she first ran away, Faerune was better off without her.

Elmerah

ELMERAH WAITED ATOP A NEARBY ROOF AS THERA returned to the shack. It seemed her fears had not been warranted, as she returned with a single cloaked figure about Rissine's height. However, the darkness obscured the face of the person at Thera's side, so she remained wary.

Thera unlocked the shack, and entered, the cloaked person close behind.

Shaking her head at her own paranoia, Elmerah lowered herself down from the roof's edge until she hung from her hands, then dropped the rest of the way, bending her knees to absorb the impact.

Fanning away the dust that billowed up, she approached the shack, then walked through the open door.

"Did you not trust me to bring her?" Thera questioned as Elmerah shut the door behind herself.

She shrugged. "Can you blame me?"

The cloaked figure turned around.

Elmerah gasped, her heart pounding. It wasn't Rissine

after all. She backed toward the door, but knew it would do her little good.

The emperor pulled back his hood, revealing his short black hair. "I must admit, I'm surprised you returned. Where is Saida?"

Her hand found the door handle behind her, but it wouldn't budge, as if the metal had been fused together. Giving the door a final angry tug, she glared at the emperor. "What do you want? Am I to believe you ventured into the slums just to see *me*?"

Egrin stepped forward past Thera. "You value yourself too little. I'm sure *any* man would venture across the Capital to see you. Now I'll ask you one more time. Where is Saida?"

Elmerah sneered. "*Far* from here."

Egrin sighed. "Of course, I expected as much, though the Akkeri will not be pleased." He glanced at Thera. "Leave us."

Thera bowed, then hurried toward the door.

Elmerah blocked her path. "You won't be going out there without me."

Thera smiled snidely, then reached past her toward the door.

Elmerah tried to grab the handle first, but suddenly she couldn't move. She would have cursed the bloody emperor, if only she could breathe.

Thera opened the door with ease, slid past Elmerah, and went out into the night, closing the door behind her.

A moment later, she could move again, and lunged for the door. She pressed down on the handle, but it wouldn't budge. Straightening her back, she turned to face the emperor. "What do you want? I have no clue where Saida is. I cannot help you."

He stalked toward her, his black cloak billowing around

him. "You're strong for a witch," he observed. "Almost as strong as your sister." She stepped further into the room as he reached her side, then spun to keep him in her sights as he paced around her. Finally, he stopped near the door, then looked her up and down. "Perhaps stronger, in some ways."

She stepped back. "What do you *want*?" she growled, debating her options. He could crush the breath from her in the time it would take her to summon a lick of magic or draw her cutlass, and running for the door again was obviously out.

"I want to learn why you've come to the Capital," he explained. "At first I assumed you were here because of Rissine, yet here you are," he gestured to her with a flip of his hand, palm up, "not with Rissine." He smirked. "Yet trying in vain to find her."

She stared at him, unsure of what to say. *I'm here to convince my sister to kill you*, didn't seem like a wise answer.

He laughed, though at what, she did not know. "I'm almost tempted to let you go, just to see what you'll do."

"I like that option," she agreed, "let's go with that."

He shook his head. "I said I was tempted, but I'm really not *that* curious. Do you remember your time in Shadowmarsh?"

She was so baffled by the question she instinctually backed further into the room, away from him.

He stepped forward, closing the distance between them. "Rissine claims to remember little of your homeland."

Elmerah blinked at him, knowing that if Rissine had actually said that, she'd been lying. A teenager when they left, she'd remember Shadowmarsh clearly. "What do you care for Shadowmarsh? Your father had everyone there killed. Is that not enough?"

He chuckled. "He was looking for something there, but was unable to find it. I've been curious about it since I was a boy."

She chewed her lip. This was going nowhere. Was he simply toying with her before killing her? "Well I don't remember it either, so I can't help you."

He tsked at her. "You Arthali are such liars." He lifted a hand toward her.

She flinched a moment before the air was crushed from her lungs.

Though he kept his hand raised, it seemed to take little effort for him to suffocate her.

She stared at him, because it was all she could do as her mind buzzed like it was filled with bees. Just when she was about to lose consciousness, he released her.

She fell to her knees, gasping for air. Her eyes filled involuntarily with tears.

His boots hissed across the floor as he moved to stand over her. "Do you care to answer my questions again, *honestly* now?"

She squinted at him as the burning receded from her lungs. "What was the question again?"

"Shadowmarsh. What do you remember of it?"

Was this man utterly mad? Perhaps his foul magic had corrupted his mind. "I remember beaches, and mist, and marshes, and my mother's mutilated body." She forced herself to her feet. "I believe your father was responsible for *that*."

He laughed. "Now that's more like it. What else do you remember?"

She blinked at him. "That's it. I was young when I was

forced to leave, and you know exactly why I left. What more is there to tell?"

He began to pace. Even when his back was turned, she didn't bother trying to escape. He'd simply crush her again, and she wanted to avoid *that*. "Did you know that the Faerune elves amplify their magic with gemstones, moonstones in particular?" He turned toward her.

"Uh, yes? I suppose I've heard that."

"And the Dreilore," he continued, resuming his pacing, "are as great in magic as the elves. What amplifies their natural gifts?"

She blinked at him. "Um . . . metals?"

He nodded. "Very good. The elves have their gems, and the Dreilore their metals. Their magic comes from the earth." He stopped pacing again. "But you," he gestured to her, "you have greater magic than either race, but where does it come from?"

She crossed her arms to hide their trembling. "I could ask you the same question."

He grinned, though it didn't reach his cool, apathetic eyes. "Yes, you could ask, but you can't *make* me tell you. I'm going to make you tell me."

"Well good luck with that," she scoffed, "considering I have no idea. There are no mines in Shadowmarsh, or any of the old Arthali provinces. We don't have gems or metals."

He frowned. "Stupid girl. You possess great magics, yet know nothing about them?"

"Well maybe if my mother hadn't been *murdered* she could have taught me more."

"Never mind," he sighed. "We'll simply have to figure it out ourselves." He spread his feet apart. "Now, *attack*."

She blinked at him for a moment, then drew her cutlass. He wasn't going to have to ask her twice. She summoned fire to her blade, then whipped it through the air, flinging it at him.

A lick of flame hit him in the chest, then dissipated. He didn't so much as flinch.

With a growl of frustration, she summoned more flame, letting it grow in strength before flinging it his way.

Just like the first attack, it faded, leaving the emperor utterly unscathed. *Anyone* else would have suffered severe burns.

He tilted his head. "What else do you have? I know Rissine can summon lightning. Can you?"

She glared at him, unwilling to admit she couldn't summon lightning indoors.

"Weaker than your sister after all," he sighed. "Oh well, attack me with all that you have, and do it quickly, I've got things to do."

Her eyes widened. He truly was insane. She had to think of another tactic, lest he make her attack him until she was completely drained and defenseless.

Thunder crackled outside, bringing with it the scent of rain.

Egrin grinned. "So you *do* have lightning." He widened his stance a bit more, bracing himself.

Should she tell him it was simply a storm moving in?

Suddenly the door handle across the room crackled with blue electricity. She and Egrin watched as it intensified, then the door burst open. Elmerah caught a flash of a figure standing outside, then lightning hit Egrin in the chest, flinging him aside.

"Run!" Rissine shouted, as she rushed in through the door.

She hit Egrin with another bolt of lightning while he was

down, the impact sliding him across the floor and into the wall. Even so, he quickly got to his knees.

Elmerah ran out the door into the drizzling rain as Rissine filled the small shack with electricity. Out in the street, she hesitated.

"Run!" Rissine shouted again as she charged out the door, framed in crackling blue light.

Elmerah ran.

The rain increased, soon soaking her clothing. Rissine ran at her side, her boots seeming to thud in time with the thunder.

"What in Ilthune is going on!" Elmerah rasped as they ran.

"Keep running," Rissine hissed. "I'll explain once we're safe."

Elmerah flung herself forward into a blind sprint, wanting to achieve as much distance as quickly as possible, though she heard no sound of pursuit. Long moments passed until they outran Rissine's storm and stumbled into an alleyway to catch their breath.

Hunched over with hands on knees, Elmerah looked to her sister, in the same position. "Now," she panted, "will you tell me what in the name of Ilthune is going on? Why does the emperor care about Shadowmarsh?"

Seeming to catch her breath, Rissine straightened and wiped away a lock of hair plastered to her face. "I do not know, but I'm beginning to think he has no intention of lifting the Arthali exile."

Elmerah leaned against a nearby wall and peered up at the dark night sky. "So was it his alliance with the Dreilore, or the fact that he's madder than a whipfish that finally gave it away?"

Rissine glared at her. "Neither, it was him privately approaching Thera and bribing her to keep an eye out for you. He didn't want me to know if you returned."

Elmerah bent her knees, sliding her back down the wall until she sat in the dirt. "You knew Thera would betray you?"

Rissine crossed her arms. "You've always been dense. How do you think I found you?"

Finally, things fell into place. "She played the emperor," she realized. "She only let him think no one else knew where I'd been led."

Rissine nodded. "Since you were seen together by guards at the gates, she had no choice but to alert the emperor of your presence, but she found me first, before going to Egrin."

Elmerah glared. "Then what took you so long to rescue me!"

"Oh don't be silly," Rissine lectured as she turned away. "I wasn't going to pass up the perfect opportunity to figure out what Egrin wants. What he *really* wants. I knew he would not kill you outright, else he wouldn't have asked Thera to lure you to a private location."

Elmerah rolled her eyes at her sister's back, then stood to follow her out of the alley. "And did you figure it out?"

Rissine sighed as Elmerah reached her side. "Well, we know he's interested in Faerune's gems, and the magical metals of Salisfait. He obviously hoped there would be something similar in Shadowmarsh."

"But what could he hope to do with the gems and metals? Only the Faerune elves and Dreilore can utilize them with their natural magics."

Rissine glanced at her, her eyes glinting in the starlight.

"I do not know. All I do know, is that we mustn't let him get them."

Elmerah stopped walking. "I thought you only cared for the fate of the Arthali. Why would you care to stop him?"

Rissine stared at her, as if waiting for her to figure it out.

Elmerah stared back, utterly clueless about her sister, as always.

Rissine sighed. "I do only care for the fate of the Arthali. I care about you and I, and Egrin wants us both dead. Therefore, it is now my mission in life to keep Egrin from getting *anything* he wants, even if that means protecting Faerune."

Elmerah smiled. "Well then, sister, I think we *finally* have something in common."

Rissine raised her eyebrows. "So you'll help me?"

Elmerah's smile broadened. This had been easier than she'd thought. "Find me a mug of ale and a warm safe place, and we'll discuss our *new* plan."

Rissine pouted. "But I liked my old plan. Little needs to change."

Elmerah gestured for her to start walking. "Your plans are always the worst. Do you remember that time you thought it would be a good idea to scare mother by filling her bed with fish heads?"

Rissine chuckled as she started walking. "She made us eat only fish head stew for *days*."

"I can't stand the stuff to this day," Elmerah sighed.

Her sister flashed her a smile. For a moment, walking side by side, it almost felt like a time long ago, before they'd both been scarred by violence.

Unfortunately, much time had passed between them, and there were some things now, despite their current partnership, that Elmerah would never forgive.

CHAPTER TWENTY

Alluin

A lluin patted his dappled mare's thick neck as she carried him south. He'd felt a bit guilty stealing her in the dead of night, but now that morning had come, bringing with it clear skies, he'd stopped thinking about what the farmer would do the next day when he wanted to take his cart to market, or plow his fields. He could only look forward, for the past held too much pain.

He stopped occasionally to check for signs of travelers, but it was impossible to tell where Saida and Merwyn had passed. The rains had washed away all but the freshest tracks, and he was yet to notice the double-pointed hoof prints of the antlioch. Even if there were prints to be found, there was no saying if they'd kept to the woods this far south, or if they'd risked the speedier travel of the road. If they were stopping for rest each night, he might even pass them by entirely.

With that thought in mind, he tugged the mare's braided

leather reins. He glanced left to the deep woods, then to the more sparse woods on his right, willing them to tell him their secrets. Beyond the sparse woods he'd find the sea, another possible area to search. If Saida and Merwyn became lost, they'd only need follow the coastline all the way to Faerune.

He said a silent prayer to Felan, the goddess of the hunt, then dismounted. While riding granted him speed, tracking on foot would grant him accuracy. He needed to find some sign of Saida and Merwyn so he would not pass them by.

As he led his horse through the quiet shadows of the woods, he was overcome by an odd feeling of unease. His instincts told him the woods were dangerous, which he already knew, but this was something *more*. It was almost as if he could sense a prickle of magic nearby.

Rubbing at the goosebumps on his arms, he continued on regardless, keeping his eyes on the earth, and his ears focused on things unseen, just as was taught to all young Valeroot hunters. That was something that would never change, despite how far removed from their homeland they'd become.

Elmerah

ELMERAH LOUNGED ON THE DUSTY WOODEN FLOOR, waiting for Rissine to return to the small warehouse they'd commandeered as their new hideout. A sliver of light cut across her black breeches from a window high in the wall. She'd watched as it slowly made its way across her legs. Rissine had been gone *ages*.

She wondered if Alluin had made any progress. If he'd managed to catch Saida's trail, he could be back on the way to the Capital within the next day or two. She needed to be ready with a plan when he returned.

She slumped a little further down the wall, splaying her long legs across the floor. While it made her nervous to work with her sister, she held hope that perhaps Rissine would be the one to kill Egrin. After her experience in the shack, she was not looking forward to facing the emperor ever again.

A key turned in the nearby lock, then the door swung inward, revealing Rissine. She'd exchanged her emerald coat for charcoal gray to better blend in with the crowds. Not that the pair of them would blend in *at all* if they traveled together. One Arthali witch with her hair covered could be mistaken for a tall, deeply tanned human. Two was just making things obvious.

Rissine tossed an overfilled satchel beside Elmerah, then turned and locked the door behind her. "I've spoken to Thera. She'll keep an eye out for your friend."

Ignoring the satchel, Elmerah laced her fingers over her stomach. "You're sure we can trust her? She won't turn Alluin in?"

Rissine approached, then sat cross-legged on the floor, facing Elmerah. "I trust Thera with my life."

"Why?"

Rissine pulled the satchel toward her, then pawed through it. "Because she owes me hers. There's a reason you don't see many Faerune elves in the Capital. They don't survive long on their own. Thera knows if she truly helped the emperor, it would only result in her death."

Elmerah smirked. "So basically you trust Thera to not get herself killed?"

Rissine nodded, not seeming to catch her sarcasm, then removed a waxed linen pouch from the satchel, handing it to Elmerah.

She took the pouch and opened it, finding it filled with dried sweet plums.

"I remember they were your favorite," Rissine commented.

Elmerah handed them back to her. "I'm no longer the girl you knew." Never mind that she still adored dried sweet plums.

Rissine sighed, then popped a plum into her mouth.

Elmerah's mouth watered. She snatched the bag back and pulled out a plum, stuffing it into her mouth. At her sister's grin, she growled while chewing, "Just because they're not my favorite doesn't mean I'm not hungry."

Instead of commenting, Rissine stood. "We should probably leave the Capital at nightfall. It will be easier to meet your friend that way, rather than bringing him into the city. You say he knows of other Valeroot settlements?"

She nodded. "You know, I'm surprised you're willing to work with the elves."

"It seems the best option," she explained. "Now that I've confronted Egrin, I must abandon my initial plan and move forward. Until we can gather the Arthali, the elves are our only logical allies."

Elmerah ate another plum, fighting her blush. Though Rissine claimed to have her doubts about Egrin previously, Elmerah knew she'd sacrificed her whole grand plan to save her. She'd sacrificed an alliance with the emperor himself to save a sister who'd abandoned her nearly a decade prior. She really was *crazy*.

Elmerah sucked sticky bits of plum from her teeth. "So

we'll leave the Capital and wait for Alluin. Once we know word has been sent to Isara, we'll begin our plan to assassinate—" She whipped her head to the side at a frantic knocking on the door.

Rissine hurried over to it.

"It's me," a voice hissed.

Rissine unlocked and opened the door, letting Thera inside. Her white-blonde hair was pulled away from her face and stuffed under a dirt-brown cowl atop a raggedy tunic and loose breeches. She looked nothing like the refined elf Elmerah had seen the previous day, and the bruised nose only added to her poor appearance.

Thera leaned her back against the wall, lightly panting as Rissine peeked outside, then shut and locked the door.

"The Dreilore," Thera said as soon as she'd caught her breath. "They've been spotted south near Port Aeluvaria. An entire army of them."

Elmerah stood. "Port Aeluvaria?" As she recalled, that was only a two-day ride south at a leisurely pace by way of the Emperor's Path. Saida had left two days prior, heading in that direction, though traveling through the woods would slow her down.

Thera nodded. "It seems the attack on Faerune will happen sooner than we'd thought."

Rissine stepped toward Thera. "What of the militia?"

Thera shook her head. "They have not yet been organized. Only the Dreilore."

"And they're heading toward Faerune?" Rissine pressed.

Thera shook her head. "No, they're camped in the deep woods, but have not advanced south according to the most recent report. It seems they're waiting for something."

Elmerah chewed her lip. If Saida and Merwyn were

keeping off the road, they might very well run right into the Dreilore, and if Alluin was tracking them, he'd be next.

"We need to go," she decided. "We cannot wait for nightfall."

Rissine raised an eyebrow at her. "Do you hope to confront an entire army of Dreilore now? Plotting to overthrow the Empire is one thing, facing the Dreilore without an army of our own is utter madness."

She glanced at Thera. The elf already knew they were waiting for Alluin, so Elmerah supposed it would do little harm to voice her worries in front of her. "Alluin is likely heading right for them, and he doesn't know that they're there."

Rissine tilted her head. "You worry for his safety? Have you fallen in love with an elf?"

Elmerah snorted. "Hardly, but he is our only connection to that *army* you're so keen to acquire. It is in our best interests to keep him alive."

Rissine stared at her for several long moments. "Fine," she decided. "It will be risky to leave the city in daylight, especially after last night's events. We'll have to leave by boat at the South Docks."

Rissine turned to Thera, who nodded. "I'll arrange it."

As Thera departed, Rissine turned back to Elmerah. "I sincerely hope your elf friend is worth all this trouble."

Her shoulders slumped with a sigh. "So do I, *dear sister*. So do I."

Alluin

ALLUIN CURSED HIS ROTTEN LUCK. HE'D FOUND NO SIGNS of antlioch tracks. Instead, he'd found many horse hoof prints and large boot prints. In places the underbrush had been cleared, and he'd even found fire pits. Large numbers had been passing through the woods roughly halfway to Port Aeluvaria, which was unusual considering the well-trodden Emperor's Path spanned down to the trade port and well beyond. Anyone staying in the woods was hiding from something. While his kin might take such a path, they would not leave behind so many signs of their passing, and they'd likely have antlioch, not horses.

He lifted his ear to the wind, but heard nothing save the chatter of birds. He walked onward, then his boot kicked up a long, thin branch. He looked down. Not a branch, but an arrow, its tip coated in blood.

He knelt down and retrieved it. While it could have been from a hunter, he doubted it. Any hunter would not have left the arrow behind, especially an arrow such as this. The point was made of gleaming silver, and the shaft dark wood with intricate runes carved along it. Instead of the common turkey feather fletching, vibrant red feathers were used. He'd never seen such feathers before.

Arrow in hand, he began searching the surrounding area, soon finding a puddle of blood, and a few strips of discarded cloth. Recognizing the cloth, he continued searching until he found the antlioch prints.

His hand gripped the arrow painfully. Saida and Merwyn had been here, and at least one of them was injured. The cloth was from the cloak he'd given Saida at the Valeroot settlement.

Noting the direction the antlioch had gone, he climbed back atop his horse, urging it to a trot. He kept his sharp eyes on the ground, following the subtle trail. Soon it became clear that Saida and Merwyn had headed back toward the Capital, abandoning their mission to reach Faerune.

He knew Saida would not have turned back without good reason. She likely hoped to reach the Valeroot settlement, only, no one would await her there. Except, perhaps, the Dreilore.

Elmerah

IT WAS MIDDAY BY THE TIME THERA RETURNED, FAR TOO long by Elmerah's estimate. Saida and Alluin were both getting farther away, perhaps walking right into Dreilore clutches, while she sat around in a tiny storeroom with her sister.

Thoroughly irritated, she stood and waited for Thera to reveal their plan.

After shutting and locking the door, Thera turned to them, her ugly cowl still covering her hair and ears. "I've managed to arrange for a boat," she explained. "Just a small rowboat manned by a single fisherman, but the skies are clear so it should get us to the southern coast without issue, as long as we are not seen."

Rissine slung her supply satchel over her shoulder, tugging her long braid out from under the strap. "Let us go before Egrin realizes where we're hiding."

Elmerah shivered at the mention of the emperor. She realized with a start that she was *scared* of Egrin Dinoba. She hadn't been actually scared of anything in a very long time.

She glanced at Rissine. A frown marred her brow, but she didn't look scared. *Nothing* scared Rissine, of that she was quite sure, but then again, she'd seen her magic in the shack the previous night. Rissine had filled the entire space with lightning. Who would be scared with powers like those?

Feeling suddenly inadequate, and therefore *angry*, she focused her gaze on Thera. "Can we trust this fisherman?"

Thera shrugged. "We have little choice but to trust that our coin, and the threat of the guilds will buy his silence."

Elmerah's shoulders slumped. She was right. A boat was the only other way to escape the Capital, barring climbing the city walls. While the majority of Alluin's tunnel might have still been structurally sound, they'd be digging through piles of burnt rubble out in the open to find the entrance.

Each of the women nodded their agreement, then Thera unlocked and opened the door before leading the way outside. Elmerah followed warily, hunching her back beneath her black coat and hood. The chances they'd run into any of the emperor's men through the poorer areas of the Capital on the way to the South Docks were slim, but she still felt nervous.

Rissine shut the door behind them, then gave Elmerah a light shove to get her moving. "Stop acting like a quavering maiden," she lectured.

Elmerah straightened her shoulders and started walking. Rissine was right. It was embarrassing to act like a helpless little girl. Something about being around her sister made her feel powerless. She'd always paled in comparison to the *almighty* Rissine.

Her thoughts dark, she followed Thera down the hard-packed dirt street. There were no other souls to be seen, but that would change soon enough. She could hear the murmur of city folk not far off.

Thera glanced back at them as they walked, nerves showing clearly on her pale, delicate face. It was actually a bit odd given Thera's usual demeanor.

Elmerah sidled up to Rissine as they walked. "Is it just me," she whispered, "or does your pet elf seem a little *too* nervous?"

"She's risking her life for us," Rissine hissed, "of course she's nervous. After last night, she'll never be able to show her face within the Capital again, lest Egrin remove her head from her shoulders."

Elmerah accepted her answer with a nod, though she was still unsure. Something felt off. Keeping her continued thoughts to herself, she followed silently behind Thera, keeping her head down.

Miraculously, they soon made it to the South Docks without incident. The wooden planking leading up to the sea was bustling with activity. Several fishing vessels were anchored to the docks with men and women unloading the morning's catch. Further down, a few larger vessels loaded up with crates of goods likely destined for Port Aeluvaria. The larger ships headed for more distant lands would all be at the more expansive Central Docks.

Few paid them any mind as Thera lead the way down the docks toward the warehouse where Elmerah and Alluin had confronted Vessa. She eventually stopped beside a tiny rowboat. An elderly fisherman sat hunched in the vessel, the sun-wizened skin of his arms and face bare to the elements. He looked up at them with foggy eyes as they approached.

His expression grew wary after observing Elmerah and

Rissine, but he still scooted to the back of his vessel and gestured for them to board.

Thera hopped in first, her elven grace barely rocking the boat.

Rissine went next, slightly less graceful, then held her hand up to Elmerah. "I know how blunderous you can be."

Sneering at her sister's hand, Elmerah hopped into the small remaining space, then had to quickly plop her rear end down to keep from toppling over into the gently lapping water.

They waited silently while the fisherman unwound the rope from the dock, then sat next to Elmerah, plastering himself against the side of the boat so as not to touch her. She glared at him while she took up an oar and started paddling. Long moments passed as they gained momentum away from the docks, but no one bothered them. It was not unusual for small boats to disembark on their own. Most would just paddle out to deeper waters where larger fish could be caught.

As the dock behind them grew distant, Elmerah exhaled a sigh of relief. They'd made it out of Galterra alive. Once they reached the southern coast, they could find horses at one of the smaller villages. After that, they would go after Alluin, and hope he had not yet run into the Dreilore at Port Aeluvaria.

Beginning to pant, she pumped her oar, anxious to reach the shore. She wished she could see Thera's face, but she sat ahead of her next to Rissine. Still, the elf's shoulders were hunched uncharacteristically, her face burrowed in the hood of her ragged cloak. *She looks like a sneaky little mouse*, Elmerah thought, or some other form of . . . vermin.

Noticing the fisherman repeatedly glancing at her, she turned to glare at him. "*What?*"

He winced. "I've never met an Arthali witch before is all. You're taller than I'd imagined."

She sucked her teeth, annoyed with Thera's choice of fisherman. "Will you be throwing me overboard then?"

"Leave the poor man alone," Rissine chastised.

Thera still didn't say a word. In fact, she didn't even look at any of them.

Elmerah lifted the toe of her boot, tapping the bench beneath Thera's rump. "Are you afraid of deep water? You're a lot more quiet than usual."

"Than usual?" Thera questioned.

"Yes, I've known you for *ages*," she lied. "I should notice if you're acting strange."

Rissine darted a questioning look back at her comment, but didn't speak.

"I'm just nervous with everything going on," Thera explained, not arguing the knowing her for *ages* comment.

"I suppose that makes sense," Elmerah agreed. "By the way, how did you get that bruised nose? Did you fall down the stairs?"

"Oh, um, yes," Thera replied. "Quite an unfortunate accident."

That did it. Not only was this Thera a fake, she'd stolen credit from Elmerah for the bruised nose. Noting a subtle nod from Rissine, Elmerah leaned back on her bench, bracing herself with her hands, then lifted both her feet. She took a deep breath, then shoved them into Thera's back with enough force to break a board.

With an *eep* of surprise, Thera launched from the boat, splashing into the serene blue sea.

When she bobbed back up, her hair was no longer white, but red, and dripping wet fox ears perked up from her head. She paddled to remain afloat. "Foolish witches!"

"Foolish Nokken!" Rissine growled back, diving toward the edge of the boat to snatch at the female shapechanger.

"Stop!" the fisherman screeched as the boat rocked violently.

"Where's Thera?" Rissine hissed, giving up her grappling efforts in favor of drawing the long, curved knife at her belt and coating it in a thin veil of flame.

The Nokken's eyes widened, then she dove down out of sight.

Rissine stood, darting her eyes around in search of the shapechanger.

Elmerah picked up her oar. "We need to go, *now*," she ordered. "If a Nokken knew to impersonate Thera, then the emperor knows we're trying to escape."

Rissine turned wide eyes to her. "Curse it all!" she spat, then sat down and picked up her oar. She turned a venomous glare back toward the fisherman. "Start paddling unless you want to end up at the bottom of the sea."

The fisherman didn't need to be asked twice, though Elmerah hoped his heart would not burst with fear. They needed him to row.

Rissine positioned herself further toward the bow so she could alternate her oar to either side of the boat, while Elmerah and the fisherman started paddling on their respective sides behind her.

All conversation ceased. Had they realized the Nokken's plan in time, or would a trap await them on shore? Perhaps they'd be better off diving into the sea and swimming up where they would not be easily spotted.

A splash signaled the Nokken surfacing. She'd swam closer to shore, and would make it there before them at the rate they were going. If the Nokken escaped them, she would take the answers they needed with her.

Rissine glanced back at Elmerah, her intent clear.

"I just finally got dried off after all the rain," Elmerah groaned.

"You always were a weak swimmer," Rissine quipped, then stood and dove into the sea, leaving her satchel of supplies behind.

Elmerah glanced at the clearly terrified fisherman, then rolled her eyes. "I hope that Nokken paid you in advance." Making sure her cutlass was firmly in its sheath, she stood.

Just as she jumped, the fisherman muttered, "She didn't."

The icy water encased her body. She used the momentum of her dive to propel herself toward shore, then came up with a ragged gasp. Too bad for the fisherman, but at least he'd gotten a satchel full of supplies for his efforts. Either way, it was no longer Elmerah's main concern. The water was *freezing*, and her coat and boots weighed her down like quicksand. Cursing both her sister and the Nokken, she started swimming, aiming herself a little further down the coast from where Rissine and the Nokken were heading. If an ambush *did* await, she wasn't about to swim right into it like her sister.

Though her heavy coat weighed her down, she focused on keeping her breathing even, and her strokes smooth, occasionally glancing over the waves to locate her sister. Hopefully anyone on shore would be focused on Rissine, and not her.

She dove below a cresting wave, then came up with her head barely above the surface, then dove under another coming wave. From what she could see of the shore, there was a long stretch of sandy beach, then jagged coral further down, peeking out of the water. Beyond the coral was a dense forest of waxy shrubs, an optimal place to come up unnoticed, but the coral would be a problem. She kicked under another wave, then was yanked back before she could reach the surface. Something had snagged on her boot, though the water below should have been deep enough to spare her from any debris jutting up from the seabed.

Her lungs searing from lack of air, she curled up underwater, reaching to free her boot, then reared away as a knife came slicing toward her, wielded by one of the Akkeri. The foul creature had been lying in wait in the waves. It was an ambush after all, just not the type she'd expected.

She kicked at the Akkeri with her free foot, smashing its hand where it gripped her boot. It let go and she shot up to the surface, sucking in a painful breath before paddling back out of the Akkeri's path.

Its crudely hammered knife shot up through the water right where she'd been, then the creature crested behind it. With a sickening grin, the Akkeri dove back down.

Panicked, Elmerah threw herself backward through the waves. Though she was a strong swimmer despite Rissine's insults, none could rival the Akkeri. She had to think of something fast.

She sank beneath the water, opening her eyes in search of her attacker just in time to nearly get a knife in the face. She shoved against the Akkeri's sinewy body as it passed. If only she had a belt knife. It would be impossible to wield her cutlass beneath the choppy waters.

As her head shot back up between the waves, she noted shouting on shore. Rissine and the Nokken must have made it out, but she couldn't spare the time to see what was happening.

A splash signaled the Akkeri lunging at her again, but she wasn't fast enough to move out of the way. The Akkeri's knife slashed across her side. A sharp sting signaled she'd been wounded, though her body was going numb with the cold.

Desperate, she dove back down, but her blood clouded her vision. Her only option was her magic, but fire would do her little good in the ocean, and she needed a weapon to focus more intricate magic like lightning.

The Akkeri's ugly face appeared before hers and she lashed out, calling lightning despite her lack of weapon. Instead of coming down from the sky, a vibrant blue bolt erupted between her palm and the Akkeri's face. The water became alive with electricity, and the Akkeri was paralyzed with it. She watched as his eyes seemed to bulge with the pressure, but she could stay under no longer.

She shot back up gasping for air. She bobbed just above the surface, panting as hot blood continued to seep from her side, warming the icy water around her left arm. She waited, but the Akkeri did not attack again.

She would have liked to take a moment to feel relieved, but there was no time. She forced her tired, aching limbs into motion, propelling herself through the water toward the shore. She no longer cared about stealth, just so long as she reached the shore before bleeding out. Distantly she noted the thunder rumbling overhead, and knew Rissine was in trouble.

Saida

"Thunder," Saida commented, her eyes scanning the clear blue sky. "That's odd."

Merwyn did not reply. He'd long since lost consciousness, and she was afraid to check his pulse.

The antlioch stumbled beneath them, clearly exhausted from lack of rest. Saida was exhausted too, but she could not afford to stop now. She'd sacrificed any chance she'd had of reaching Faerune in time. She would not let Merwyn die along with her hopes of helping her people.

A deep rumble sounded again near the coast, followed by a bolt of lightning cutting across the sky. As she watched, dark, angry clouds rolled in across the sea, moving too quickly for a natural storm.

She knew the storm could only mean one thing. Elmerah was still near the Capital, and she was in trouble.

Guilt twisting her gut into knots, she tapped her feet against the tired antlioch's sides. The creature hesitated, but finally began to trot, carrying Saida and Merwyn toward the Emperor's Path, and the growing storm beyond.

CHAPTER TWENTY-ONE

Elmerah

Elmerah flopped onto the shore like a dying moss seal, though instead of deadly shark wounds she had an Akkeri to thank for her blood loss. She'd evaded any more Akkeri while in the water, but only because they'd been busy swarming the shore, and the very angry witch that awaited them.

Elmerah staggered to her feet, taking in the score of Akkeri surrounding Rissine as the Nokken who'd posed as Thera stood off to the side. Next to her dripping wet figure were two more Nokken. They must have been waiting further down shore. Someone else waited a little further inland, and Elmerah gawked as she recognized him. It was bloody Daemon Saredoth. Rissine's arms were extended skyward, beckoning the darkening storm overhead, but he seemed none too worried about his position.

The hairs on Elmerah's arms prickled with electricity. Her sister was far stronger than she remembered.

"Kill her!" one of the Nokken ordered, her gaze on Rissine. "Keep the weaker one alive."

Elmerah frowned. She might have just been thinking it, but she did not appreciate others referring to her as *the weaker one*.

Lightning struck near the three Nokken, tossing the two females aside, then the mob of Akkeri attacked.

"Ugly muckdwellers," Elmerah grumbled as she shucked her heavy wet coat, then withdrew her cutlass, wincing at the pain in her side. Though rain had begun pattering across the ocean, she still managed to summon flame to her blade. She would have liked to add to her sister's lightning, but she had been worn out *before* her underwater fight with the Akkeri. She could barely manage flame now.

She staggered across the beach as Rissine whirled like a dancer, tossing Akkeri aside with bolts of lightning that flung harsh sprays of sand into the air. The two female Nokken, who'd now righted themselves, turned their attention toward Elmerah, leaving the remaining male to watch Rissine fight the Akkeri.

Elmerah's hand trembled around her cutlass as the pair of Nokken neared, their fox ears pinned back and their mouths snarled to show pointed canines. Elmerah knew little of their magic except that they could shapechange, and had superior senses. They might have other tricks waiting for her, and it was already two against one.

Oh well, it wasn't like she had much choice but to face them. She whipped her cutlass through the air, flinging a string of flame long enough to hit both women, though one darted out of the way in time. The other hissed as the flame hit her, then dropped and rolled through the sand to extinguish it. Soon enough she was back on her feet, and the pair approached cautiously.

"Use your lightning you fool!" Rissine shouted, still fighting the oncoming Akkeri.

The little whelps were ridiculously hard to kill.

Seeming to sense her weakness, the wet, uninjured Nokken smiled. She crouched, then pounced forward like a wolf.

Elmerah slashed at her with her cutlass, the movement viciously straining her wounded side, making her stomach lurch. She repressed the urge to vomit. For all her effort, the cutlass barely grazed the Nokken, and her flame only managed a weak sizzle as it hit the Nokken's wet clothing.

Elmerah backed away. "I'd like to remind you both that you're supposed to keep me alive."

"Alive, yes," the wet Nokken said in the thick accent of the Dracawyn Province, "but perhaps severely mangled is acceptable."

The Nokken stepped forward. An arrow thunked into her leg and she staggered, letting out a loud shriek.

Elmerah watched in shock as blood blossomed on the Nokken's tattered wet clothing, then she staggered back, realizing the archer might have been aiming for *her*. Her shock only increased as she spotted a Faerune elf nearing from the dense shrubs, a short bow held at the ready. At first she thought it was Thera, but the elf was too short.

"What in Ilthune are you doing here?" she gasped.

As Saida neared, Elmerah noted her eyes were a bit too wide, and her hands trembled slightly on her bow. She obviously wasn't used to shooting people with arrows.

The injured Nokken cursed in her native tongue, then

the uninjured one stepped forward with a whispered comment to the other.

Saida's bow shifted to point at her chest. "Do not move," she ordered.

The uninjured Nokken spoke again in her foreign tongue, then lightning struck down directly on top of her. She made a guttural *oof* sound as she was flung forward into the sand, then remained motionless.

Elmerah looked beyond the still conscious Nokken to see Rissine approach. Daemon and the other Nokken stood back, *watching*, but why?

Her hands raised in defeat, the female Nokken crept back, dragging her injured leg in the sand.

Once Rissine arrived near Elmerah, she turned and faced Daemon and the male Nokken coming toward them. Her storm still crackled overhead, but it was quickly dissipating. Her power must have been nearly drained after her fight with the Akkeri, who now lay strewn across the beach.

Clutching her wounded side through her loose blouse, Elmerah moved to stand shoulder to shoulder with her sister. "Have your bow ready," she muttered to Saida.

Daemon and the male Nokken stopped roughly ten paces away, leaving the female to sit in the sand and nurse her wounds.

Elmerah pointed her cutlass toward them. "What do you want? Why stage such a pitiful ambush?"

Daemon smiled coldly. "You and the elf, of course. We only meant to tire you out first." He drew a jewel-encrusted rapier from his belt.

"It's enchanted," Rissine muttered. "It is why he would risk himself so near our magic."

"That is correct," Daemon replied. He flicked his gaze to

Saida. "Now kindly lower your pathetic little bow and I won't kill your friend. We only need one of the witches. Either one will do."

Elmerah flexed her fingers around her cutlass as the Nokken who'd been struck by lightning groaned, then slowly got to her feet. *Wonderful*, Elmerah thought, now they'd be entirely dependent on Rissine's sword skills and Saida's bow against three opponents, because she was just about ready to topple over.

Without warning, Saida loosed her arrow. It sailed right toward the male Nokken, though she may have well been aiming for Daemon. The Nokken darted aside, rolling through the sand, then coming to his feet as the arrow plunked harmlessly into the ground where he'd been standing.

Before she could draw another arrow, the Nokken who'd been hit by lightning tackled her, and the two startled tussling over the bow.

With a cruel smile, Daemon stepped forward, raising his rapier in an offensive stance. "Now, who would like to test their sword skills first?"

Elmerah glanced at her sister to find her looking far paler than usual, and her eyes seemed unfocused. Curse it all, she'd used up too much of her magic. It was a wonder she was still standing.

Just then, Rissine fell to her knees and fainted.

"I guess that would be me," Elmerah sighed. She stepped forward, then lifted her cutlass, though the movement pained her greatly. She wavered slightly, feeling like she was on a ship in choppy waters. She glanced at the male Nokken. "Let's make this a fair fight, shall we? I'll kill him first, then I'll kill you."

With a smug smile, the Nokken raised his hands, showcasing long, thick black nails, then stepped back.

Elmerah turned back to Daemon, then charged.

He parried her first swipe easily and she cursed her sluggish movements. She tried to spin around, but stumbled, slashing awkwardly.

He made a stab for her heart, which she managed to duck, then lifted her leg and kicked him in the chest. He staggered back, then resumed his stance.

She tried to lift her cutlass again, but her arm trembled horribly. That last kick had taken every ounce of strength she had left. She would not be able to fight off his next attack. They would kill her, then they would take Rissine prisoner, returning her to Egrin so he could experiment with her magic like he had hers. She heard the distant sound of hooves, and knew then that Daemon had reinforcements on the way. Saida's struggle with the female Nokken ended as the male Nokken closed in, snagged the bow, and kicked Saida aside, ending the fight. Saida curled up on her side, guarding her abdomen against another kick.

They were utterly sunk.

She considered surrendering as she spotted the horse in the distance, just a lone rider atop its back. Probably stupid Egrin, here to crush them all to death . . . but then why did Daemon look suddenly surprised?

He turned just as the horse hit the beach, its cowled rider leaning low over the dappled mare's neck. It was a stocky thing, made for plowing fields. It plowed right into Daemon Saredoth, trampling him.

Beyond the trampling horse, Saida rolled to her feet, using the distraction to elbow the male Nokken in the gut. He doubled over with a grunt, then she kneed him in the face, propelling him backward. As he fell, she darted in and stole his belt knife, then pointed it at the female Nokken.

The female raised her hands in surrender, slowly backing away.

Elmerah put pressure on her wound as she blinked blearily up at the rider. Sunlight cut across the beach, let in by the dissipating clouds.

Though she was about to topple over, she smiled. "Took you long enough, you stupid elf."

Alluin

IT SEEMED ALLUIN HAD ARRIVED JUST IN TIME. RISSINE was lying motionless in the sand, and Elmerah was looking at him like she was drunk, though he suspected she was actually just delirious from the wound in her side.

He dismounted and drew the twin blades at his belt as the male and female Nokken backed away toward their remaining companion, a female sitting in the sand with an arrow in her leg.

The male raised his hands in surrender. "It seems our plan was not the wisest," he said, his thickly accented voice a deep rumble in his chest.

"Perhaps not," Alluin agreed as Saida reached his side.

The two Nokken reached their companion and helped her to her feet. Supporting the injured female between them, they all looked at each other with subtle nods, then turned and hurried away.

Alluin's shoulders slumped. They needed to leave the beach before anyone else arrived, but first he wanted to make sure Daemon Saredoth was dead. He approached the crumpled form lying beside his waiting mare.

"Curse it all!" he growled. Red hair, fox ears, and a badly bruised Nokken body lay in the sand. The shapechanger had only made himself look like Daemon Saredoth.

As Alluin watched, the Nokken's eyes opened. "Don't kill me," he groaned, wincing at Alluin.

Alluin pointed a dagger downward. "Why not?"

"We only thought to improve our standing with the emperor," he muttered, wincing in pain. "He knows not that you are here. He knows nothing of this encounter. We thought—" he gasped, "thought if we captured the witches, we would be as valued as the Dreilore."

Elmerah staggered up behind Alluin. "Well that was a stupid plan, now wasn't it? You planned this with the Akkeri."

The Nokken closed his eyes. "They hoped you would lure out the Moon Priestess."

Alluin peered down the beach toward the Akkeri corpses littering the sand. "Let's get out of here," he sighed. "There may be more of them coming."

Elmerah placed a hand on his shoulder, an unusual display of affection . . . no, wait, she was just using him to keep herself standing.

He looped his arm beneath her shoulders and helped her toward his waiting mare. She hung onto the mare's saddle, relieving him of her weight. He turned at the sound of Saida's whistle.

Good, she hadn't lost the antlioch. He wasn't sure how they would have all gotten out of there quickly with just one mount. He glanced at Rissine, still unconscious in the sand. Even two mounts would be difficult.

The antlioch approached cautiously, and Alluin realized Merwyn was atop its back, his small body leaned forward on the creature's neck. The antlioch stepped lightly, careful to not topple its seemingly unconscious rider.

What he'd found in the woods clicked together in Alluin's mind. Merwyn had been shot by an arrow. Saida had bound his wounds with the cloak, and turned back toward the Capital to find him aid.

The antlioch reached Saida, who in turn led the creature to Alluin.

"The storm drew you?" he asked Saida.

She nodded. "When I saw how quickly it was moving in, I knew it was likely caused by Elmerah."

At that moment, the witch in question fell over with a soft *thunk,* landing on her side in the sand.

He looked to Saida. "We need to get out of here. I have no idea how I'm going to balance two unconscious witches on one horse, but I'll have to try."

"I'm not unconscious yet!" Elmerah called out. "Just not exactly standing."

Saida glanced at Rissine. "Two? Why would you want to take *her?*"

While it was tempting to leave her behind, he could reluctantly admit they needed her. "I'll explain everything later. Just help me lift her."

Though Saida looked unsure, she obeyed. After some awkward attempts, they managed to slide Rissine over the base of the horse's neck, belly down. Then they helped Elmerah into the saddle, which proved less cumbersome as she was still conscious enough to hold on, but just barely. Once she was in place, she hunched over her sister. "Don't forget to fetch my coat," she groaned.

Alluin peered down the beach, spotting her crumpled black coat in the sand.

Saida waited near the antlioch while he fetched the coat, then they both led their respective animals and unconscious riders down the beach.

"Will we go to the settlement?" Saida asked as they walked, one palm on the antlioch's neck as it ambled beside her. "We need a healer."

He shook his head. "We cannot go there. For now, we must simply find a place to hide and look at Elmerah's wound."

Saida nodded. "Yes, I suppose that is the first thing we should do, though I'm quite confused how everyone ended up here."

Bile threatened to creep up his throat at the thought of mentioning his kin, but it was the easiest way to explain how they'd all ended up on this deserted beach. "My kin were killed by the Dreilore. The other elves have moved on to more distant encampments. I was tracking you to give you more information, but it seemed you had turned around. I was following your tracks back when I saw the storm, and knew it must be Elmerah."

Saida shook her head in disbelief. "Your kin?"

His head drooped. "It is best not to speak of it now. There is much more I need to say to you. I can only hope we are not too late for Faerune. If only that Nokken had truly been Daemon . . . " he trailed off, letting go of the elation he'd felt at trampling the man.

"Daemon?" Saida questioned. "He was present during the attack?"

He furrowed his brow at her. "No, but the Nokken was posing as him."

She shook her head. "I only saw four Nokken, and the dead Akkeri."

He lifted his brows. "Perhaps you are skilled at seeing through the Nokken's disguises, as I was entirely fooled."

Saida looked down at her feet deep in thought, then shook her head. "It doesn't matter. We have more pressing matters to discuss. We encountered one of the Dreilore in the woods," she replied. "If Faerune is their target, we will not make it there before them."

He'd thought that had been the case judging by the arrow, but just hearing it made everything feel utterly hopeless. "Then perhaps we are too late."

"Hey," Elmerah groaned, still leaned forward in the saddle atop her unconscious sister. "I did not get stabbed in an Akkeri water fight just to cry and give up. *You* two dragged me into this war, so in the name of Arcale, or Cindra, or whoever in Ilthune you elves worship, we will be finishing it. That son of a Dreilore wench who calls himself Egrin Dinoba picked the wrong *witch* to mess with."

Alluin raised his eyebrows at Saida, who smiled in reply. "Perhaps not *all* is utterly lost," she offered.

He laughed. Perhaps Saida was right, though they needed to get the witch to a healer soon, lest her bluster prove more than her bite.

CHAPTER TWENTY-TWO

Elmerah

Elmerah propped herself up with several hard pillows in her less than comfortable bed . . . the same bed she'd slept in after she and Saida escaped the pirates. *Of course* the nosy innkeep was part of Rissine's guild, a perfect spy to gather information from the frequently visiting militia. She'd been forced to forgive the old man his gruff attitude when he'd taken them in, allowing an injured Arthali, and a more gravely wounded Akkeri to hide at his inn. Rissine had been given a room of her own, fortunately, granting Elmerah time to recover both her strength and her pride.

She reached for her nearby cutlass as footsteps sounded outside the door.

"It's me," Alluin called.

With a groan, she rose from the bed, then padded barefoot across the room to unlock the door. Though she wore black breeches, her loose, sleeveless undershirt exposed the bandages circling her wound whenever she lifted her arms.

She hesitated at the door, then decided Alluin had seen her in a far worse state, namely slung across a horse pinning down her unconscious sister. She twisted the lock, then the knob.

Alluin waited outside. Though he'd had time to rest, deep bags marred the skin beneath his green eyes, and his long hair was mussed. He'd found a clean forest green tunic, a few shades darker than his eyes. "You look like one of the Akkeri," he commented, eyeing her bedraggled condition as he walked past her into the room.

She shut the door behind him. "Speaking of, how is our diminutive friend?"

Alluin shook his head as he turned to her. "Still breathing, but there's no saying if he'll live. His wounds have been properly tended, and he's been given herbs for his fever. It is all we can do."

She walked back to her bed and sat. "They're a tough race, I'm sure he'll recover." She was actually not sure, and rather annoyed to find she cared.

Alluin sat on the bed beside her. "I thought we'd go over our plan before we spoke to Saida. We should be prepared to leave come evening."

She cringed. He was right, they couldn't tarry, but the wound in her side begged her to argue. "You mean you haven't told her about Isara?"

He shook his head. "As much as she now detests the emperor, it will be difficult for her to believe that we plan on overthrowing the Empire entirely. I thought it might help to hear it from her friend."

"I'm not her friend," Elmerah snapped.

"Yes you are," he stated matter-of-factly. "She'll trust what you say, just as your sister trusts you."

She snorted. "I've no clue *why*."

He raised an eyebrow at her. "You know, you're really not as terrible as you make yourself out to be."

"Just give me time."

He laughed. "We'll see. For now, we need to convince Saida to reach Isara. We can only hope she'll still be alive by the time we reach Faerune."

It was her turn to raise a brow. "So we're going to Faerune now?"

He nodded. "Splitting up did not work out well for us the last time, and it is imperative that we reach Isara. We'll stop by some of the Valeroot settlements along the way to make sure they are prepared."

"Well," she sighed, "I suppose anywhere is better than here. That will give Rissine time to rally the Arthali . . . *if* she can find them."

He looked down at his hands resting in his lap. "Yes, the Arthali. Hopefully they'll keep their sights on the Empire, and will not turn on the elves."

She smirked. "Oh trust me, as much as I detest the Arthali, they know who their true enemy is. While the elves might fear or sometimes detest us, you have never been our enemies."

Another knock sounded at the door.

"Come in," they said in unison, each reaching toward their respective weapons.

The door opened to reveal Saida, dressed much like Alluin in a fresh tunic and breeches done in forest hues . . . though both were a bit too large for her small frame. "You're looking much better," she chirped, hurrying into the room before closing the door behind her. She approached the bed. "I fear I cannot say the same for Merwyn."

Elmerah nodded. "So I'm told, but like it or not, we'll have to move him soon."

"Yes," Saida agreed, glancing to Alluin. "I'm told we have a plan, but not exactly what that plan is."

Elmerah smiled, then crooked her finger for Saida to lean in toward her. Once she was close enough, she whispered, "We're going to murder Egrin and Daemon, then put Isara Saredoth on the throne."

Saida straightened, her eyes wide.

Alluin sighed. "When I said she'd take it better coming from you, I failed to consider that you're . . . well, *you*."

Ignoring him, Elmerah looked up to Saida. "Well? What do you say? Want to help us overthrow an empire?"

Saida's expression grew serious. "The Empire has broken its treaties with my people, sending Dreilore to attack us, and framing us for horrible deeds." She crossed her arms. "Of course I'll help."

Elmerah turned to Alluin. "Perhaps you were right in letting me deliver the news."

"There's only one problem," Saida added.

They both turned back to her.

"Isara Saredoth left Faerune last winter. No one now knows where she is."

Elmerah hesitated, then turned to Alluin. "Could your scouts not tell you this?"

He frowned. "Because Valeroot elves are so often allowed within the crystalline walls? We had no way of knowing this."

She turned back to Saida. "Did she say why she left?"

She nodded. "She wanted to study the old Akkeri temples to continue her father's research. As far as I know, she has not been heard from since."

Alluin stood. "We must find her. Our entire plan is dependent on her taking the throne. If we assassinate Daemon and Egrin without knowing where she is, we might end up with one of their allies as ruler."

Elmerah hunched her shoulders. Could nothing be easy? "Do we at least know where these Akkeri temples are? Perhaps some nearby villages might know of her whereabouts, or if she even still lives."

Saida nodded. "Yes, I know where they are, though not what we might expect upon our arrival. Perhaps once Merwyn is awake, we can ask him."

"That seems our only option," Alluin agreed. "For now, we will make for the nearest Valeroot settlement to find fresh mounts and supplies, then we will head south."

Elmerah moved to the head of her bed, then slumped against the pillows. "Just when I thought the situation could grow no worse, we add in Akkeri temples. Aren't they supposed to be filled with traps and monsters?"

Alluin chuckled. "Oh come now, I'm sure they're no match for an Arthali witch."

She smirked. "That's true. It's the two worthless elves I'm worried about."

Alluin and Saida both laughed.

It was an odd feeling for Elmerah, laughing with two elves who'd somehow become something akin to friends, but she found she didn't really mind it. She also didn't mind embarking on a bit of an adventure, her lonely swamp not quite carrying the appeal it once did.

Now, Akkeri temples on the other hand, *those* she minded, but perhaps they'd be filled with jewels, and she could live out her life a rich woman with Egrin Dinoba's head on a pike outside her front door.

Rissine

LATER THAT EVENING, RISSINE PREPARED TO LEAVE. Elmerah escorted her out the inn's back entrance. Once she knew whether Thera still lived, which was unlikely, she'd take the sleek black horse she kept housed at the inn's stables to Port Aeluvaria, where a ship awaited her.

Yes, she'd been planning this for a very long time, if not in this exact manner.

Elmerah glanced at her as they walked over crunchy pine needles toward the waiting horse, tethered to a tree by the innkeep far from where any militia men might notice.

Reaching the horse, Rissine stroked its sleek black mane, then turned to her sister. "Are you sure you don't want to come with me? It will be easier to convince the Arthali clans with you by my side."

Elmerah shook her head. "I told you already I want nothing to do with the Arthali further than using them to overthrow the Empire."

Rissine pursed her lips. "But Akkeri temples?"

"Are you worried about me, *dear* sister?"

Rissine chuckled as she untied the horse's reins. "I've never had to worry about you a day in my life. Even as a child you could protect yourself."

"Yes," Elmerah sighed, "and you made me prove it."

Rissine frowned. If anyone knew how to hold on to old grudges, it was Elmerah. "Will you never forgive me?"

Elmerah stared at her for a moment, then replied, "Probably not, but at least now that you've made yourself useful, I won't have to kill you . . . at least not yet."

Rissine laughed, then put her foot in her stirrup and swung her leg up over her saddle. "Oh my dearest sister," she turned her horse toward the distant road, "I'd like to see you try."

EPILOGUE

Later that evening, four more travelers left the small inn under the cover of night. One wished to lift his peoples' curse, though he knew he might not survive. One wished to save her homeland, though she feared she hadn't the strength. One had lost everything, but would fight for what was right, no matter the cost.

And the final traveler, though she had lost much, and had many wishes yet to be fulfilled, was simply glad to feel the wind in her hair, the weight of a cutlass at her belt, and the promise of adventure ahead.

Or so she kept telling herself.

The story continues in Curse of the Akkeri, now available!

ALSO BY SARA C. ROETHLE

The Tree of Ages Series

Tree of Ages

The Melted Sea

The Blood Forest

Queen of Wands

The Oaken Throne

Dawn of Magic: Forest of Embers

Dawn of Magic: Sea of Flames

Dawn of Magic: City of Ashes

The Duskhunter Saga

Reign of Night

Trick of Shadows

Blade of Darkness

Heir of Twilight

The Will of Yggdrasil

Fated

Fallen

Fury

Forged

Found

The Thief's Apprentice Series

Clockwork Alchemist

Clocks and Daggers

Under Clock and Key

The Xoe Meyers Series

Xoe

Accidental Ashes

Broken Beasts

Demon Down

Forgotten Fires

Gone Ghost

Minor Magic

Minor Magics: The Demon Code

Printed in Great Britain
by Amazon

65219520R00190